Wolf Hook

MICHAEL
WALLACE

CHAPTER ONE

JIM HEYDRICH TOOK THE STAGE before the third act, knowing that whatever he glimpsed as the lights came up would condemn someone to death. The man sitting next to his uncle in the audience would be wearing either a green tie or a yellow tie. A yellow tie meant Jim's own death. A green tie, and he would live, but it meant death for his friend Nigel standing next to him on the darkened stage. And a green tie meant death for the rest of them, too. His fellow actors. The stage crew and the producer. Maybe even the new girl at the lights—all of them would suffer so Jim could skulk away and save his own neck.

Jim and Nigel waited at the front of the thrust, where the set of the English drawing room intruded from the stage almost into the very laps of the audience. He couldn't see the audience, but he heard them, shifting in their seats, rustling to put away programs, a few dying conversations in German or Dutch as they leaned forward in expectation. It was conspicuously quiet directly in front. Both his uncle and the Irish diplomat sat in that hushed zone. Several seconds passed, but the stage remained dark.

"Bloody hell," Nigel Burnside whispered next to Jim.

For a moment Jim thought the poor Dutch girl had unplugged the light board. This was only her third performance—they'd grabbed her from a cabaret show after border agents seized the previous technician at the crossing from Belgium. Irregularities in his papers.

What a time for a lighting foul up, with half the theater filled with humorless agents of the Reich, while the usual audience stayed away in droves, no doubt enjoying the more relaxed surroundings of one of Amsterdam's semi-licit whiskey bars.

But then the lights came up. In that moment between darkness and the full glare Jim saw the audience clearly. A wedge of officers and Gestapo agents in black uniforms and swastika armbands carved out the middle of the theater. The Dutch officials of the occupied government stretched from stage left, while various foreign civilians made a smaller clump in front of stage right. The previous two nights, audiences had packed the theater, but tonight the edges were ragged with empty seats. Jim's uncle, SS-Obergruppenführer Reinhard Heydrich, sat in the front middle seat, severe in his black uniform, his blond, neatly parted hair, and his icy blue stare. The Irish diplomat sat on Heydrich's left side, staring grimly ahead. He was a small, unimposing man, eyes too small and closely placed together, his face dominated by a bushy white mustache. If he enjoyed the irony of watching the work of an Irish-born playwright while on the German-dominated soil of the continent, it didn't show on his face.

But it was the man's brightly-colored tie that drew Jim's attention. It stood out among all the blacks and grays and swastika armbands, the Nazi flags draped around the theater. Jim had his answer.

Nigel Burnside, playing Lord Goring in Oscar Wilde's play, held up the carnation that was his opening prop of the scene. His lines came to Jim's ears in a blur that may as well have been Dutch. Jim responded on pure instinct.

"Got my second buttonhole for me, Phipps?" Nigel said.

"Yes, my Lord," Jim—or rather, Phipps, the butler, said. The lines emerged automatically, even as his mind reeled.

"Rather distinguished thing, Phipps. I am the only person of the smallest importance in London at present who wears a buttonhole."

"Yes, my lord. I have observed that."

"You see, Phipps, fashion is what one wears oneself. What is unfashionable is what other people wear."

"Yes, my lord."

The dialogue continued in this fashion for a couple more exchanges before Nigel's character said something that required an actual response: "Don't think I quite like this buttonhole, Phipps. Makes me look a little too old. Makes me almost in the prime of life, eh, Phipps?"

And with that, the lines evaporated from Jim's head. His response was simple, he knew, some dry counterpart to Lord Goring's foppish, affected wit. The straight man whose well-timed lines brought the most laughs. But the Irishman's brightly colored tie drove away everything else.

It was green. Not yellow, but green. Jim would live. All he had to do was get himself to a certain bridge over a certain canal in Haarlem by six A.M. The Irish would smuggle him from Europe.

"Eh, Phipps?" Nigel tried again. Was that a strain in his voice?

Nigel would be the first to suffer. Never mind that he was a fascist, driven from his home country for cozying up to the Germans. He was a Brit from his toes to his tea and crumpets, and head of a theater company performing *An Ideal Husband* in English. How suspicious was that? As soon as Jim disappeared, Nigel would be the first to suffer the iron gaze of the Gestapo.

My lines. What the hell are they?

A few nervous coughs from the front row. Only seconds must have passed, but in the curious stage time, where a disaster came on suddenly, and then lingered as thick and inescapable as black tar, it may as well have been minutes. Nigel's face twitched.

I don't observe any alteration in your lordship's appearance.

That was his line. But before he could stutter out the words, Nigel improvised out of the jam. "What is that expression, Phipps? Does that mean you *don't* notice a difference? Hmm, I am not quite sure. For the future a more trivial buttonhole, Phipps, on Thursday evenings."

There were laughs from the English speakers in the audience and, thank God, Jim remembered his subsequent lines, which brought more laughs. A few more exchanges, words correctly delivered but the timing off, and then they fell into a comfortable rhythm. By the time Jim's character introduced Lord Goring's father, the Earl of Caversham, who had arrived to humorously throw Goring's plans into chaos, he'd recovered his stage presence. In every other way, he was a wreck.

He came backstage and found a garbage can. His supper came out stained red, mystery fish and poorly-seasoned potatoes dyed with the cheap, acidic wine served up in the restaurant on Warmoesstraat. He turned to find Lula Larouche watching him. She wore an elegant green dress that showed a swell of bosom. Her golden hair was piled elegantly on her head, and a string of fake pearls glittered around her long, graceful neck. She wore a touch of lipstick — which cost the company a fortune on the black market — that made her lips so red and full they looked almost obscene. The former film star still had enough beauty and stage presence to make her an effective foil for Nigel's Lord Goring.

Jim wiped his mouth and pushed the garbage can away. "Looks like supper didn't agree with me."

"Even if your audience is full of Nazis, you can still picture them naked," she said.

"I *almost* got them naked, but wouldn't you know, underneath those uniforms they're all wearing red and black codpieces with swastikas?" He tried to smile. "How bad was it?"

"It was only a moment. You recovered."

"*Nigel* recovered. I'm just lucky I didn't fall off the stage."

"And land in your uncle's lap? *Quelle horror!*" She squeezed his arm. "Don't worry, it's not like he'd deport you. Wouldn't that make Christmas dinner awkward?"

"Reinhard isn't the deporting type. He likes to stretch your neck instead."

"Ah, yes. The Hangman. I almost forgot."

He found himself staring. Lula was a survivor and a hell of an actress. Could she convince his uncle's men that she was innocent? Maybe. They'd grab Nigel first, then the man's sister, Margaret. Guilt by association. He mentally ran through the cast, giving them odds of survival. The best he could come up with was fifty-fifty for any one of them.

A smile spread across Lula's face. "What a look. Do I need to lock my dressing room door? Or maybe leave it open until you come in and *then* lock the door." She pinched his cheek. "But maybe you don't like the ladies. God knows how you keep your hands off Margaret."

He shrugged. Yes, Margaret was a beauty, but she was so silly and so blindly fascist in her outlook that she held no fascination for him.

Onstage, Lord Goring rang the bell that was the cue for Phipps to reenter. Jim came around the curtain, delivered his few lines, and then returned offstage. Lula had dropped her easy manner, and wore her Mrs. Cheveley face as they both waited for the next cue.

What if Jim warned his friends? Would they try to stop him? They'd have to. The instant he defected, the English-language troupe would transition from specially favored of the Ministry of Public Enlightenment and Propaganda to prime suspects of the Gestapo. He knew what Uncle Reinhard thought of him, that he was weak and effete. Send him east to shoot partisans and Jews. That would toughen him up. Meanwhile, he was certainly incapable of planning or plotting on his own. Jim's own friends no doubt felt the same. That wouldn't make his betrayal any less cowardly.

By the time Nigel gave him his next cue, Jim had decided. At the end of the show, after he gave his stiff gratitude to his uncle and performed his obligatory Nazi salute, he would track down Nigel to warn him about Uncle Reinhard's letter and Jim's plans to meet the Irish diplomat and flee the country. Maybe his friend would beg him to stay. Maybe he'd come up with some clever way for Jim to elude his duty to the Fatherland without putting the rest of them in danger.

And what if he didn't? What if he reacted badly?

Jim tightened his jaw. Then to hell with them—his uncle, the theater company, all of them. Nothing would deflect him from his goal, to get out of Europe alive.

CHAPTER TWO

THE PLAY FINISHED WITHOUT DISASTER. Jim joined the cast for a curtain call. The previous two nights, the audience had risen in a standing ovation, which had become the default reaction as the company took their show across the continent. Even in Vichy, where they'd performed one night without a single laugh, leading Nigel to declare that there were more English speakers in Mauritania than in Marseilles, the audience sprang to its feet the instant the lights came back up. The poor sods were so starved of anything that resembled uncensored, apolitical entertainment that they were perfectly primed to rise and cheer, drunk on *bon humour.*

Tonight, however, the audience stayed in its seat, applauding politely, but with little enthusiasm. Only when SS-Obergruppenführer Reinhard Heydrich rose did the applause grow, the cheers of "bravo!" and "*goed gedaan!*" cry out. But Heydrich was only approaching the stage to greet his nephew, not out of any great enthusiasm for the show. That much was obvious from his expression. He looked like a younger version of Jim's father, if you erased the laugh lines at Vater's mouth, replaced his spine with a steel pole, and tailored a starched uniform around his trim figure.

Jim held out his hand, only remembering to stiffen

it into a Nazi salute at the last moment. "Thank you for coming," he said in German. Jim's heart was pounding, and he felt certain his uncle could read his thoughts, pry the treachery from the depths of his brain.

"I was in Holland already. Your play is decadent. I did not enjoy it."

"It's not decadent. It upholds traditional Germanic values we share with the Anglo Saxons. The decadence is a trick, only what you see on the surface. What is the word?"

"A veneer?" Uncle Reinhard said.

"Yes, a veneer. Exactly."

"The Germanic values are the veneer. The decadence is subtext. And when did your German get so weak?"

He gave a half shrug. "All those years in Ottawa, I'm afraid. Vater spoke to me in German, but he never insisted I answer in the mother tongue. And my Mutti—"

"Yes, of course," Heydrich interrupted. One of his lieutenants handed him his hat and he put it on. "A deficiency in your education. Still, it has been three years since you came back. That is long enough." He glanced up at the stage. "Or do you only speak English in this morally suspect company you keep?"

"I'm working on my German. I'm sure a few months in Prague and it won't be so..." He paused again to think of the word or how to talk around it. "So rusty."

"I shall assign you a German tutor when you arrive."

Margaret Burnside had sidled over to shake hands with a young Wehrmacht colonel, who had taken her hands with a bit too much enthusiasm and was now trying to coax her into joining him and his fellows for drinks, while she pretended not to understand his Schleswig-accented German. Jim caught her watching with a sidelong glance.

If she had any sense, she'd stick with the colonel. Not that Uncle Reinhard might not be interested — he had a certain reputation as a philanderer — but she might find it difficult to extricate herself when her ardor cooled.

But no, she didn't have the sense. "Herr Heydrich, it is so wonderful to meet you. I'm Margaret Burnside and it's so, so...*wonderful!*"

Heydrich raised his eyebrows at the blushing girl with her vacant look and her thick English accent, but then his attention caught the Wehrmacht colonel, who suddenly discovered something critically important to discuss with one of his companions. A scowl crossed Heydrich's face.

"Yes, well," he said. "I must go now. Perhaps some other time, *fraulein.*"

He snapped his fingers at his aide, a pale-skinned young man with hair the exact length and cut of Heydrich's. The man pulled out a letter and handed it to Jim, and then turned on his heel and followed the SS-Obergruppenführer up the aisle and from the theater.

Margaret caught up with Jim as they made their way backstage. "Your uncle is so handsome," she said in English. "Is he married?"

"I've answered that question about ten times. Yes, he's married."

"Oh." Her mouth curved into a disappointed pucker, then she brightened again. "I wanted to tell him how much I admire him for his heroic struggle against the communists. If we ever go to Prague, would you—?"

"Oh, I will," Jim said.

I'm not going to Prague, you silly hen.

But that only reminded him of the whole awful business and the crushing guilt of what he was about to put on Nigel, Lula, and the rest. Even Margaret, silly as she was, didn't deserve that.

"Aren't you going to look at it?"

"At what?"

"The letter. What does it say? Maybe it's an invitation to a party. Wouldn't that be exciting?"

"I'm sure it's nothing." He looked down to see that he still held it in his hand and tucked it quickly into his pocket. "Family business, no doubt. Excuse me. I'm not feeling well."

"Wait a minute," she said, but he was already pushing through the curtain and down to the musty basement of the Grote Huis theater.

No private dressing rooms in Amsterdam, and so he pushed into one of the curtained stalls. He stripped out of the butler's jacket, took off the cummerbund. Underneath, his shirt was stained yellow and tattered, but it was difficult enough to replace the collar, let alone defy wartime rations for a sharp, well-kept dress shirt. Jim reached for the cuff links and found he couldn't get them off because his hands were trembling.

No doubt other cast members had found it nerve-wracking to perform in front of a theater infested with the SS, not to mention one of the most powerful, ruthless men in the Third Reich. But if pulling off an English-language, decadent play felt like juggling swords, surely nobody but Jim had faced such an acting challenge as that last bit, after the lights came up. More like juggling live grenades, chatting with his uncle as if there was nothing wrong. And all the while thinking of the bicycle he'd stashed around back, while he tried to remember what he knew about the roads between Amsterdam and Haarlem.

"A heart of iron," Jim's mother had said over Christmas dinner, when he'd returned to the family house in Halle an der Saale and received the awful summons. "The Führer said that himself."

Jim had stopped with his fork in mid air, the stringy piece of underfed chicken dangling off the end. "Wait, Adolph Hitler said that Uncle Reinhard has a heart of iron? The Führer himself implied that Reinhard is a hard man?"

"Leave the boy alone," his father said. The telegram sat in the middle of the table, a fine, thick paper with twin, jagged SS marks on the letterhead. "He knows what must be done."

"Do you want Jimmy to work under that man?" his mother asked.

"He has been working under Reinhard for two years now," Vater said.

"No I haven't," Jim said.

"You know what I mean," Mutti said to Vater as if he were still twelve years old, off at the children's table, and not twenty and sitting right in front of them.

"No, I don't. The boy has been hiding since we left Canada, relying on the family name to protect him. His mates are on the Russian steppes, fighting for their lives against the Bolsheviks."

"My mates are in Canada and England," Jim said quietly. "They fight for the other side."

"You, be quiet," his father said.

"Do you want our son to grow a heart of iron?" Mutti asked. "Is that what you want? Do you want him to be like those other men?"

"Ooh, maybe they'll give me my own concentration camp," Jim said. "What a great reference for after the war."

Vater pushed away his plate and stood up. "At least maybe then we would be eating goose for Christmas, and maybe there would be wine in my glass, and butter on my bread. How about that?"

He stormed away from the table, but later that evening he'd knocked on Jim's bedroom door as the young man repacked his battered suitcase for the following morning's train trip to Munich where he would reunite with the company. Father and son sat on the edge of the bed and talked for a few minutes about their old home in Ottawa, a life that seemed far away and magical now. At last his father cleared his throat. "Follow your conscience, son."

"So long as I answer the summons, you mean," Jim said.

"You have no choice. You know that."

"Then what do you mean, follow my conscience?"

"Don't let them change you. Be a force for good, if you can."

"There's no conscience on the Eastern Front. There's no force for good. There are only iron hearts."

"James."

"There's a reason they call Uncle Reinhard the Butcher of Prague, Vater. Why they call him the Hangman."

"You've been listening to British propaganda. I'm sure it's not that bad. A few incidents, that's all."

Jim scoffed and turned away to finish packing. A few minutes later, he heard his father slip away. They hadn't spoken again except for an awkward embrace at the train station.

And now, sitting in the dressing room after the show, struggling with his cuff links, Jim thought about this conversation, only two weeks old now, but receding quickly into some distant period of freedom that was quickly becoming no more real than his years in Canada. He was walking down a tunnel that grew darker behind and more brightly lit and narrow in front.

He got the cuff links off and then reached into the pocket of his butler's jacket for the letter given him by Heydrich's adjutant. He unfolded it.

The page was dominated by a stiff-winged eagle that clutched a swastika in its talons. Below, in a severe font, from a typewriter that no doubt had sent many men to their deaths beneath the same letterhead:

> *I shall send my staff car to pick you up at 0700. The train leaves at 0725. Be ready.*
>
> *SS-Obergruppenführer Reinhard Heydrich*
> *General Government*

Jim was supposed to meet the Irish diplomat right before dawn, or roughly the same time the staff car would come around to the hotel. It wouldn't take long, maybe a half hour or so, before they discovered he was missing and began the search. Maybe another hour or two to spread the search as far as Haarlem. But first it would hit the theater company.

Jim had to warn Nigel.

Every member of the cast had his or her own way to unbuckle the stress after a show. Some chatted for an hour or two, until they had to scurry off to the hotel before curfew caught them out, while others found an underground lounge and drank until dawn. Jim read

English novels, when he could get them, or something in German when he could not. French poetry would serve in a pinch, and once he'd found himself in Bruges, ogling a pre-war cookbook as if it were smutty pictures, and trying to decipher the Flemish ingredients. Nigel unwound by climbing to the roof to smoke a cigarette (or a cigar if he could get one), and sometimes he invited Jim up to discuss the dangerous subject of politics. Nigel called himself a humane fascist, but sometimes tried to pin Jim to the viewpoint that extreme measures may be necessary to stop the spread of international communism. It was all theoretical. Nigel rarely raised his voice except to yell at actors who didn't hit their marks.

After dressing, Jim grabbed his coat, declined the wine offered by Lula and Dunleavy, and made his way through the empty theater, so dark that he had to find his way up the aisles by touch. He moved as quietly as he could. Margaret hadn't been downstairs and he didn't want to burst into the lounge to find her still flirting with some German officer, or worse, wanting to chat with Jim about the best way to ingratiate herself with Uncle Reinhard. But the only person in the lounge was a tiny, hunchbacked Dutch woman, scrubbing with a brush at the mud tracked onto the carpet by a hundred pairs of German boots. He made his way through the box office and climbed the ladder to the light booth. It was empty.

He crawled out the window of the booth onto the catwalk that stretched around the perimeter of the theater. The slats were wooden, the metal stripped out for wartime salvage, and it creaked beneath his feet. He made his way to the far side, above the stage, where he found the staircase to the roof. He pushed the door open silently and stepped into the darkness. A sharp breeze knifed in from the ocean and he clutched his coat tight against the chill.

Nigel sat near the roof line, face turned in profile, hunkered down in his great cloak, with the glow of a cigarette at his lips. Amsterdam stretched below, buildings hulking shadows in the blackout. Crescent canals glimmered with reflected moonlight. West of the city, a pair of spotlights swung across the sky to penetrate the gloom against attack from the North Sea. The distant hum of airplanes vibrated against Jim's ear drums, but there was no gunfire, or any other sign that an Allied raid was targeting the Dutch coast.

Jim was about to cross the distance to Nigel when he realized his friend wasn't alone. There were two other figures with him, a man sitting flat on the gravel-covered roof with his legs stretched in front of him, and a second figure crouched by the man's feet and gripping his ankles.

"This is your ticket home, mate," Nigel said. He held out his cigarette, which lit the tip of a second cigarette at the sitting man's mouth.

Two quick puffs, and the sitting man said in a shaky voice, "Bloody hard way to go. You're sure there's no other way?"

It was Kristiann Janssen, who played Nigel's onstage father, Lord Caversham. Janssen, like many of the men who made up a typical audience for their show, spoke English with an upper-class Eaton accent, having been educated almost entirely in England between the wars.

"What do you suggest, simply getting on the next train home?" Nigel asked. "We raise suspicions and the Gestapo will come down on your replacement like rabid wolves. Your story must hold up to scrutiny."

There was something so unexpected about the situation and strange about the hard edge to Nigel's voice—a tone that sounded almost like an English version of the way Uncle Reinhard spoke, that Jim froze in the shadows near the door. He still held the doorknob in his hand.

"And when I arrive in Copenhagen with no money and no job?" Janssen asked. His voice climbed the register until it sat a half-octave higher than Lord Caversham's pleasant onstage baritone. "And a bloody broken leg? Who is going to feed my lady and my three children?"

"We'll take care of that," Nigel said.

"*Lort!*" Janssen took a drag. The tip shook. "Let's get this over with."

"Hold him," Nigel said to the third figure, who hadn't said a word. Nigel rose and picked up something near his feet. It was long and heavy, but Jim couldn't see exactly what it was in the darkness.

"*Lort! For helvede!*" Janssen sounded truly panicked now, but he didn't try to escape.

"Look away," the third person said. "It will be over in a second."

The voice belonged to a woman. Margaret Burnside. The silly, giddy girl who had practically thrown herself at one of the most ruthless men in the world, oblivious to what that would do to her life expectancy, held Janssen's ankles while her brother prepared to break his leg. And Janssen, complicit in the whole, insane scheme.

Nigel swung his arms around. He held a wooden sledge, like the kind they used in windmills to knock slipped gears back into place. It slammed into Janssen's leg with a crack and the man let out a stifled cry. He bucked and Margaret cursed as one foot caught her in the jaw.

Meanwhile, Jim's hand had grown numb on the frigid doorknob and it slipped from his grasp. He flailed for the door as it swung closed, but he didn't get it in time. The door clanked shut.

Nigel whipped his head around. Margaret sprang to her feet and reached into her jacket. Her hand emerged with a dark lump that could only be a gun.

"Who is there?" Nigel said in a sharp voice.

Terrified, Jim grabbed for the door handle. He got the door open just as Nigel and Margaret sprang after him.

CHAPTER THREE

J IM RACED ACROSS THE CATWALK above the theater, while
Nigel and Margaret Burnside came after him through
the darkness. He squirmed through the window into the
light booth and slammed the shutters behind him. It took
them a second in the darkness to find the window and
get it open and by then he was down the stairs into the
ticket booth. He yanked the ladder away to buy himself
a few more seconds. He went to the front door. It was
locked. In fact, the theater manager stood on the front
porch, turning the big skeleton key in the lock. Instead
of pounding for the man to open and let him out, he
turned around, burst through the lobby doors and into
the theater itself. He ran down the aisle. Pursuit sounded
at his back.

What the devil?

Margaret had a gun. She must have seen who he was.
Nigel, too. Were they going to kill him?

Jim had one advantage. He had been organizing
this escape since their arrival in Amsterdam six days
earlier, even before he dropped the note at the Irish
consulate, addressed to Mr. Gordon Gaughran, chargé
d'affaires, Irish Legation. He had purchased a bicycle
on Zeedijk Street, paid for it with ration coupons and
four hundred Reichsmarks, and then hid it in the shed

behind the theater. He had slipped a few hundred more to the needle-nosed Dutch fellow who worked in the ticket booth, who then produced a road map of central Holland. Jim compared the map with his memories of Amsterdam — his family had spent six weeks in the city after their ill-fated return to Europe shortly before the Wehrmacht invaded the Low Countries and incorporated them into the Reich.

He'd already planned for flight in case Gaughran turned his letter over to the Gestapo. Jim had imagined the hard knock on his door while he slept, the Gestapo arresting him at night as was their way — fog and mist as his uncle called it. Jim would climb out the hotel window, jump into the rubbish bin, and sprint the two blocks to the theater for the bike. Or, if they came for him at the theater, he figured out how to hide beneath the stage or how to escape from the building through the costume room.

And so when he got backstage, he ducked into the costume and prop room. Nigel hissed something at Margaret, and moments later they pushed in after him.

It wasn't much of a room, more the conglomeration of all the leftover nooks and crannies of centuries of interior remodel jobs, cobbled together into a dark, winding passageway. The theater company had arrived to find it already stuffed with props and costumes, most of it rubbish, and the clothing smelling of mold and mothballs. A few days ago, Jim had explored the costume room, and now he groped for an upright coffin to his left, reached from there until he found the light bulb and unscrewed it. Hands grabbed for him and he fled deeper into the room.

Moments later someone found the chain and pulled

on it. Nigel cursed when the light didn't come on.

"We know you're in here, Jim," Margaret said. "We saw you come in. We're not going to hurt you, we just want to talk. We can explain what you saw, or thought you saw."

She sounded calm, her explanation reasonable. But then again, Margaret was an excellent actress. Forget her work onstage as Miss Mable. That silly naive English girl act *offstage* had been pure brilliance. She'd played the role for six months and fooled him completely. And now he didn't know who or what she was. He didn't care to find out.

"Get in there and find him," she told Nigel when Jim didn't answer.

Jim bore left in the darkness. The passage wrapped to the right, where it followed the building until it ended above the dressing rooms. But here about waist high he'd found a window, had gone around outside to scrape away paint from the frame that kept it sealed shut, and then slid it up and down several times. His fingers found the window now and he got it open before Nigel seemed to hear him and flailed in his direction. A cold draft poured into the room.

"Jim!" Margaret called. "Talk to us. That's all we want."

He climbed out the window, dropped the few feet to the ground, and then turned around and yanked the window shut again. He didn't stop to see if Nigel had found the window, but ran for the shed. The bicycle was still there, thank God, hidden behind a stack of crates. His biggest fear had been that someone would come for the crates to burn them — the Dutch would even enter shaky, bombed-out buildings to strip them for firewood — and then discover and steal the bicycle. He got it out of the shed, jumped on, and wobbled into the darkness, tires bouncing over cobblestones.

Nigel came out the theater window as he passed, dropped down and sprinted after him. By now, Jim already had some speed and he quickly pulled away.

"Don't shoot, you fool," Margaret snapped, her voice sounding from the window above and to his rear.

Jim braced for a gunshot. But there was nothing. He emerged from the alley and flew past the front of the theater. A moment later and he was pedaling furiously down the thin gray strip that marked the road. Margaret and Nigel spoke in raised, angry tones to his rear, already moving as if they planned to cut him off.

Jim rode east at top speed, toward the cathedral-like Oude Kerk, as if he meant to cross the canal bridge to its east, but two blocks later cut down a narrow alley to loop north. There were no signs of pursuit, but he knew they'd be looking for him. Why? The hell if he knew what was going on, but it had to be one of two things. They were either Nazi agents or enemy spies.

Either way, Margaret's gun and her command that Nigel hold his fire—but *not*, he supposed, out of concern for Jim's life so much as fear of being heard—left little doubt what they'd do if they caught him.

Gradually, as he darted from one alley to the next, his heart rate slowed, and he became convinced he'd lost the pursuit. But he was hardly out of danger. The police would be out and harassing curfew violators. If they stopped him, he didn't speak Dutch. If he ran into Germans, he could trade on his uncle's name, as surely every German in Holland knew that Heydrich was in Amsterdam. That assumed they didn't drag him off the bike, shove him against the wall, and gun him down before he could explain. But even if they didn't, there would be an awkward moment when his uncle demanded to know why he'd been riding a black market bicycle around Amsterdam on the night before the train would carry him east.

The bicycle alone could get him arrested, as all Dutch bicycles had been confiscated by the authorities. This one was an ugly thing with mismatched tires that kept throwing its chain. One of the tires was bald rubber, patched again and again, and the other a wood hoop taken from a barrel. There was a basket tied above the front tire, made from a broken wooden crate. He had stashed a burlap sack with a bit of food inside. The bicycle clanked and rattled, a sound that was surely audible for a hundred feet in every direction.

There were other curfew violators: an old lady with a basket; a girl who was probably a prostitute coming out of the seedy alleys north of Slaperssteeg, a purse clutched to her chest; and two young boys who ducked into a doorway at his approach. He rounded a corner at one point to see a German soldier, and his heart flopped in his chest, but the soldier leaned his back into the shadows of a building as if he, too, didn't want to be seen. As Jim clattered by, the German held back his arm to shield—or was that restrain?—a young woman in a long wool coat pulled up around her ears.

He took the canal bridges with extra caution, knowing that he'd be visible from dozens of apartments along the canal, if anyone should glance out at this late hour and see the glint of moonlight on metal spokes. The canals stank of sewage and glistened with a sheen of oil. He passed one that was clogged with boats on both sides, with only a narrow passage opening in the middle. People on the boats wore blankets and huddled around fires that burned in open metal barrels. The apartment block on the other side lay in ruins, some buildings two-story piles of rubble, while others lay sheered open with kitchens and bedrooms and staircases exposed like the heart of a giant's dollhouse. Faces turned up from the boats as he crossed the bridge, and someone hissed at him in Dutch. Jim was glad when he left them behind.

When he became sure that he'd escaped the riskiest stretch of his trip, he slowed to get his bearings. A sudden, unwelcome realization struck him. In his flight from the theater, not only had he left behind such useful possessions as his gloves, an extra pair of socks, and what money he had left, but his map. It was still at the theater, hidden in a stage credenza in the costume and prop room. He'd studied the roads around the theater so many times that he'd initially forgotten that once he left Amsterdam he didn't know exactly how to get to Haarlem. And when he reached the outskirts of the city, he discovered that the Germans had torn down the road signs, perhaps to confuse the British commandos who sometimes raided the Atlantic coast.

He forced himself to remain calm. It was still early at night. Haarlem was only ten or fifteen miles west of Amsterdam, if his memory held true, but the key was not to cut across the heavily militarized Marken Penninsula, but to go north, then turn west above the town of Edam. If he kept the dunes and the sea to his right and hugged the coast, he'd be sure to find the road leading into town. He could take his time, pick his way as slowly as necessary whenever his instincts raised suspicions.

Jim shortly found himself crossing the Dutch countryside, a flat expanse of fields that began without preamble, as was common in Europe, unlike towns in Canada that seemed to bleed from the outskirts of a city for miles until turning to forest or farmland. He made good time for about twenty minutes, pedaling slowly by moonlight to keep from driving off the road, and then he threw the chain again. He pulled off the road to fix it, and was lucky to have done so; moments later a motorized patrol of German Kübelwagens came down the road, headlights scooping holes in the fog that drifted across the road. He kept his head down until he no longer heard the rumble of engines.

The chain wouldn't fit. He'd fixed it easily enough in Amsterdam, but it would no longer stretch over the front sprocket, almost like the damn thing had shrunk or deformed. His frustration mounted with each passing minute. Doubtful the chain was meant for this bicycle in the first place, although he supposed that someone with better tools and mechanical skills could get it on again. As it was, with no tools, no light, and hands that were numb with cold, the bike had turned into a lump of metal and wood. Jim took out the burlap sack with a half baguette and two apples from the basket, and then abandoned the bicycle with a curse and continued on foot. Someone would have a valuable find on their hands when they discovered it lying in the ditch.

Calm down. You've got time.

Several hours until dawn and he must be halfway to Haarlem already. And without the bicycle, there was no reason to stick to roads. Instead, he decided to make his way across open countryside, directly west.

Apart from feet and hands, he'd stayed warm pumping along on the bike, but on foot, with the damp fog that kept drifting inland, he was soon shivering. He tucked the sack under one arm and shoved his hands deep into his pockets. He walked at a brisk clip, but he was tired and found himself eying farmhouses with half a mind to seek refuge in a barn. He even imagined giving up the whole endeavor and might have done it if he could have thought up a way to get back to the hotel in time for his uncle's staff car by 7:00 A.M.

He ate the bread, and this revived his energy and spirits, but as he crossed a field, the ground turned waterlogged, and his boots, the soles thin and restitched, took on water. His feet throbbed. A light glowed in a farmhouse window and he thought again about stopping, but was glad he didn't, because about an hour later, through some stroke of luck, he stumbled into Haarlem. At first he wasn't sure it was the right town, but the cobbled road took him straight to the Grote Markt, right in the shadow of the Grote Kirk, the huge brick church with its giant tower overlooking the city. The air above the square was a spiderweb of electric trolley wires, crossing to many of the eight or ten streets that led into the Grote Markt, but the open space itself was empty of stalls or carts at this hour.

Jim had taken the train to Haarlem with his parents three or four times before the invasion of the Low Countries, and he recognized the sights even in the dark. His knowledge of the compact, canal-riddled town, together with its proximity to both Amsterdam and the sea, was the reason he'd proposed that Mr. Gaughran meet him here in the first place. The only thing to do was to wait out the night, and then make his way to a bridge that crossed the canal off Koudenhorn.

But it was still only three or four in the morning and his feet were numb, his hands and his cheeks ached with cold, and he couldn't stop shivering. What he needed was to find the red light district and pay a prostitute, not for sexual favors, but to share the warmth of her bed for a few hours until dawn. Unfortunately, as he dug through his pockets, all he could find were a pair of two reichsmark coins. Maybe in Warsaw or Kiev he could find a woman desperate enough to shelter him for that kind of money, but the Dutch weren't quite so miserable. Not yet, anyway. Give it a few years, and his uncle would probably serve as *Reichskommissar* of Holland, too. And then he'd set about squeezing blood from a turnip here, too. Or blood from a tulip, as the case may be.

Movement caught his eye on the far edge of the square. He shrank against the wall of the boarded-over shop at his back, but as he stared across, his eyes picked out shuffling shapes. Not a German foot patrol, he decided, but the old, the homeless, and the indigent. He made his way around the edge of the square toward them. There were at least a couple dozen in all, sleeping or huddled in boxes, covered in layer after layer of rags, from their bundled feet to the strips of cloth that wrapped turban-like around their heads. A lucky few had blankets. It stank of vomit and unemptied chamber pots, but he could feel the warmth of huddled bodies already and he was so cold that he didn't care about the smell. Jim took out his two remaining coins and clinked them together. Eyes pulled in his direction, and a woman of indeterminate age waved him over. The others turned their backs as he approached. The woman snapped up the coins and jerked his arm to draw him into her blankets, where she pulled down her blouse and tried to put his hand on her breast.

"You're too kind," he said as he withdrew his hand, "but didn't we just meet? Besides, I like to pee without it burning."

It took gestures, exchanges in broken German, Dutch, and English, and Jim pushing away her hands before she stopped groping him in an attempt to get his ardor up and finish the deed. She was younger than he had thought, probably no more than thirty, and though she was filthy and stank, and was all bones and angles, she still had her teeth. In a different time and place she might have even been pretty. She stared at him with a confused expression.

"I don't want that, you understand. Just the blanket. No touch."

At last she seemed to understand and let him share the blanket and the shadows in which she hid without trying anything more. He was hungry again, and felt the weight of the burlap sack with its two apples where he'd tucked it into his jacket. He reached in, fetched one out and had it halfway to his mouth before he saw the woman staring.

"Here, you can have this one."

She took it with a quick gesture and fished into her blankets while he removed the second one for himself. To his surprise, she produced a small paring knife, which she used to cut the apple in two. It struck Jim as such a strange gesture that he watched without eating, expecting her to cut her apple in quarters and then eighths. But to his greater surprise, a small child scrambled out of the shadows to their rear. A girl, he guessed, though she was so young and filthy that it took a moment until he was sure. She'd been hiding in the boxes not three feet away, and she snatched the half apple from the woman and devoured it. Jim had the awful thought that had he taken the woman up on her initial offer, the daughter would have been back there watching.

He no longer felt hungry. After all, he'd eaten half a baguette a few hours earlier and it wasn't eight hours since his last meal, even if he'd thrown most of it up backstage. "Here, why don't you have this one, too?" he said.

The woman took the second apple, cut this one in half, too, gave one portion to her daughter, and then offered the final half to Jim.

"No, I'm fine. You go ahead."

The woman and the daughter finished the apples, and then the three of them huddled together beneath the blankets, where Jim drifted in and out of sleep for about an hour. He woke to the sound of two soldiers clomping around the edge of the square. All shuffling and movement from the huddle of indigents stopped at once. The Germans slowed their pace and one flashed a light into the shadows. Faces froze with downcast eyes.

"Filthy beasts," one of the men said, and then they crossed to the church side of the square and disappeared.

Haarlem started to wake not long after that. A man came up and down the streets, banging on a cowbell with a mallet. He clanked six times, walked a half block, and then clanked six more times. A light came on in one window, a woman shuffled off the stoop of an apartment building. A man crossed the square with long, brisk strides. A few minutes later another man came by pushing a cart loaded with broken table legs and dresser drawers and a separate box containing salvaged brass handles, nails, and screws. Another man carried a wicker basket covered in cloth. It smelled like bread and the indigents stirred and muttered until the man was out of sight. The church bells didn't ring. The Germans had probably stolen them for their metal.

Much warmer now, Jim pulled free from the woman and rose silently to his feet. The square was gray now, and if Gordon Gaughran planned to keep his promise, he'd already be in Haarlem by now, no doubt making his way to the bridge. Time to find his way there himself.

The woman pulled on his arm and held out her hand. "*Alstublieft. Ik ben erg honger.*"

"No, I'm sorry." He slapped at his pockets to show they were empty. "No money, no food."

But he could see the woman's features more clearly now, her sharp cheekbones and her eyes drawn back in their sockets, the naked desperation on her face. Her daughter stared from the shadows. The salvage man clattered by again, his cart empty this time, and it gave Jim an idea.

He took off his belt and handed it to the woman. "Take this. Italian leather and American brass. You know, like bomb casings. You can sell it."

"*Dank u, vriendelijke meneer.*"

Jim was aware as he walked away that he didn't actually need a belt to hold up his pants. In spite of the gnawing in his belly, he was well fed enough that they stayed up perfectly well on their own. And whether he'd stayed in the theater troupe, joined his uncle in the east, or ended up as a refugee in Ireland, he would likely stay well fed, while those people on the edge of the Grote Markt would shiver and starve until this ungodly war ended, if that day ever came.

There were enough people on the street now that Jim made no attempt to conceal himself. If someone demanded his papers, he'd be in trouble, but curfew had lifted and there was no reason anyone would do so. He had to find Gaughran and trust that the Irish had some way of smuggling him out.

He found the bridge a few minutes later, stretching over the largest canal cutting through the center of Haarlem. Nobody was crossing as he approached. He climbed to the top and looked up and down the canal as well as into the streets on either side. Still nobody.

Dammit.

Now what? It was a green tie, right? Yes, yes of course. And Jim's note was clear enough. Yellow tie meant Gordon Gaughran had no interest in helping him. Green tie, and the diplomat from the officially neutral Irish Republic would meet him on this bridge with a plan to escape from the continent. The tie last night was green. It was the right bridge, the right time. So where was he?

Boots clomped in the deep shadows of the alleys on the other side of the canal. A voice laughed, said something in German. It was the two soldiers from before. Jim stood on the bridge, idling. Any moment they'd come out, mark his behavior as suspicious, and demand his papers.

"Heydrich!" a voice said. "Down here."

The man's voice came from the shadows beneath the bridge, and Jim leaned over to see a ledge a few feet wide where the bridge met the street. A homeless couple squatted on one side, wrapped in blankets up around their heads, paying no attention to the man in a long wool coat with a hat pulled over his eyes who gestured for Jim to come down.

"Who is that?"

"Who are you expecting?" the man said. An Irish accent. "Franklin Roosevelt? Now get down here before you get us both killed."

Jim's heart was still pounding as he came off the bridge, swung his legs over the edge of the canal and then slipped below. His eyes fought to pick out the features of the man standing in front of him. "Mr. Gaughran, is that you, old fellow? Or is it the president of the United States?"

"Quiet!"

Gaughran — if indeed that's who it was — squatted next to the pair of derelicts and pulled his collar up around his face. Boots sounded across the bridge overhead and Jim fell into the shadows with his back pressed against the slick, damp-smelling moss that grew on the brickwork beneath the bridge. Words in German caught his ear. "She has the face of a dog," one man said.

"A dog with mange, maybe," the other one said.

"Still, as my father always said, a poor man will eat a burnt crust and call it a feast."

"Ah, so the preference for ugly women runs in the family. What does your mother look like?"

"*Dumpfbacke*," the other man said, but the insult came out with a good-natured laugh.

The voices faded. Beneath the bridge, nobody moved for several seconds, and then one of the homeless pair stood and threw off the blanket. The second derelict slumped forward with his head twisted at an awkward angle. His pockets had been turned out, his jacket was missing, and his shirt torn and stained with blood across his gut, dripping. His eyes stared straight ahead, dark and glassy. White hair, mustache.

Dead. My God, it's Gaughran and he's dead.

Jim looked up in alarm to see the first man level a submachine gun at his chest. It was Nigel Burnside. His sister Margaret moved to his side, holding a knife which she was wiping clean on the edge of the blanket they'd wrapped Gaughran in.

"Hello again, *old fellow,*" Nigel said, his Irish accent gone.

CHAPTER FOUR

CHIEF INSPECTOR WULF KATTERMAN PAUSED outside the front door and wondered if he should draw his pistol first or simply knock. Success, he decided, depended upon respect for the law, not the superior application of force. He reached for the knocker.

Lieutenant Scholl put out a hand to stop him. "Perhaps we should..." He cleared his throat. "That is to say, we could write a strongly worded letter to the Gestapo District Headquarters."

"The evidence leads us to Fritz Wenck, does it not?" Katterman asked.

"Indeed, but—"

"And this sort of disgusting, depraved behavior is still a crime in Saxony, is it not? Indeed, throughout the Reich?"

"That's the part I'm not so sure about," Scholl said. "One hears stories."

"Yes, one hears stories."

Indeed, one heard the most awful sorts of stories, and it seemed to Katterman that there had never been a more lawless period in German history, with more examples of the egregious miscarriage of justice. If he needed a reminder, all he had to do was drive past the factory camps at Birkhahn and Amendorf where he saw the faces of hungry, resentful Poles staring back through the chain-link fences, where they worked and lived as virtual slaves. But they were foreigners and under SS control, and not his concern. Here in town itself, however, the old laws still applied. And the laws, as they now stood, did not permit even a man of Wenck's position to commit such heinous crimes without fear of prosecution.

"So perhaps it's not illegal after all," Scholl said. "For someone of Wenck's stature, that is."

"Thus necessitating your strongly worded letter to the Gestapo District Headquarters."

"Precisely." Scholl sounded relieved.

"I shall make note of your advice in the case file, that you suggested a complaint instead of arrest, due to the political status of the accused."

Katterman took the knocker and let it fall with a thundering boom. The door was solid oak, with a brass knocker the shape and size of a lion's head. He waited a few seconds and then let the knocker fall a second time. The door opened.

He expected to see Wenck's adjutant and was surprised to see a Gestapo agent in a black uniform with the rank of Obersturmbannführer — the SS equivalent rank of colonel. The man had red hair, cropped close to the skull, and a strawberry-blond mustache, walrus-like rather than the paintbrush style popular at the moment. He had a ruddy complexion, a square jaw, and sharp, intelligent eyes.

The man held out his hand. "I am Klaus Hossbach. Katterman and Scholl, is it?"

"Yes," Katterman said, surprised. "Were you expecting us?"

"Yes, of course, and I thought I should be here when

you came with your evidence. Sturmbannführer Wenck works under me, after all. I am fortunate this case came to my attention."

Katterman looked pointedly at Scholl, who must have been the informant, as Katterman hadn't taken anyone else into his confidence about the case. So Scholl had already taken his own advice and contacted someone within the Gestapo to tell them that an overeager local police inspector was sticking his nose into state affairs. Why? To curry favor or simply to save his own skin? Katterman studied Scholl's face, but the man wouldn't meet his gaze.

"Does this mean the case is already decided?" Katterman said to Hossbach. "That is, will Wenck be set free regardless of his guilt or innocence?"

"Let's hear your evidence first." The Gestapo agent gave a wolfish smile as he stepped aside for the two men to enter. "If you've got any."

Katterman entered and gestured for Scholl to follow. The man blanched, looking like he would rather be anywhere, even back at the morgue with the mutilated child's body, than entering Wenck's house. He only came when Hossbach turned his piercing gaze on the young lieutenant. Hossbach shut the door and the warmth enveloped them at once.

The door opened into a grand foyer decorated with Belgian tapestries, marble busts from Greece, and a melange of Dutch portraits and Byzantine iconography. There was a gilded grandfather clock and a sitting room to the left filled with a mixture of Wilhelm-era and Louis XIV furniture. Katterman had only entered the manor on one other occasion, and that was in 1923, during the inflation, when he was a young police inspector, coming at the request of the count in whose family the manor had remained for generations. The count lost the house at the height of the crisis, but it remained boarded and unoccupied until 1935, when it came into possession of Wenck, a man with wealth and power, but apparently little taste.

The library looked and smelled largely the same as it had under the count, except for a certain degree of Nazification. Leather-bound books filled the bookshelves that stretched to the second floor, where they could only be accessed by a rolling ladder. The count had mounted the heads of rhinoceros, lion, and other big game from his African safaris, but Wenck had replaced these with portraits of the Führer, a colorized photo of himself standing next to Heinrich Himmler and Reinhard Heydrich, and banners with swastikas, wolf-hooks, and other Nazi runic emblems. A fire cast off heat from the massive fireplace. There were four burgundy wing-backed chairs arranged in a half-moon in front of the fireplace, where Wenck sat in a silk robe, smoking a pipe and watching them enter with the smug expression of a man who believes himself untouchable. He was a tall man, and he draped over the chair with the lean, muscular ease of a great cat.

A servant with white gloves took Katterman and Scholl's jackets, at which point Wenck told them to sit down. Scholl moved to obey, but Katterman put a hand on his arm to stop him. "We prefer to stand."

"Of course you would," Wenck said. "Easier to run for your life that way. Want your coats back so you can get a head start?"

"Yes, let us send for all the coats. Yours as well as ours. Do you need time to dress before I take you to jail?"

"Jail?" Wenck laughed. "Did you hear that? Jail!"

"Please," Hossbach said. "Sit down, Inspector Katterman. Nothing will happen until we've had a chance to hear the evidence."

"I'll deliver my evidence to the magistrate," Katterman said. "We only came here to arrest the major, not to debate the facts of the case."

"I'm not, uhm, not sure that is entirely accurate," Lieutenant Scholl said. "We know you are busy men, and perhaps this is not the best time. If we could —"

Hossbach held up his hand. "Scholl, why don't you leave? This doesn't concern you."

It most certainly did concern the lieutenant, and Katterman wanted a witness should these men murder him or take him into protective custody. But Scholl leaped to his feet, and over Katterman's objections Wenck called for his manservant, who returned with Scholl's coat. Moments later, he disappeared toward the front door, leaving Katterman behind.

"I had no idea Scholl could be so craven," he mused out loud. "Never mind. The law is on my side. And my lieutenant knows of my intent to arrest Herr Wenck for the murder of Lisle Zansen. Should anything happen to me, others will take up the case."

"Others have *already* taken up the case," Hossbach said. He touched a folded piece of paper on the end table next to his chair. "These are my orders. They give me extrajudicial control of this situation. If you have an objection to how I wish to proceed, it is with the law of the Reich, which means that your objection is to the Führer himself. Do you understand? Good, now sit down. That is an order."

Katterman obeyed. Hossbach took his own seat

between the inspector and the accused. Wenck puffed from his pipe and looked into the fire as if bored by this whole affair. The servant came a few moments later with a tray that held snifters of whiskey. Katterman took his with reluctance, pretended to take a sip, and then set the drink on the end table.

"Now," Hossbach said. "I've heard about the atrocity and I understand you believe the major is the guilty party. And I find myself wondering why you'd bother."

Katterman blinked. "Bother? A young girl died under horrific circumstances. I'm the chief investigator in Halle-Merseburg for non-political crimes — it's my duty to solve the case. My investigation has led me here. What else would you have me do?"

"You have no evidence," Wenck said. He set down the pipe and took up the snifter, but still didn't bother looking in the direction of the other two men. "This is politically motivated. This man is a communist. I denounce him."

"I have no political motivations. I pursue justice and enforce the law. The law continues to prohibit the sexual assault and murder of children, even by a man highly placed within the regime. Herr Wenck is guilty and I intend to see justice done."

"Rubbish," Wenck said. He started to say something else, but Hossbach cleared his throat and the major fell silent.

Hossbach said, "I have seen photos of the body. Nasty, awful business. But why do you think this man did it?"

"I don't have my evidence files. I didn't expect to need them."

"You don't need the files. Give me your evidence. I'll

hear you out."

"Very well," Katterman said. "Lisle Zansen disappeared on October 11, 1941. The community organized a massive search that failed to find the girl. She was last seen hunting for mushrooms in the woods outside this man's estate."

"Lots of people search those woods for mushrooms," Wenck said. "And anyway, you know she wasn't found anywhere near my land."

"Go on," Hossbach said.

"We found the body six weeks later, stuffed into a barrel in the basement of the old textile mill."

"Ten miles from my property. As I said, nowhere near here."

"Quiet, please," Hossbach said. His lips drew into a thin line and Wenck fell silent. "And I understand that the cold had preserved the child's body."

That was accurate, Katterman agreed. He continued. Community suspicion fell on the usual suspects: a mentally defective farm boy, an old man once accused of molesting children, even Gypsies said to be camped in the ruins of a castle in the woods. Katterman's own gaze turned toward those most likely to have committed the crime. He looked first at the girl's father, and then at other relatives and neighbors, and finally to where the girl had last been seen. At last, he found a tantalizing trail of clues.

The crime had not been covered very well, as if the perpetrator had been either a stupid man or a powerful one, convinced he could not be implicated for the murder of a peasant girl who local gossip had was one-quarter Italian anyhow. A boot print found in the woods near where the girl disappeared was matched with a boot print near the mill. The print was notable for both its large size — and here Katterman noted with satisfaction that Hossbach's gaze drifted down to Wenck's slippered feet — and the good repair of the boot's sole. How many men in the district had the money or connections to acquire new footwear these days? Generally they were executives or SS officers at the factories.

"A boot?" Hossbach said. "Is that all?"

"No, there is more. Two men spotted Herr Wenck riding on his estate that day, less than a mile from where the girl disappeared. A third man positively identified Wenck's Horch Cabriolet at the old mill on two separate occasions between the girl's disappearance and the discovery of her body."

"Who are these men?" Wenck demanded. "Where are these liars?"

"They remain anonymous."

Wenck sneered. "We'll see about that. I'll bet one is that idiot who works at the mill. The retired night guard they kept on to chase off vandals — what's his name? The old fool is nearly blind, everyone knows that. And stone deaf, too."

"Go on," Hossbach said.

"I corroborated this second testimony with tire tracks found at the mill that matched the cabriolet. I took the liberty of making a cast and taking photographs last week when Wenck's driver brought the vehicle in for service." Katterman didn't mention that he'd arranged for defective petrol to be delivered to the Wenck estate in order to assure timely engine troubles.

"As for motive," he continued, "there was a complaint filed against Fritz Wenck in 1927 when he was a pupil in the gymnasium. A schoolmaster caught him molesting a younger student. In 1931, when he was attending Reinhard Heydrich's SS-Junkerschule in Bad-Toelz, he was almost expelled when he was accused of raping a child. The mother of the child was a war widow and later withdrew her complaint. I suspect Wenck's father paid her off. He was a member of the Reichstag."

"Slander and lies," Wenck said.

"I am aware of these accusations," Hossbach said. "But he was never officially charged with a crime or expelled from the party. Just this past year, Heinrich Himmler awarded him the SS-honor ring for his service in Moravia. He has also acquired commendations from Rudolph Diels and Reinhard Heydrich. Not many men can say that."

"I'm not sure that the recommendations of highly placed men within this particular regime are a mark of a man's moral standing."

"Be careful, Katterman," Hossbach said. His voice held a dangerous edge. "I wouldn't follow that path if I were you."

"I apologize, colonel," Katterman said. "And politics are not my concern, in any event. But let me continue. In addition to the aforementioned accusations, we have two similar, unsolved crimes in the district—a nine-year-old girl who disappeared from the village in 1936 and a ten-year-old girl who disappeared in 1938. Their bodies were never found, but I have acquired proof that Wenck purchased large quantities of sulfuric acid within three weeks of each disappearance. He purchased acid on a third occasion in 1937, I suspect to dispose of a third body, although I cannot find record of another missing child."

"And did he acquire sulfuric acid this time?"

Hossbach asked.

"I do not know, but he certainly has access. He is over the forced labor at the Amendorf factory, which manufactures mustard gas and other war chemicals. We were fortunate to discover the body before he had a chance."

Wenck got up from his chair with a snort and walked over to stand in front of the fire with his back turned to the two men. "Let me know when this farce is over."

"So you think Wenck has been killing children for some time?" Hossbach asked. "Have there been any other disappearances or complaints since 1938?"

"No, but the major was posted in Prague from the spring of '39 until July of 1941, when he received his latest promotion and returned to Saxony. Who knows what crimes he committed while under the military regime of Bohemia-Moravia." Katterman rose to his feet and walked over to where Wenck stood with his back turned. The other man towered over him and Katterman felt the comforting weight of his sidearm. "So you see," he said in a low voice, "there is little doubt that Fritz Wenck is guilty of not just one, but several murders of young children. As for Lisle Zansen, the evidence suggests that he used her sexually both before and after he strangled her with his bare hands."

Wenck turned with a snarl. He snatched the iron poker from next to the hearth and brought it around like a club at the inspector's head. Katterman had carefully kept distance between himself and his suspect, but between the taller man's long reach and the poker, he had miscalculated. The weapon, he could already see, would crush him a blow across the skull.

He couldn't remember drawing his Walther, but

suddenly it was in his hand. He must have reached for it even before issuing his final denunciation. He fired three times. Wenck jerked like a skewered boar. The poker fell from his hand and clattered to the flagstones. His hand slammed back against the hearth and pulled down the fire screen on top of him as he fell. Wenck slid off the edge of the hearth and came to a final rest on the floor in front of the fireplace. The fire screen fell across his face, and the smell of charred meat rose into the air.

Obersturmbannführer Hossbach rose to stand by Katterman's side. He looked down at the body with a thoughtful expression. "Unfortunate, but he really was a monster, wasn't he?" He looked at the gun in the other man's hand. "You can put that away, inspector."

Katterman did as he was told. "Should I go home and wait for the Gestapo, or would you like to arrest me now? I have done my duty and will not resist. If given a chance, I will explain why I found it necessary to confront the man."

"You already explained." Hossbach bent and pried something from Wenck's right hand, and then handed it to Katterman. It was a silver ring decorated with the totenkopf — the death's head — wreathed with oak leaves, and elaborated with the swastika, the sig, the hagal, and the double rune.

Katterman rubbed his thumb against a fresh scratch in the silver from where Wenck had flailed against the edge of the fireplace as he fell. It was a sinister, ugly thing. "This is the ring Himmler and Heydrich gave him?"

"That's right." Hossbach retrieved the ring and pocketed it. "The SS-honor ring. Himmler will want it back." He looked around the room, at the busts and the tapestries and the paintings on the wall. "I find myself appalled by so much wealth, both acquired and displayed in such a vulgar manner. Let's find somewhere else to speak."

"If you wish," Katterman said.

The servant appeared at the head of the library. If he was shocked to see his master lying dead on the flagstones, it didn't show. Hossbach took Katterman's elbow and led him away. "The manservant works for me. He is prepared to dispose of the body."

"You already knew this would happen?"

"It was not unexpected. Scholl sent a strongly worded letter to Gestapo district headquarters."

"I shouldn't have trusted him."

"Don't be too hard on the young man. He left enough hints that I took the liberty of inspecting your files and saw for myself that Wenck was guilty."

"Then Wenck was right. It was a farce."

"How so?" Hossbach asked.

"If you knew, why didn't you have him arrested and tried for murder?"

"The court system is not my preferred method. Once I'm convinced of guilt, there is no reason to delay justice." They entered the main hall and made their way toward the front door. Their coats lay across the Louis XIV divan in the sitting room, and they put them on. "Besides," Hossbach continued, "Fritz Wenck was incidental to my visit. What I really came for was to see how you operate. I was pleased to see you dispatch Wenck so efficiently. You goaded him into an attack and then gunned him down without remorse. Very effective."

"That isn't exactly what—wait, you came to see *me*? Whatever for?"

"I am pursuing a suspect of much greater worth—

you might say infinite worth — to the Reich. But he is also more dangerous and better protected than Sturmbannführer Fritz Wenck." Hossbach opened the front door and gestured for Katterman to follow him into the dark winter night. "And I think you might be the man to bring him in."

CHAPTER FIVE

J IM CAME TO WITH A cough. His head pounded and he squinted at the shards of light that poured in through a window to his right. His stomach churned and he thought he was going to be sick.

"He's coming around," a man's voice said.

"Close the blinds," a woman answered.

The light diminished, but Jim's eyes still wouldn't focus and he felt like he was swirling around consciousness, unable to fully awaken, and not entirely certain that this wasn't a bad dream. But then someone shoved something beneath his nose and noxious fumes hit him like a bucket of ice water to the face. He sputtered and coughed and tried to back away. A hand withdrew and screwed the lid back onto the bottle that was giving off the smell.

Gradually, as he grew more alert, he recognized the gentle sway beneath him and the clack of wheels on rail tracks. Nigel and Margaret sat across from him in the private train compartment. Nigel's face had the iron expression he'd worn beneath the bridge, while Margaret looked disgusted, as if she'd discovered something foul stuck to the bottom of her shoe. They had changed clothing, Margaret into a trim gray dress with black leather gloves, and Nigel into a tan suit with his jacket laid carefully across his lap, his right hand beneath. He had a gun hidden there, Jim guessed.

"Let me put it to you straight," Nigel said. "Answer our questions and you might live. Or you might not. It depends on your answers. Realize, too, that Margaret wants to kill you now. She thinks bringing you onto the train was a mistake. She says we should have cut your throat and dumped you into the canal with the other guy."

Jim tried to clear the cotton taste from his mouth. "By other guy, you mean Gaughran, the Irish diplomat?"

Those last few moments beneath the bridge crawled up from the depths of his memory, blurred, as if he'd been drinking hard the night before. After Nigel leveled the gun at Jim's chest, Margaret tied a block of cement to Gaughran's ankles and pushed him into the canal. He sank and didn't come back up. Jim was still trying to decide if he should scream for help when she wheeled on him and kneed him in the groin. Nigel slapped a rag over his face and then he couldn't remember anything more, only swooning, and then blackness. How had they got him on the train while unconscious?

His hands tingled painfully. They were bound behind his back. They'd bound his feet, too, and a gag sat next to him in the fourth, empty seat of the train compartment. If he screamed for help, would someone hear him before the gag came up? Possibly. But he wouldn't be sitting here without complicity from officials at the station and on the train. It appeared that these two were not merely Nazi-sympathizers, but full-blown spies for the Reich.

"Now talk," Nigel said.

"Talk about what? Okay, I admit it. It was me who was putting on Margaret's unmentionables. But I have no idea where those used condoms came from. I'm allergic to sheepskin."

Margaret leaned over and slapped him across the face. His head rocked back and he gasped in pain. What the hell was that, a lead lining in her gloves? And the hard look in her eyes matched the weight in her gloves. He could scarcely believe that this was the same young woman who giggled and pranced her way across the stage or flirted with government officials and Gestapo agents. For the first time, he was alert enough to realize the depth of his trouble.

"Listen to me carefully," Nigel said. "You will speak when spoken to. I ask the questions, not you. Do you understand?"

Jim stared back without answer. He was terrified, but didn't see any good in admitting it.

"And no more clever answers, you understand? Well, do you?"

Jim refused to respond. He braced himself for another blow, but it didn't come.

"Why were you spying on us last night?" Nigel asked.

"I wasn't spying on you."

"No, then what were you doing?"

"If you must know, I went to the roof to radio my review to the Times. I'm afraid I panned the show. Your performance was wooden, and I don't buy your motivation in that scene with the hippopotamus."

This time he was prepared for the attack and tried to duck out of the way before Margaret hit him. But he was still sluggish, and she moved faster than he thought possible. His head rocked back again, and the pain rang all the way into his ears.

"Damn you!" he said.

"Easy," Nigel said. "We might need him unbruised."

"I didn't hit him that hard."

"You bloody well did," Jim said. He flinched in anticipation of another attack, but Nigel grabbed Margaret's hand before she could hit him.

"Listen, old fellow," Nigel said. "I'm trying to help you out here, but you're making my job difficult."

"You'd be difficult, too, if your friends turned on you. Fine, you want to know? I went to tell you I was leaving. That's what I was doing on the roof, you bastard."

"Curious timing. And curious how you sat there quietly instead of announcing your presence." Nigel shook his head. "You don't flee the city in the middle of the night, you don't make a secret rendezvous with foreigners, if you're not playing a game. Now I want to know what it is. Why were you spying on us?"

"Go to hell."

"So that's the way you'll play it."

"I can say 'go to hell' in German or French if that will help you understand."

"Very well." Nigel sighed and rose to his feet. He put on his jacket and tucked what looked like a gun into his inner pocket. "I'll be waiting in the dining car," he said to Margaret. "Come get me when you finish." He reached for the door handle.

Margaret smiled and reached a hand into her pocket.

Panic took hold of Jim. "Wait! I'll talk, I'll tell you everything. Just listen to me."

Nigel hesitated. "I don't know, is it even worth the hassle? How do I know you'll come clean?"

"Tell her to stop hitting me and I'll tell you everything I know."

Nigel came back in and shut the door again, locked it.

He nodded at Margaret. "That's enough for now."

She shrugged her response.

"Let's try something different," Nigel said. "How do you know Gordon Gaughran?"

"I met him in Amsterdam before the war. We were part of the same English-speaking expat community for a few months. Gaughran once had too much to drink at a party and made impolitic remarks about the Nazis. I remembered that when Europe hit an iceberg and started taking on water. Ireland seemed like a good place for a drowning rat to climb ashore."

"And why did you leave Canada? Your father lost his job or something?"

"Are you trying to trip me up? It's not made up — I'll tell it the same way every time. Father was too pro-German, too pro-fascist. He made enemies at the university, and my uncle's letters didn't help matters. My mother resisted for a while. In the end, she gave in."

"But why Holland?" Nigel asked.

"I told you that a long time ago."

"And I forgot."

"You didn't pick up something from that French dancing girl, did you? I've heard syphilis can go to the brain."

An edge of anger hit Nigel's voice. "Don't toy with me."

"It wasn't as easy to come back as we'd thought. There was some struggle within the SD or the SS at the time. Someone had accused Uncle Reinhard of having a Jewish ancestor — politically motivated, of course — and he needed to resolve it before bringing us back to the glories of the Third Reich. That, and we needed to build up our shoulder muscles for all that saluting."

"And you were making contact with Irish diplomats, too, apparently."

"Oh, I see. You think my father was a spy. Of course not. He—" Jim stopped, suddenly unsure. There had been a lot of contact with Gaughran, but very little with the Irish legation itself. His father, especially, spent a good deal of time at private parties with the diplomatic staff of various countries. It was a frantic time, with everybody hearing the heavy footfalls of war, but the upper classes formed a coherent expat community in capital cities, both in Europe and North America. It was a polyglot fraternity that kept its own rules and made its own narrative. Even the Germans, in the long, painful process of Nazification, had plenty of old blood, the career diplomats and businessmen who couldn't imagine that Western Civilization would be so clumsy as to stumble into another disastrous conflict.

A curious look spread across Nigel's face. He turned to Margaret. "I do believe he's only now putting together the pieces. Tell me, Jim. Why were you meeting Gaughran last night?"

"My uncle summoned me to Prague to work with him in the occupation government. I don't want to go, so I asked Gaughran to smuggle me out of Europe. I thought he might do it as a favor to my parents. He said he would." Jim licked his lips. "My uncle will be looking for me. He sent a staff car this morning to pick me up at the hotel."

"As it turned out, he has been summoned himself, and is on his way to Berlin for some important conference. A man delivered a message to the hotel this morning. You have ten more days and you are to find your way to Prague yourself. Tell me, how did you get to Haarlem?"

Jim explained how he'd purchased and hid the bicycle, how he'd planned his escape from the theater, how he'd improvised when things went wrong. Margaret raised an eyebrow at how he'd huddled with the refugees on the Grote Markt, but overall they seemed to accept his story. They stopped him once when someone knocked twice on the door, and Nigel knocked three times in return, and then urged him to continue.

When Jim finished, Nigel turned to Margaret. "It appears that we have been lucky."

"Lucky by ten days," she said. "We can't let him fall into Heydrich's hands. Even if Jim is telling the truth, he's a naive boob and not particularly bright. He'll blab."

"Ten days is enough time to settle matters."

"And what about Gaughran?" she asked. "Did he tell anyone? Surely he did. The trail will lead back to us rather quickly, don't you think?"

"The two services don't talk. Heydrich might never find out. And if he does, it will take time to work its way through the system. With any luck, we'll be in Italy by then."

"What are you talking about?" Jim asked. "Wait, you're not working for the Gestapo, are you?"

Margaret snorted. "Like I said, not particularly bright."

"You thought he was bright enough when you had him working for the SD," Nigel said. "You thought he was a master spy."

"I'm not a spy," Jim said. "I'm only an actor."

"And not a very good one," she said.

"Like that flouncing you do across the stage is high art?" Jim said. "Besides, either of you would have done the same thing in my shoes. Obviously, I was right not to tell anyone."

"You *did* tell someone," Nigel said. "The wrong someone. Fortunately for you, Gordon Gaughran wasn't working for the SD — that would be the Sicherheitsdienst, your uncle's spy network — but for German military intelligence, the Abwehr. It is a slightly less evil, slightly less competent parallel structure within the German regime. But don't fool yourself. If you'd fallen into the hands of the Abwehr, things would have gone poorly for you. Maybe your father has pull, maybe not, but at best, you'd have been used as a tool against your uncle. No doubt they would subject you to rather stern interrogations to get everything out of you. The kind of interrogation that would make Margaret's slaps look like love tickles."

"Why would Gaughran do that? The Irish are neutral."

"Officially. Unofficially, they're about one-third neutral, one-third pro-Allies, and one-third pro-Axis. Rather, not so much pro-Axis as anti-British. Gaughran's father died in the Irish troubles. Gaughran labored under the delusion that he would be set up as military dictator after Britain capitulated. No doubt the Germans made him promises they did not intend to keep."

Margaret said, "We have about five minutes until Arnhem. Last chance to ditch this one. After that, they'll want to see papers at the German border."

Jim didn't like the sound of being "ditched." He suspected Margaret meant that in a rather literal way, that he'd be taken off the platform, murdered, and stripped of anything that might identify his body to the authorities. "I'm an actor, remember? I can play along in whatever you're doing."

"I don't think so," Nigel said. "You're an amateur." He slid the shade open. The terrain was still flat outside. The train rolled along at a leisurely pace, and it felt like they were slowing. Trim brick buildings rose along the canal, their roofs glistening white with frost. A man pulled a handcart and two girls in wooden shoes carried baskets on their heads. They watched the train as it passed.

"Nigel?" Margaret said.

"Don't punish me for being in the wrong place at the wrong time," Jim said. "Listen, our next shows are in Florence, right? Get me a little money. The Italians are easily bribed. I'll disappear and you'll never hear from me again. By the time you get back to German-controlled territory, I'll be off your hands. No more worries."

"Here's the stop," Margaret said. "Hurry up and decide."

"Maybe it's safer to take care of matters now," Nigel said, "but I don't have the stomach for it."

"We have other worries than your delicate constitution."

"And you want to do it? Kill him in cold blood?"

She hesitated, and then sighed. "Very well." She moved to the empty seat by Jim's side and twisted his hands around to get at the knots, which she began to untie. "If that's what you want to do, you'd better start improvising."

Margaret had the cords off his hands and feet by the time the train screeched into the station, puffing smoke and blowing its whistle. Nigel and Margaret made their way into the aisle while Jim remained inside the compartment, rubbing circulation back into his hands and looking out the window at the shabbily dressed families who boarded second-class cars further up the line. Lula Larouche and Ursula Becher stepped onto the platform to stretch their legs while smoking.

Were they all in on it? Had he been traipsing around

Europe for the past year with a bunch of spies? How in God's name did a bunch of native English speakers and others who spoke the language without foreign accent manage to avoid the attentions of the Gestapo?

But to ask the question was to answer it. Why, *Jim* was the answer. His father was a spy with Abwehr and his uncle the head of the SD and military ruler of Eastern Europe. It made Jim almost untouchable. They were traveling under *his* protection. He was their cover.

And once he realized that, he understood two things. First, that he'd never been in particular danger from Nigel and Margaret Burnside. Second, that they sure as hell wouldn't let him slip away in Italy, because if they did, their spy games would come to an end.

CHAPTER SIX

J IM NEEDED TIME TO PLAN his escape strategy, so he
played his part as the train left Holland and rolled
into Germany. He was first off the train, and he showed
his papers to the border guards, joked with an officer
who asked if he was related to *Reinhard* Heydrich.
*Why yes, he's my uncle, as a matter of fact. Can we have
the first-class service or do I need to send a telegraph to the
SS-Obergruppenführer?* He said this with a smile, and the
officer laughed. Jim noticed that the inspection of both
the passengers of the private car and their documents and
personal belongings passed with only cursory attention.
The soldiers even helped unload luggage and move it to
the next platform.

The cast and crew milled about on the train platform,
smoking, sitting on steamer trunks and footlockers,
waiting for the Lyon-bound train. Every once in a while
a uniformed guard would come to practice his English on
Lula or Margaret. The latter played her coquettish role,
touching their arms and laughing with delight at any silly
thing they told her. Kyle Dunleavy pulled out a German
phrasebook and chatted with a group of soldiers. The
Germans grinned and laughed at his abysmal German.
Jim was gregarious by nature and might have sidled
over to needle his cast mate, but he was of a mood to

observe. He started to lean against a sign before he saw the warning letters in German, Dutch, and French.

HALT!
Wer Weiter Geht Wird Erschossen!
Wie Verder Gaat Wort Doodgeschoten!
Qui Dépasse Cette Limite Sera Fusillé!

Move beyond this line and be shot!

A soldier with a submachine gun scowled at him on the other side of a painted red line, while other soldiers pushed a half dozen shackled British airmen in torn and filthy uniforms toward a prison car at the back of the train. One of the prisoners wore a blood-soaked bandage around his eyes.

Jim glanced at Nigel for his reaction. The man stood ten or fifteen feet away reading a copy of *Das Reich,* and didn't glance either at him or the British airmen.

More drama played out farther up. An elderly couple shared a tearful separation. The cuffs of the man's pants and shirt were dirty and worn and he wore safety pins in place of two buttons. The woman wore layer after layer of clothing and struggled with a single, stuffed carpet bag. Her husband tried to help her carry it, but he didn't have a ticket and they wouldn't let him onto the platform. He wouldn't stop arguing and a soldier knocked off his hat. When the man reached for it with shaking, blue-veined hands, the soldier kicked it away. Jim ignored Nigel's warning scowl and helped the old woman wrestle her bag down to the platform. Soldiers rifled through the bag, but at that moment Jim's attention fell on an altercation near the ticket booth on the opposite side of the tracks. A man with four small children raised his voice, waving papers at an unsmiling woman behind the metal grille who snapped her fingers. Two guards with submachine guns broke off from their chat with Dunleavy, faces growing stern. They pointed and made threatening gestures.

"Some people don't know enough to keep their mouths shut," a voice said over Jim's shoulder. It was Margaret, her smile bright and pretty — her *public* face, he thought of it now — but her tone suspicious.

"He must have been desperate," Jim said.

"He's more desperate now, poor bastard. Look."

The man was still carrying on and suddenly one of the soldiers snatched away his papers, folded them, and put them in his jacket pocket. Too late, the man's tone turned supplicant, and he looked back at his children where they remained in a cold, huddled knot near the ticket window, as if only now realizing that he was responsible for four other people. Two more guards came up behind him and jabbed him with their gun barrels. When he resisted, one of them shoved him forward. He sprawled, they dragged him to his feet, and ordered him to get moving. A woman in a gray uniform stepped from the offices behind the ticket window, bent and spoke to the children, who stared after their father. The youngest one began to cry.

"Bring them with me!" the father cried out in German. "Please, for the love of God."

"Dammit," Jim said.

"Stay where you are," Margaret said. "There's nothing you can do."

He had started forward, but checked himself. The soldiers hustled the man through the crowd, which parted fearfully, and then forced him through the doors and out of sight. The hole carved through the crowd closed again and all was silent. His eyes followed the female guard as she led the children in the opposite direction. He reminded himself that he didn't know what was going on with this particular drama. Maybe the man was recently divorced and trying to make off with his children without the permission of his ex-wife. It could be something like that. Yes, hopefully.

"It's been this way all along, hasn't it?" he asked.

"What, this is the first time you've noticed that train stations and border crossings are exciting places?"

"Of course not. There were those Jews in Brussels. And that Polish guy last year they dragged off our car and shot. Hard to miss that."

"And yet?" she said.

He wanted to say more, but grew cautious, unwilling to give away the thoughts that had stirred since he woke in the train compartment with his hands bound. He was reframing the entire course of his experience with the theater troupe. It wasn't only the way they criss-crossed Europe with such ease, it was every step of his involvement, beginning with his recruitment in Halle an der Saale. It had seemed innocent at the time. Now, he was not so sure.

To begin with, the Canadian branch of the Heydrich family couldn't have picked a worse time to return to Father's home town. Three weeks after leaving Amsterdam, German negotiations with the French and British broke down, there was a border incident with the Poles, and the Wehrmacht swept into Poland. Even in their quiet corner of Saxony, war fever swept through the town. By the time the Germans invaded France the next summer—coincidentally on Jim's 20th birthday, May 10, 1940—he couldn't step into the street without some stranger telling him to do his patriotic duty. Teenage girls flirted with him, but their interest evaporated the instant they learned he was not a soldier on leave from the front. The nine-year-old neighbor kid called him a coward, a pair of Hitler Youth threw rocks at their windows, and a bent old man accosted him one day when he came out of Mass. The man claimed he'd fought in the Franco-Prussian war. That had to be what, almost seventy years ago?

"Them French ladies is very accommodating," he said with a wink. "Very accommodating." And then, when Jim tried to pull away, he leaned in and added on sour breath, "Better to join up than face conscription, son, believe me."

Jim's mother deflected criticism by claiming they were still trying to resolve citizenship. Born in Silesia, she'd moved with her parents to Toronto at the age of ten, and found the war hysteria bewildering. Fighting Poles and French was one thing, but war against British and Commonwealth troops? Who, for God's sake, thought that was a good idea?

And then one day a man showed up in town who Jim knew from the University of Ottawa. An upperclassman when Jim was a freshman, Hans von Steidle had been both the president of the German-Canadian Friendship Club — a beer-swilling fraternity that devolved into factional brawling by the time Jim left two years later — and an amateur thespian who goofed around on- and offstage in the theater department. He was also an accomplished rower and high jumper. Jim didn't go out much for sports, apart from skiing. He barely knew the guy.

But Hans acted as if they'd been best friends in college

and dragged him to the beer garden to chat about old times. After he toasted the Führer and made a second, sarcastic toast to King George, Hans said in English, "Can't believe you're not in France, getting ready to invade Old Blighty."

Jim stared glumly into his beer. "I'll be there soon enough. Either there, or in the blasted Gestapo with my uncle."

"I heard about old Heydrich. Hell of a family you got there, buddy." He raised an eyebrow. "All the more reason they'll want you in London. English speaker, nephew of the SS-Obergruppenführer. Could be exciting. First invasion since 1066. They'll speak your name in the same breath as William the Conqueror some day."

"Hah. Believe me, that is the last thing I want."

"Hmm. So you're not interested in the war? Or is some Canadian gal still tugging your heartstrings?"

Jim was not so big a fool as to express sympathy for the enemy, and he didn't answer. There was no girl, not at that time anyway, but it was true that the thought of fighting Canadians (or even Brits or Aussies, for that matter), was depressing beyond measure. Hans quaffed the last of his beer and waved for the barmaid. "*Zwei weitere Biere, bitte.*" He pinched her bottom as she left, and laughed at the exasperated look she gave him in return.

"What about you?" Jim said. "You're what? Twenty-four, twenty-five? Don't tell me you're sitting on the sidelines."

"Unfortunately not. I have, in fact, been called up. Bloody conscription."

"Wehrmacht? Kriegsmarine? Luftwafte?"

"No, nothing like that. You think I'd be drinking beer and pinching shapely bottoms if I were? There's a war in

France, you know—last I heard the army is sixty miles from Paris."

It was true, wasn't it? It was surreal, sitting in the warm sun, with honey bees buzzing among the purple wisteria that grew from cracks in the ancient stone wall to their backs. At the next table sat several veterans of the Great War in their uniforms and medals toasting the Führer, while at another table, two elderly men with bushy white mustaches and wearing lederhosen—the kind of men who brought their own steins to a beer garden—played chess with shiny wooden pieces. Three nuns sat at another table, sipping foam from half-pint glasses of lager. The war seemed quite distant.

Hans chuckled. "No, I wouldn't be here. I'd be with those poor blighters getting killed on the front."

"Oh, I see."

"No worries, mate, it's not the Gestapo, either, if that's what you're getting at," Hans said. "At least not directly. It's certainly a better gig than taking your chances as cannon fodder." The beer arrived and he switched temporarily to German. "You know, there's a chance I could get you on board, too. It's right up your alley, now that I think about it. You were one of my best college mates—putting your name forward is the least I could do."

Jim thought about his recruitment as Nigel and Margaret herded him onto the new train. None of what had happened had been what it seemed. It was twenty months behind him now, a period that saw the capitulation of France and the Low Countries, a delayed invasion of Britain, the remarkable assault on the Soviet Union, and now, in the past few weeks, the entrance of the Americans in the war. These last two developments struck him as fairly ominous, but he had to admit that things seemed to be going well on the Eastern Front, so maybe he was overly pessimistic. In any event, he'd stayed well-fed, well-rested, and largely out of harm's way, all thanks to Hans von Steidle, a man he'd never seen again.

But he had seen Nigel Burnside, who arrived in Halle an der Saale two weeks later that same summer, looking for him. There weren't many Englishmen roaming Germany in the summer of 1940. Those few left on the continent were, in fact, trying to flee Dunkirk, from what they boasted on the news reels. Nigel had a remarkable offer, an opportunity so fortunate, so wonderful, that if Jim hadn't been such close friends with Hans von Steidle, the theater company's patron in the Reich's Ministry of Public Enlightenment and Propaganda, it would have gone to a more experienced actor. Jim tried not to act overeager, and he certainly did not mention that he'd only been Hans's casual acquaintance in Canada, that maybe time and nostalgia had built the relationship into something bigger than it had been. No, he wasn't dumb enough to say that. Besides, that would be ungenerous. And Nigel soon became a genuine friend, the best he'd had since leaving Canada. Or so it had seemed at the time. He didn't recognize this hard-faced stranger who now shared his train compartment.

Later that day, the train crossed the border into France. The rail yard at Pont-à-Mousson was a mess of twisted, smoking tracks, and the train sat for three hours before it finally chugged out of the station. He caught

Nigel looking at his wristwatch with a scowl.

"Are we supposed to have a show on Thursday?" Jim asked.

"Yes. I don't want to cancel. It would be a disaster."

"You seem more anxious than usual. It's not like the delay was unexpected."

Nigel grunted. Margaret said, "Our friend has been thinking."

"Oh, has he?"

"You knew all along, didn't you?" Jim said. "Hans von Steidle didn't just run into me that day in Halle, did he? Old college chum — hah! I barely knew the guy. What an ass I was."

"Read your book, Jim," Nigel said. "Better yet, run your lines. You're my understudy. Could you go onstage Thursday as Lord Goring?"

"We might have to cancel, remember?"

"We're not canceling. And if I were you, I'd doublecheck those lines."

"Why, is there a reason why you might not make the show? Nobody is going to break your leg, are they?"

"Jim," Margaret said. "This ends badly, you know that. You keep pushing and — "

She stopped as someone knocked on the compartment door. Nigel unlatched it and Kyle Dunleavy leaned his head in. He was a young, handsome man with a Victorian-style mustache and, together with Nigel, one of the leading men of their production of *An Ideal Husband,* playing the role of Sir Robert Chiltern. Dunleavy played a sympathetic character onstage, a warm, cheery sort off it, but when rehearsals went poorly he turned stiffer than a Prussian Junker dipped in plaster of Paris. Dunleavy was Scottish on his father's side — his father was an ace in the last pointless European slaughter, shot down near the front lines, and then pitchforked to death by Flemish farmers enraged that his downed Sopwith Camel was presently burning their farmhouse to the ground. Kyle's mother remarried, and the boy spent the rest of his childhood in India, British Africa, and later, German-controlled Windhoek, where he took on German citizenship without ever learning the language.

Or so went the story; Jim was no longer sure of anything he'd heard about these people.

"We're going to run lines with the new fellow," Kyle said. Hints of Scottish brogue and boarding-school English came through in his accent, with the odd North American idiom creeping into his vocabulary. "Margaret, fancy coming down to the lounge car for a spell?"

"What new fellow?" Jim asked.

"Our new Lord Caversham. He boarded the train in Metz. You've not met him yet?"

"No, I didn't hear what happened. Is Janssen out for good, then?"

"Afraid so," Nigel said. "Far as I know he's still at the hospital. Hell of a way to go. He's lucky the sandbag didn't land on his head."

It was all Jim could do not to raise a skeptical eyebrow. "Sandbag?"

Dunleavy gave a disappointed shake of the head. "One of the pulleys jammed. I don't know what possessed him to take the curtain down himself. That is what the stage crew is for. Anyway, we are running act 4," he told Jim, "but you are welcome to come down if you would like to meet the chap. He has his lines memorized already, if you can believe that, but his accent needs work. Lula said she'd tackle that."

"You two go on," Nigel said. "Jim and I are talking about understudy stuff."

Margaret rose hastily to her feet and pushed Dunleavy into the hallway, while Nigel pulled the compartment door shut after them and latched it again.

"Who is this new guy?" Jim asked.

"An actor from Hungary. Nothing special, but he was available. Finished up some cabaret thing in France and was on his way home to Budapest. We were lucky."

"That *does* sound lucky. Almost an amazing coincidence, in fact."

"It's better to accept the story at face value," Nigel said.

"Is Dunleavy in on it, too? Janssen knew. I'm guessing Lula, since the two of you were lovers last year. Is there anyone in the cast and crew besides me who *doesn't* know?"

"Very few know. They go about their business, oblivious. Pretend you're one of them, and you'll be fine."

Fine? Jim didn't believe that. It was a stroke of luck that called his uncle back to Berlin, or he'd be lying at the bottom of a Dutch canal with Gordon Gaughran. But that was a reprieve of a few days. Nigel and Margaret wouldn't let him go off to Prague to work for the head of the SS spy network, a man he was related to by blood. And if he escaped, if he found a way to tell the authorities his plight, not only would they crush the theater company, guilty and innocent alike, Jim would still find himself working with Uncle Reinhard, which sounded no more appealing than it had last night.

Any way Jim looked at it, he was in trouble.

CHAPTER SEVEN

"**H**YPOTHETICAL QUESTION," HOSSBACH SAID. HIS breath came out in puffs. He had traded his Gestapo uniform for a charcoal suit and a gray tie, with brown riding gloves. His hair looked even more crimson in the morning light, and there were flecks of gold in his green eyes. He had freshly trimmed his mustache and his lips were now visible.

"Go ahead," Katterman said.

"The Reich has outlawed the keeping of Rhode Island red chickens and given orders to the local prefects to arrest and detain violators of the new law. Priority urgent. You know that a certain important man in the village has been known to raise these animals as pets, as he claims the Rhode Island red has the most beautiful plumage. What do you do?"

Katterman's bladder was bursting and his joints were stiff from the cold that seeped up from the metal chair. "Hypothetically? I rise before dawn, secret myself on or near his property, and listen for the sound of a cock crowing."

"You wouldn't wonder why?"

"I always wonder why. Every crime must have motive and opportunity. Your important man of the village clearly had opportunity—having been seen keeping these animals before — but does he have motive sufficient to violate a law that might cost him his life? I would find out."

"But the why of the *law*?" Hossbach said. "What about that?"

"That doesn't concern me so much."

"No? But if you had to guess, how would your reasoning go?"

Three hours now the colonel had kept him on the terrace. Last night, Hossbach had driven Katterman south from Fritz Wenck's chateau in the dead man's own automobile. Upon arriving in the Gestapo-owned chalet, Hossbach told him to telephone his wife and warn her he would be away for a few days. She was alarmed, but he reassured her that he was not under protective custody, but on official business. Oh, and if he hadn't returned home by Friday, could she keep his appointment with the headmaster at Hermann's school? After that, Katterman settled in for the night in comfortable quarters and read for a while from a French book taken from the library. It concerned a Dr. Beaurieux, who studied postmortem consciousness by attempting to communicate with condemned criminals in the seconds after their decapitation in the guillotine.

After breakfast the next morning, Hossbach led him outside to the terrace for questioning. The man set a thin green portfolio on the coffee table, but never unwound the twine to consult it. He would occasionally stand up and go inside under some pretense or another — probably simply to warm his hands by the fire. He instructed Katterman to stay in place, but made a point to tell him that he was not guarded or restrained in any way. He left the file in place, within easy reach, but with no instructions not to touch it. Katterman refrained.

The sun was out, and there was no breeze to amplify the chill, or he would have insisted on going inside, instructions or no. Under other circumstances, he might have enjoyed the terrace. It stretched to the edge of the hillside behind the chalet and overlooked a tiny Bavarian valley. A village of a dozen or so timber houses sat a few hundred feet below, next to a swiftly flowing mountain stream. There was a trim little church that chimed the hours, and a ruined monastery to the south, collapsed except for one sheer wall that stood precariously, from this angle seemingly unsupported. Snow flocked the pine trees that climbed the mountainsides both above and below them.

"I'd prefer not to speculate about the law itself," Katterman said. "But if compelled to do so, I suppose I would say that the Rhode Island red must be a vector of some poultry-killing disease. The state decided to eradicate this particular breed in order to preserve the value of the entire poultry industry."

"A good guess. Any others?"

"Rhode Island is an American state, is it not? So this must be an American breed. Now that we are at war with the United States, it is unpatriotic to keep this particular chicken when there are so many more benign and equally productive birds. Eliminating the Rhode Island red could improve the national morale."

Hossbach lit a cigarette and set the ashtray on top of the unopened file. "Now that would be a silly reason, wouldn't it?"

Yes, indeed. Senseless, like so many other diktats from Berlin these past few years. He kept this thought to himself and answered with a shrug.

"Anything else?" Hossbach said. "No? What do you suppose I'm really getting at?"

"More guessing? Let me see. The Rhode Island red is a metaphor for a Jew. The Hebrew race is a foreign element that the state has decided is hazardous to the health and well-being of its citizenry. Keeping of Jews — friendship and business associations, let us say — is no longer merely frowned upon, it has become illegal."

Hossbach looked taken aback by this. "What makes you say that?"

"I'm surprised by your surprise," Katterman said. "Isn't that what you're getting at? Wasn't this entire line of questioning an extended metaphor about the Jewish question?"

The colonel was silent for a long moment, and then said, "You are a perceptive man. And yes, I have taken criticism in recruiting you because of your lack of zeal in discovering hidden Jews within your district. But no, the chicken question was a frivolous example with no hidden meaning, except to determine your desire to uphold the law, even when you don't fully understand it."

"If you say so," Katterman said.

"Would you like to answer the Jewish question while it is on the table?"

"Not particularly. Like I said, I'm not interested in politics."

And propaganda, even less. But he imagined Hossbach's eyes widening in horror and rage at the word and kept this thought to himself.

But there was no other word for it. Facts, loosely gathered, mixed with speculation and polemics, and then twisted like a carnival contortionist until it fit a preconceived narrative, and then fed to a gullible public.

"You are not a member of the party?" Hossbach asked.

"Well, yes," Katterman admitted. "I could no longer avoid that responsibility and still maintain my position as inspector."

"So you are a member of the party, yet you profess no politics. That itself is a political statement. As is your disinterest in the Jewish question."

"I make no judgment on the matter. That is not my interest. But I have developed an ear for the truth in my job, and recognize when people are lying to protect themselves or cast guilt on innocent parties. Now, given the considerable resources directed by the Gestapo toward this question, and its lack of interest in the more general lawlessness of the state of Saxony, I prefer to expend resources on the later. As soon as I eliminate theft, rape, murder, and strong-armed robbery, I'll turn my attention to finding Jews."

"Do you voice these opinions often, inspector?" Hossbach asked.

"Only when directly questioned. This rarely happens."

"Thank God for that."

Neither man spoke for a long moment. Hossbach seemed to be reconsidering the entire — well, whatever reason he'd brought Katterman here to propose. "You have been sitting a long time," he said at last. "Would you like to visit the washroom?"

"Yes, please."

When Katterman came back a few minutes later, less irritable now that he'd relieved the pressure on his bladder, he found a servant delivering a tray with coffee and slices of Kürbiskernbrot with berry preserves. Hossbach had composed himself and poured the two men coffee. "Now, where were we?"

"The proper regulation of poultry, I believe."

This brought a smile. Hossbach tamped out his cigarette and leaned back.

Katterman said, "Is this about finding Jews, Obersturmbannführer?"

"No, it is not."

"I didn't think so."

He fell silent. Let the other man speak first.

"One more question. And then I'll give you answers."

"I have my answers, Obersturmbannführer. Give me details, and I can start work."

"You do?" A smile crept across Hossbach's face. "What hubris. Go ahead, share by all means."

Katterman shrugged. "You've given plenty of clues. Clearly, you want me to participate in a political struggle within the regime. You saw my willingness to confront Fritz Wenck as indicative that I could be trusted, as an outsider, to pursue a powerful figure within the government with little regard to politics or, for that matter, to my own life."

Once more Hossbach looked caught off guard. Katterman found himself enjoying the colonel's discomfort. The Gestapo liked to awe with secret tactics, with so-called *Nacht und Nebel* operations—night and fog. A man would disappear in the middle of the night with no warning, no charges filed, no notice given to friends or family. Such tactics left a general feeling of terror in their wake. But in the past twenty-four hours he had received confirmation that even their highest officials were human. Wenck foolishly attacked him with a poker, and now Hossbach probed with questions that revealed as much about the interrogator as about the subject of the interrogation. If there had been any doubt,

Katterman had confirmation these were not *Übermensch*, they were flawed and could be outwitted.

"So why are you looking to me, in particular?" Katterman continued. "Plenty of ruthless, cunning men in the Gestapo. So your target is either high in the regime — untouchable — or he is easily enough tracked and destroyed. Two guesses. First, you decided I'm incorruptible. That is accurate, I would say. Second, your target is beyond the control of the Gestapo somehow. Somewhere like Hungary, Vichy France. North Africa, the Eastern Front. He is a German, perhaps a high-ranking diplomat or military official."

Hossbach let out his breath. "Thank God for that."

"Obersturmbannführer?"

"I was beginning to think that you either had supernatural abilities, or that someone had tipped you off. That you were working for an enemy and I'd been set up."

"Then my guess is wrong?" Katterman asked, disappointed.

"Oh, it's close enough. A little too close for comfort, in fact. The first thing I need to teach you is discretion, heaven help me."

"I can be discrete. But I was standing above the dead body of one senior official, in the hands of a second, with no witnesses. Even my pathetic junior inspector was gone by then, and no one else had seen me enter the Sturmbannführer's chateau. My best defense was candor. Show my qualities."

"I understand." Hossbach moved aside the ashtray and slowly unwound the twine on the file. He opened it, flipped over a couple of sheets of paper, some photographs, and then settled on a typed report, running a gloved finger down the page. "You speak French, Italian, and some Latin. Yet you have never been outside of Germany."

"We went to Vienna on honeymoon."

"Ostermark is a German state."

"It wasn't in 1931. It was a foreign nation."

"True," Hossbach said. "But a German-speaking nation."

"I study languages as an intellectual exercise. Italian because I enjoy the opera, Dante, and Petrarch's writings in the vernacular. French because of the many useful writings about criminology and medical science. English because it is the only way to read Shakespeare. Apart from language lessons, I am not particularly interested in meeting modern French and Italians."

"And the English? Would you like to meet them?"

"Not particularly. But I suppose they are better than Americans."

"I've heard enough." Hossbach shut the file. "You will go to Italy tomorrow."

Katterman kept the distaste from showing on his face. "Rome?"

"Florence."

"I suppose that is better. The land of the Renaissance, after all."

"We're not in Florence to sketch the *David*."

We. Katterman noted the pronoun.

Hossbach lit another cigarette. "I will provide you all the papers you need. Once we leave the Reich, you are not to call me Obersturmbannführer, or refer to the Gestapo or the SS in any way. When questioned, you will say you are on official business, but will decline any additional information. If we receive resistance from the

Italians, the military attaché will resolve matters on our behalf. Any questions?"

"Yes," Katterman said. "I would like to know who we're investigating, this quarry so powerful and dangerous that we don't dare to make the inquiries and arrest on German soil."

"Our target," Hossbach said, "is an English-language theater troupe operating under the authorization of the Reich Ministry of Public Enlightenment and Propaganda."

"English language? In the Reich?"

"Curious, isn't it? The elites of Europe, the businessmen, the nobles, and even generals within the Wehrmacht, have become Anglophiles. They have studied in British schools, made business contacts in London and New York, traveled throughout the British Empire. And they love English theater, sufficient to provide steady work for this company of actors."

"That would be ideal cover for recruiting British sympathizers," Katterman said. "If one were a spy, that is."

"Indeed."

"Then why not arrest, interrogate, and prosecute?"

"The Gestapo does not prosecute. They detain without trial. But here is the problem. Our hypothetical keeper of chickens is the nephew of a man placed very highly within the regime. I need to be one hundred percent certain. I need to lay evidence, to set a trap." Hossbach smiled. "And that is why you're coming with me to Florence."

CHAPTER EIGHT

THERE WAS TROUBLE AT THE border, east of Nice, as they left nominally Vichy-controlled territory to enter Italy. Nigel warned Jim that the German guards here would be alert and aggressive, on the lookout for criminals, spies, traitors, Jews, and anyone else who thought they'd have an easier time bribing their way out of Europe via Italy than territory under Nazi control. The German-controlled side of the border was on the west side of a series of tunnels that cut through the French and Italian Alps. When the company lined up on the station, he waited with the others and their trunks, baggage, theater sets, and equipment unloaded for inspection. It was temperate, almost warm in the south of France, even for the time of year, and they stood with jackets unbuttoned and hands out of pockets while they waited.

A guard with a German shepherd on a leash walked up and down the platform, the dog sniffing people and bags, while three more guards inspected luggage. Two more questioned people and examined papers down the line. These last two wore black uniforms.

"Fabulous, it's the Gestapo," Lula muttered. She stood with Nigel, Jim, the Hungarian and his servant, and Margaret, who chattered about the weather and the terrible food in the dining car. He couldn't decide if she was keeping up appearances with either Lula or the servant, or if she was simply getting into character before the inspection came their way. Both women and the Hungarian, a man named Károly Weil, were smoking.

"Look at the tall one," Margaret said. "Ooh, he's handsome. I wonder if he's married."

"Come on, Megs," Nigel said in a good-natured tone. "Be serious."

"You're worse than Father," she said. "I have no intention of being an old maid, you know."

"Or any kind of maid, for that matter," Nigel said.

Margaret sniffed, and then turned to Lula. "What do you think, Lu? He's a real looker, that one. Don't you agree?"

"Maybe if she gets in his trousers we'll get out of here quicker," Lula said. "They're taking their time."

"Listen up, both of you," Nigel said. "This is not one of the easy crossings. Either here or on the other side. No games, you understand."

"Oh, fine," Margaret said with a pout.

Jim kept his face blank as he listened to this ridiculous exchange between the brother and sister, none of which had been sincere, but now he asked, "They *are* expecting us, right? So there's no reason to be jumpy. Other than the random chance of getting dragged away and lined up against the wall, I mean."

They never traveled without sending advance notice. Their group was too unusual, singular, even, with its collection of English speakers. Papers alone wouldn't be enough to keep them from all manner of delays and interrogations. But they had a new member of the company, and Jim suspected that it was working on Nigel's nerves. Hard to say if Weil and his man would handle the crossings as well as Kristiann Janssen until they'd done it several times. And Jim was aware for the first time that yes, they really were hiding something, and not innocently taking a show on the road.

"Of course they're expecting us," Nigel said. "But the lot of you act like you need a reminder that this is tricky business. Especially you," he told Margaret. "Be serious, please."

Ten minutes passed as the Gestapo agents made their way closer. Nothing unusual happened until the end of the second-class passengers, where the agents stopped in front of three men, who they questioned in French. Their attention soon focused on one of the men in particular. Jim couldn't pick out the words at first; it started calmly, but shortly the questions grew sharper, more direct, and the lead agent raised his voice. "You hesitated," the man snapped. "Why? You don't know? You forgot?"

"I do know, I do!" the man said. "27 July 1905."

"What is it?" Jim asked his companions in a low voice. "What's wrong?"

"The agent asked his birth date," Lula said. "He didn't answer quickly enough. His papers might be forged and he forgot what was written. Look at him. He's a bad actor. He's guilty of something."

Or maybe being scared out of your wits was enough to make a bad actor of anyone. The three Germans had isolated the man and now they ordered his hands up.

Jim had seen a hundred dramas play out over the past year — an old man beaten by police with truncheons, Jews being loaded onto trains, respectable housewives offering to lift their skirts for a bag of potatoes to feed their children, entire towns turned to rubble by allied bombs. But there was something about this particular man, caught on the wrong side of one of these dramas, that tore at him.

"We have to do something," he said.

"Are you mad?" Nigel asked.

"Maybe we could help. What if I — ?" He stopped as the soldier with the submachine gun glanced his direction.

"Don't say another word," Nigel said. "Look away, *now*."

But Jim couldn't. For a moment the poor fellow at the end of the interrogation looked like he was going to bolt. He turned for help from his companions, who showed their backs as if they didn't know him, and then he glanced up and down the track. Ahead, the tunnel to Italy, and a squat brick building snug against the mountainside that flew a swastika, together with a pair of concrete gun emplacements manned by soldiers. On the opposite track, the line continued back into France in the direction from which they'd come, hugging the mountain, with a steep drop of a hundred feet or more before the tops of pine trees that grew all the way down the slope to the valley below.

Where could he run? He could hurl himself off the edge, or make for the tunnel, or run back down the tracks toward France. You could see the thoughts going through his mind, but finally the man stumbled back toward the brick building as instructed. A German soldier shoved him in the back with the snout of a submachine gun when the man didn't move quickly enough. Another man kicked at the back of his legs with his boot, and the man staggered forward and nearly fell. *Macht schnell!* the lead Gestapo agent yelled.

The Gestapo agents came back a few minutes later, moving more quickly now. The company stood stiff and quiet as they handed over papers and let the border guards paw through their belongings. Even Margaret fell silent, dropping the nonsense about flirting with the Gestapo agent, who paid her little attention in any event. And then the inspection finished, and the border guards gave orders to reload the train and board for the crossing.

"Thank God," Lula said, as they watched the stage crew heft boxes. Normally, Jim helped the crew reload, but this time he stepped back to watch, so he could consider each man and woman and ask himself what, if anything, they knew. "On to Italy," she added, "where the wine is good, the men have charm, and even the fascists have a sense of humor."

Twenty minutes later they were in their seats. The train whistled, jerked into motion, and Jim settled back with the assumption that the most difficult inspection was behind them. The train passed through a series of tunnels, long and poorly ventilated enough that the smell of coal soot seeped into the cars. He supposed they were still in France, but would cross the border into Italy somewhere beneath the mountain.

Nigel ordered the company to the lounge. He frowned pointedly at an elderly, well-dressed German couple who appeared to be traveling into Italy on holiday, until they left for their own compartment. When they were gone, he gave instructions for second crossing.

"Don't be fooled. We'll be treated like visiting dignitaries on the surface, but these Italians are prickly about their rights. And the locals have a certain... *autonomy* from Rome. Don't get in trouble. By the time our attaché wires his outrage to Mussolini's government, you may have already been dragged away, dangled upside down, and had your ankles broken."

Jim raised his hand and made his voice as innocent as possible. "But they're all fascists, right? Even the locals. I'm sure if you talked to them, they'd see we're all allies."

Nigel fixed him with a hard look, then continued over the interruption. "Florence is a nest of spies. Don't trust anyone who speaks English, for one. Better stay away from French speakers, too, even if they claim they're from Vichy or North Africa. In fact, now that I think about it, German is dangerous. Anyone who speaks German to you is likely to want something."

"Then how do we get around the city?" one of the stage crew muttered.

"Maybe it's better if you don't. Not alone, anyway. We'll go out together, it's safer that way. We can see the Duomo and the Uffizi. And there is the opening night party at Count d'Angelo's villa—that will give you a chance to get away from the hotel and the theater."

"I don't want to be a tourist," Margaret said. Her lips scrunched into a pout. "I want to come and go as I please."

"Me, either," Lula said. "Why are we taking the show to Tuscany if it's not to stretch our legs, drink wine, eat good food, and relax without the ministry looking over our shoulder and wagging their finger every time we step out of line?"

"I don't know," Nigel said, his tone peevish. "The ministry said go to Florence, so we're going to Florence. The country is full of Wehrmacht advisers of the Italian Army, and some general must have pulled strings. Whatever the reason, I don't want to make a hash of it."

"That's no reason to treat us like enemies of the state," someone else said from the back of the train car. Mutters and frowns passed through the rest of the company.

"Listen," Nigel said, "if any of you want to petition the government to put you in charge of the company when we get back, by all means, go ahead. Until then, I don't care if you like it or not, I'm setting the ground rules."

But Jim saw his opportunity. There was enough irritation at this unexpected personal intrusion that he thought he could make something of it.

"Be that as it may," he said, "we're not goose-stepping across the border, we're actors for God's sake. Everyone knows what actors are like when they're not onstage. We drink, we carouse, we gamble. And we speak our mind. Maybe not like we would in Paris before the war, or, say, Cairo. But this isn't Berlin, and we're not performing at the Reichstag. It's not even that last show in Holland, with half the damn audience SS officers. It's Italy, and we're guests of the Italian state. They have to expect a little free living on our part."

"And what's your plan, Jim?" Nigel said. "Let's hear your brilliant thoughts on the subject."

There were raised eyebrows at this and Jim caught people looking back and forth between the two men. Nigel and Jim were famously best friends, after all. Jim marked the ones who looked surprised and tallied them as ignorant fools in the whole operation, much as he'd been. That included most of the crew and some of the cast as well, including Kyle Dunleavy, who he'd assumed was another spy. Dunleavy didn't look like one now; he looked peeved.

"My brilliant plan is that you trust us to take care of ourselves until we prove otherwise. Don't take us for idiots. We won't mess up."

"I don't know," Margaret said, sounding suddenly thoughtful. "Maybe my brother is right. Maybe we shouldn't take risks."

"That's not what you were saying a minute ago," Jim said. "Why are you changing your mind now? Care to explain yourself?"

She didn't have an answer. That's because her pout was fake; she'd never intended to go against Nigel in the first place. It was all theater, just like Nigel's sudden decision that they should herd together like a clump of elementary school kids on an outing to the zoo. Hold hands, children, we don't want anyone to get lost.

"I agree with Jim," Dunleavy said. "Besides, I'll note that you are the head of the company, but according to my contract, I only owe you one thing when I'm offstage, and that is that I do not bring dishonor to the Reich. I trust my own judgment on that score."

"Hear, hear," Lula said.

"What is this, a *putsch*?" Nigel said.

"We'll make a compromise," Jim said. "Nobody leaves the city without permission. Inside the city, we manage ourselves as we see fit. If anyone behaves badly, we all lose our privileges."

"Sounds reasonable," Dunleavy said. "It puts a certain onus on the rest of us to keep an eye on our fellows."

"Very well, I accept those terms," Nigel said, a little too quickly. "With one additional condition. Nobody is alone. I'll assign everyone a minder. You watch them, they watch you."

"Good idea," Margaret said.

"Fine, fine. Let's see, I'll take Weil, since he's the new chap. Jim, you're with Margaret. Lula —"

"Hold on," Jim said. "I didn't think we were settled."

But Nigel continued over his complaint, and quickly the discussion devolved into who did or didn't want to be with whom. The strongest mutters of protest came from the younger, more reckless members of the crew, but they were the most likely to need supervision, and wouldn't get anywhere with the rest. At that moment, light streamed through the window of the car as they emerged from the tunnel, and the train lurched as it slowed. They had arrived at the Italian crossing. People turned to hurry back to their compartments to gather papers and personal effects for another tedious unloading and inspection.

Nigel and Margaret flanked Jim as they returned to their private compartment. "Clever work there," Nigel said. "What was your intent, to escape into the Tuscan countryside?"

"More like I wanted breathing room from a pair of traitors."

"Traitors?" Nigel said. He slid open the compartment door and gave a sweeping gesture for Jim to enter. "So you're loyal to king and country now, is that it?"

"I'm talking about our friendship, you idiot. You stabbed me in the back."

Margaret entered, closed the compartment door behind them, and said, "It wouldn't have worked, anyway. This isn't Holland, and if you couldn't get away there, what makes you think you'd have any more luck here, where you don't know the countryside and have no contacts to get you out of the country?"

"Whatever you're doing," Jim said, "I don't want any part of it. Leave me alone. Is that too much to ask?"

"If that's what you truly want," Nigel said, "stop scheming."

"While you figure out whether to poison me, strangle me, or simply toss me from the train at fifty miles an hour? Yes, I see."

The truth was, he hadn't thought far enough ahead to formulate a plan of escape. He didn't know the first thing about Florence, for one, and figured it might take a few days simply to learn the lay of the land. But it would sure as hell be easier without these two watching his every move.

He looked out the window glumly as they pulled into the Italian border station. It stood on the edge of a village that climbed the mountain on either side of a narrow valley. Streets zig-zagged between timbered buildings, some of the roads so steep and narrow they were more like staircases. Lining the tracks outside the station, children in ankle-length coats watched the train jerk to a halt until a man driving a scrawny mule loaded with baskets of coal jostled them out of the way. Two pretty women, most likely prostitutes, if his eye was any good, came down one of the staircase-like roads. Other people stared from back yards or balconies, and still more trickled toward the station. Half a dozen Italian guards, wearing belted jackets and caps tilted at angles, seemed as concerned with keeping the unruly villagers off the platform as in turning their attentions to the passengers from the trains.

"Don't leave his side during the inspection," Nigel said to Margaret when they stepped down to the platform. "If he tries anything—if he *says* anything funny—you know what to do." He took out his introductory papers together with his identification, and made his way toward the man who looked like the chief border agent.

"What does he think I'm going to do," Jim said when he was alone with Margaret, "pull out a trumpet and toot 'God Save the King?'"

"Something befitting your lowly intelligence, no doubt." She shrugged. "Go ahead and try something, if you'd like. Sooner or later we have to deal with you. It may as well be now."

And with that she fixed him with a look not very different from the one the Gestapo agent had fixed upon the captured Frenchman on the other side of the border. If there had been any doubt before, it was gone. Margaret wanted him dead.

CHAPTER NINE

A MAN HAD ARRIVED AT THE Heydrich house in the summer of 1940. It was only days after Jim's chance meeting with Hans von Steidle and a pleasant afternoon drink at the beer garden chatting about the folly of war. The newcomer was tall and clean-shaven, with his blond hair parted down the middle. He waved papers and said simply, "James Heydrich, *bitte*." He wasn't dressed in a uniform, but his regal Aryan appearance and official bearing had Jim's mother in a panic by the time she found Jim reading Huxley in the shade of the stone wall out back. Jim's heart was pounding before he got to the front door. The arrival of well-dressed strangers had a way of chilling the blood.

To Jim's astonishment, the man addressed him in English, and a crisp, upper-class pronunciation to boot. "So you're the Canadian fellow I've heard about. I'm Nigel Burnside, Reich Ministry of Public Enlightenment and Propaganda. Thespian and Booze Division." He held out his hand and grinned at the expression that came over Jim's face. "Pack your bags, my dear chap, we're on the next train to Berlin. Unless you'd rather take your chances with the conscription board, that is."

"But what? Why?"

Nigel turned to Jim's parents and two younger

sisters, who had come running as soon as the man started speaking English, and now clustered behind them. "Pay is lousy, about what a Wehrmacht corporal draws, but Jim will be well fed and far from the fight." He unfolded his orders. "Thanks to Jim's best college mate, he has been recruited into a special company of actors, headed by yours truly."

His parents were delighted, of course. Only two days earlier, several formerly exempt professions had been stricken from the lists, and he'd spotted a queue of several dozen young men lined up outside the military recruitment offices to receive their Wehrpasses in preparation for induction. The metronome of advice and criticism had picked up tempo, and last night he'd heard Father on the phone chatting with someone — possibly even his Uncle Reinhard — about joining the S.S. His father had cleared his throat that morning at breakfast, and suggested that working for his uncle might be better than storming the beaches of England. This, however, was an unexpected and entirely welcome development.

Nigel consented to a quick drink of schnapps, as Father unlocked the liquor cabinet and took out one of his precious few remaining bottles. The newcomer drank and laughed, shook hands all around, and flirted with Jim's sisters, who blushed at first and then flirted back with abandon. And then Nigel looked at his watch, made a dismayed sound, and snapped his fingers. "Good heavens, we're going to be late. And we still have to pick up my sister at the hotel. Quickly, Jim. Quickly." He held up his glass to Jim's parents as the young man rushed from the room. "One more drop for the road?"

Nigel had a car, a beat-up Opel Olympia that was nevertheless topped off with petrol, its trunk stuffed with boxes and suitcases and roped closed. Costumes and props, Jim would later discover. The two young men heaved Jim's trunk into the back, climbed in, and then Nigel pulled away with a puff of smoke, a roar, and the squeal of worn tires on slick cobblestone. Jim barely had time to wave to his mother, who stood crying on the doorstep, before the car was out of the alley and careening past the church and the boarded-over storefront of the Jewish butcher.

"No doubt you're wondering who the devil I am," Nigel said, "and how the blazes it is that an Englishman of good breeding is wandering through Germany without an escort while my compatriots brace themselves in pillboxes on the beaches of Dover and Hastings."

"Right now, I'm trying to keep my head from popping off, it's spinning so hard."

"No doubt, no doubt. Well now, here's the whole foolish business. I'm an Englishman through and through. Loyal to king and country, and I'd sooner be hung by the neck with a Union Jack than salute the bloody swastika. No doubt you feel the same."

Jim didn't answer. He wasn't so disoriented that he'd blunder into a political discussion with a stranger.

"The truth is, I fell afoul of the London regime. Yes, it's a regime, too. They're all regimes these days, all caught up in politics."

"I try to keep my politics to myself," Jim said. "Safer that way."

"I know, I know, and I shouldn't even be telling you this nonsense, but von Steidle says you're a good egg. Says you know how to keep your mouth shut. That's why we nicked you for the company, after all. Of course von Steidle vouched for your acting chops, too."

What did von Steidle know about that, either? Jim had been onstage with the man for all of ten minutes, during a session of experimental one-acts two summers ago. But again, Jim decided to keep his mouth shut on that score. If Hans von Steidle wanted to claim him as the best of chums, who was he to put the poor guy in his place?

"My politics, as it turns out," Nigel continued, "have more in common with National Socialism than with the Liberals or the Tories. What the old country wants is a kick to the whole rotten foundation, and it would come crashing down. London needs to get beyond England and empire. Our true enemy is east, anyone can see that. That's where the real war is going to start, mark my words. Hell, even the Yanks should see that, if they ever set foot outside Fortress America and took a look around. We have to stop the Bolsheviks, or Western Civilization is finished." He jerked on the wheel to take them onto a side street, and Jim's luggage in the back seat slid to the other side of the car. "I hope to serve in the military government after London gives up the fight. Meanwhile, it's the theater for me. I've got money from the ministry, and more importantly, I've got important men on my side, opening the right doors and closing the wrong ones."

Nigel kept up the chatter, occasionally leaving an opening, but Jim declined to jump in, still suspicious. By the time they screeched to a halt in front of the hotel, he didn't exactly trust the Englishman, but decided he liked him. Certainly he felt more comfortable and less suspicious than he had with Hans von Steidle, who had still been a German beneath his English-educated veneer. Some of Jim's best friends at college—his *real* friends—

had been big, brash, but competent men much like Nigel Burnside. His suspicion at his incredible fortune began to fade, replaced by gratitude and something that had been absent since the Canadian branch of the Heydrich family returned to Germany — optimism.

Margaret Burnside was another question. Oh, his first glimpse was favorable enough. More than favorable, in fact. She stood with her bags in front of the hotel, wearing a white hat which she held in place against the gusts of wind that threatened to blow it away and billowed her sun dress to expose a pair of shapely legs. Everything about her was shapely, in fact: her cute face, her lips, her hips, and especially her pert breasts.

Jim, feeling comfortable with Nigel and forgetting momentarily that she was his sister, let out a low whistle of appreciation as he saw her waiting.

"Steady on," Nigel said.

"Oh, I'm sorry."

Nigel laughed, dispelling any worries that he was offended. "My sister has that effect on men. One flash of that electric smile and they start drooling."

"But I guess you don't need any more reminders."

"Wouldn't you know I'll be playing opposite her onstage?" Nigel said. "Bloody strange, but there's no other way to cast the show."

"I suppose that's one way to keep an eye on her. Long as you don't have to kiss her, because nobody wants to look at that."

"Hell no."

Margaret waved and gave a cheerful smile. The two men hopped out of the car and helped her with her bags. "So this is the infamous James Heydrich." She had a light, breezy voice.

"It's Jim, thanks. But why infamous?"

"Your uncle, silly." She turned to Nigel. "You never mentioned he was cute as a button."

Nigel grunted and loaded the bags in the back seat on and around Jim's trunk. "The boot is stuffed with props and the like. You'll have to cram in with Jim until we get to the station."

"Ooh, I barely know him." Her laugh was like the tinkle of a bell, and then she was pushing Jim back in his seat and sitting on his lap.

Margaret squirmed around as she got her legs tucked in beneath the glove compartment, and then she pulled the door shut. Jim caught the scent of apple blossoms from her blond hair as it brushed him in the face, and then Nigel was peeling away again. He rounded the corner and Margaret squished against Jim with a burst of that charming laughter again. More squirming on his lap as she tried to get comfortable. Jim did some twitching of his own to avoid any embarrassing pressure on his groin. He'd never been so instantly aroused in his life.

"Now that we're properly acquainted," she said, "you really must tell me about your uncle. He must be the most handsome, most clever man in Germany. I simply must know *everything*."

Jim's arousal died.

They were only a mile from the train station, and so he put her off with the story of how Reinhard Heydrich's letters to Ottawa led to Jim's father losing his job at the university as the Dominion followed the British Empire into war. Only in the telling he toned down the aggressive nature of the letters, how they insulted the Jewish dean at the school, accused Canadians of being alternatively puppets of the British and lapdogs of the Americans, and instead told how Canadian officials were steaming open Vater's letters and intercepting his transatlantic calls.

"Ooh, that's terrible," Margaret said. "They spied on him? Who would do such a thing?"

Yes, who would do such a thing? Who would possibly read someone else's mail and fire someone for unpopular political connections? God, where did she think she was?

Nigel snorted. "Isn't that just like the English? Canadians, I mean, but practically the same thing. Yanks, Aussies, Kiwis — throw them in for good measure. We're always grandstanding about this universal right or that civilized behavior, and always the worst of the lot. Hypocrites. Still," he added. "I'm surprised Heydrich didn't anticipate the effect his letters would have on your father's career."

Yes, of course. That was obvious to everyone in his family. Even Jim's teenage sisters knew it had been intentional. Father thought Uncle Reinhard was facing political pressure to get his family back to the Fatherland. Not that Father was suspected of being a spy, so much as others might use him to do their spying. And so the overly belligerent tone designed to turn the Canadians hostile against Jim's family.

He figured that would be enough to keep Margaret until the station, but they came upon a political parade. Hundreds of people crowded the street in a field of beige and black, while a long snake of soldiers in gray, eight abreast across the width of the road, goose-stepped past to the sound of drums and trumpets. Two uniformed police officers wagged their fingers and motioned for them to turn the car around and go back. Nigel did so, grumbling that they were going to miss their train.

Meanwhile, Margaret kept asking questions about

Jim's uncle, mainly personal stuff. She didn't seem put off that Uncle Reinhard was married, but wanted to know if he was as handsome as he looked in the pictures. It was almost as though she'd heard the rumors about his philandering ways — he'd been drummed out of the navy once over allegations of improper behavior with another woman while he was engaged to Aunt Lina. Or was that backwards?

But Jim didn't see how Margaret could know, as she'd been unaware of his marriage in the first place. In fact, she asked again about whether Uncle Reinhard had a girlfriend before they broke free from the parade route to find a different path to the station, and Jim wondered how she would possibly memorize her lines since her memory was obviously rubbish. She did all of this while paying no attention to her surroundings. Instead, she pulled out a compact to dab at her lipstick, admiring herself in the mirror, filing her nails with an emery board, and then pulling a stick of gum from her purse, which she chomped even as she kept chatting. Her accent was elegant and precise, what they called the King's English in Canada, but the chatter and gum smacking reminded him of a bored secretary.

By the time they reached the station, Jim had formed an equally fast appraisal of Nigel's sister, but this one altogether unfavorable. She was stupid, but not particularly dangerous.

It turned out, of course, that he'd been wrong on both scores.

CHAPTER TEN

TWENTY MONTHS LATER, CHUGGING THROUGH the rugged countryside of the Piedmont, on his way to Florence via Milan, Jim had plenty of time to reflect on his false early impressions of Nigel and Margaret Burnside. They'd played him perfectly, like two veteran actors who had come onstage and established their characters in a line or two and a bit of stage business. Nigel—cheerful, friendly, competent, and strong-willed. An outsider who not only survived in a turbulent world, but thrived. His sister Margaret was just as cheerful and friendly, but without her brother's other redeeming qualities, or even the ability to notice what a hash the world had made of it. She'd be a danger to herself and the company. Indeed, she'd come close to self-destruction at least a dozen times, blurting things that would have merely raised eyebrows under other circumstances, but in these times threatened a late-night knock on the door. Only luck and the quick thinking of her fellow cast mates kept her out of trouble, or so he'd thought at the time.

Now he recognized it as one more part of the scam. Everything he thought he knew about these two was a lie. In reality, Nigel was a hard-nosed backstabber. Margaret competent, ruthless, and clever. About the only thing the new Margaret had in common with the old was that Jim hated her. Now he feared her, too.

After the initial trap in Halle an der Saale, they'd rushed Jim to Berlin to join the cast of the theater company, already in rehearsals and blocking scenes. The company set up in a *fin de siecle* theater turned American-style speakeasy, which had been abandoned when the French burlesque and American jazz musicians fled the city under Nazi harassment. Jim arrived to discover the company constructing sets, sewing costumes, and planning an extended tour of Europe.

What a cast and what a show. It was in English, for one, the language of the enemy. Their audience, Nigel explained, was the thousands of officers, officials, and businessmen who had studied at Oxford and Cambridge, who had grown up in America or some other expatriate enclave where they'd learned English. Much as the French tried to preserve their linguistic dominance through sheer snobbery, or the Germans or Russians impose theirs by the tip of their bayonets, the English language had conquered half the world with empire and commerce.

As for the show itself, Oscar Wilde, the playwright, was nominally Irish. *An Ideal Husband* was superficially about Victorian England — not the modern belligerents across the Channel — and apolitical. Its themes were the German virtues of honor and honesty, while the play simultaneously lampooned the nonsense of British class structures. Or at least that's how it was pitched to censors from the ministry. There were always two official minders at every rehearsal or cast meeting, one who watched with a scowl, seemingly understanding nothing, and the other who understood everything, laughed at the jokes and offered his opinion about blocking or line delivery.

Nigel made a point of coming down from the stage to ask this second man's opinion.

"There's a subversive element to this play, you know," Jim told Nigel one day, when the two men sat on the roof haggling about set design, three days before tech. Nigel had called a halt to rehearsals while a victory parade rolled past the theater on Tiergartenstrasse. The entire building shook with the clank of panzers, the rumble of truck engines, and the cheers from the crowd. It loud enough even on the roof, and Nigel started to respond, but fell silent while a row of Messerschmidt fighters roared over the city and waggled their wingtips at the mobs below.

Three nights earlier, on August 25, 1940, RAF bombers had struck Berlin for the first time. They hit the Tempelhof Airport, with a few small bombs falling astray in residential neighborhoods, which sent the city into a panic. That called for a parade. Not the typical preening, but a full display of the military might of the Reich. In any event, the coming invasion of England was the gossip on everyone's lips. Soon the war would be won, assuming the squabble with the Soviets didn't progress beyond words.

Nigel and Jim smoked in silence until the fighters finished their run.

"Subversive how?" Nigel said.

"Robert gets away with it in the end. He's reformed, sure, but he never pays the price for selling the cabinet secret. And Goring helps him."

"Is that really subversive? Here, I mean?"

Jim lowered his hand from shielding his eyes as he watched the fighters disappear to the east. "No, I guess not."

"You've been studying the play."

"It's good. Deeper than it seems."

"Glad you think so. I've been meaning to ask, will you be my understudy for Lord Goring?" Nigel let the cigarette dangle between his lips. "I have a feeling I might need one."

"Too many lines? Think you'll lose your voice?"

"Looks like I'll be summoned to London after the invasion."

"Really?"

"They'll need turncoats to run the government." He shrugged and looked at his hands. "I don't want to see the show die — I've put in too much time."

"It must go on, as they say."

"Yes, exactly. Will you do it?"

"Of course," Jim said. "You don't think it's all talk? The invasion, I mean? Napoleon couldn't do it. Can Hitler manage?"

"He's not lacking for confidence."

"No, he's not." Jim snuffed out the half cigarette on the heel of his shoe, carefully so as to preserve the butt, which he tucked into a silver-plated cigarette holder. "Hate to see it happen. Englishmen will die. A lot of them."

"They're already dying. Sooner the war ends, the better. Isn't that what you think, too?"

"Sure, but I'm not crazy about losing my friend to the regime, either."

"You could come with me," Nigel said.

"I prefer the stage to war and politics. And I could be wrong, but I don't think it will be another repeat of France or Denmark."

"You think the English will fight on if they're invaded?"

"To the last drop of Scottish blood," Jim said. "If England falls, the government will relocate to Ottawa, where they'll be better positioned to badger the Americans to take up the fight." He turned from watching the spectacle to look at his friend. "And send assassination teams to murder members of the collaboration government. Like you."

"I know." Nigel had smoked his cigarette down, and looked at the smoldering tip for a long moment before flicking it over the edge of the building. "But once the Nazis put your name on the list, it's hard to get it off. Not unless you want to be moved to a different list. The *wrong* list." He sighed. "Why did everything change? It wasn't so bad before, was it? We had our differences, the Germans and the English, but was that any reason to demand a duel with pistols at dawn?"

A great cheer sounded from the streets below. The waving of tiny flags grew frantic and uninformed men pushed forward to keep the mob from surging into the street. Three long, open-topped Mercedes broke the giant snake of marching men. A man stood in the middle car with his hand upright while thousands of arms jutted forward in worshipful salute. The roar pulsed and spread and Jim imagined women crying, girls screaming, children's faces upturned in rapturous delight. On the roof, neither man spoke until the cars had passed, replaced by more soldiers marching, marching, marching.

"The gods come down from Olympus," Jim said.

"Isn't it Valhalla with these blokes?"

"Only after they die. But I suppose we're mixing metaphors."

"That's curious," Nigel said with a change in tone. He squinted to the northeast, along the Tiergarten. "See that glint? There, that building next to the bank dome."

Jim followed his gaze to see a light reflected from a rooftop. And then it was gone. "Was that binoculars? Do we have watchers?"

"Or a rifle scope. Either way, I'd rather not sit here exposed."

They came downstairs into the darkened theater. It had a damp, unhealthy smell, overlaid with cigar smoke that permeated the curtain and the carpets in the lobby. But it was just rehearsal space; they wouldn't have a single performance here.

"Where is everyone?" Nigel asked as they came off the darkened stage. The houselights were up and illuminated a field of empty seats, without a single cast member studying lines or sitting with feet propped on the chair ahead of him, smoking.

"Watching the spectacle, no doubt," Jim said. "You'd think the thrill would wear off. How much strutting and boasting can a man suffer in one life?"

"Strutting and boasting?" a voice called from the balcony in German-accented English. "Is that what you call it when we honor our Führer for leading us to victory?"

Jim looked up, alarmed to see one of the minders from the ministry sitting in the darkened balcony. Nobody went up there — the theater had suffered a fire in speakeasy days, which left the balcony damaged and unsafe. The man leaned over the railing, which creaked like it would give way and send him crashing to the floor below. A familiar red-haired head with a bushy mustache peered over the edge. Klaus Hossbach, from the ministry. Hossbach had some sort of connection to the Gestapo, and took notes. Someone who took notes was someone who paid attention.

Jim switched to German. "My apologies, Herr Hossbach. I spoke out of place."

"Yes, you did. Remember, James Heydrich, no matter who your relations, this is Germany, and you are no longer a British subject."

"I am truly sorry, Herr Hossbach. Please forgive me."

"I'll note your apology. Do not let it happen again."

"Good heavens," Nigel whispered, as the two men retreated back to the stage. "You need to be more careful. At least until we're on the road and out of sight of the ministry."

"They're not coming with us?"

"No, thank God." Nigel hesitated. "Well, not in occupied countries. If we leave the Reich, say to Spain or Italy, you can bet they'll be there. Watching."

Jim gave a final glance over his shoulder at Hossbach, who still leaned over the railing on the balcony, watching. He wore a wolfish smile, as if he had reached across the distance to pluck Nigel's warning from the air. As if he knew.

By the time the theater company arrived in Italy, Jim had long since stopped worrying about Klaus Hossbach, or the ministry itself. The man would appear when they did shows in Berlin, or materialize in some foreign city, but Jim wasn't thinking about him when the train pulled into a dingy rail yard on the edge of Florence that belied the city's reputation as one of the most beautiful in Europe.

No view of palaces, gardens, piazzas, or the famous

Duomo from the window, only trains and tracks, coal hoppers, water towers, and mule-powered cranes. Italian soldiers in a mismatched array of khaki and gray uniforms loaded boxes onto one car, while stevedores unloaded carts of artillery shells and repacked them onto a separate train. A filthy child with a basket collected pieces of coal from between the tracks. Jim couldn't tell if the boy worked for the rail station or if the guards merely tolerated his freelance scavenging. Another coal gatherer set down his coal basket, squatted over the tracks with pants down, and defecated. A girl tapped on the window of their compartment, held up a jar of olives, and waved three fingers.

Margaret shook her head and shut the blinds. "Welcome to modern Italy."

"Not every day you see donkeys hauling artillery," Jim said.

"And where do you suppose they are shipping their forty-year-old field guns?" Nigel said. "It isn't the Italians beating up on the British Empire, is it?"

The cry came to disembark the train. Nigel and Margaret flanked Jim as they stepped onto the platform to join the rest of the company.

Half a dozen porters were unloading luggage and footlockers filled with props and costumes. A short Italian man not much taller than a child but with forearms the size of Jim's calves held Margaret's red carpet bag in one hand, his half of a heavy chest in the other, and had a rucksack slung over one shoulder. Two men added them to the back of a cart being pulled by a blinkered mule.

Jim started toward the gate, but Margaret stiffened and grabbed his arm. He followed her gaze. Two men in dark suits were talking to members of the theater company, including Lula Larouche, the Hungarian, and his assistant.

"Germans," she said in a low voice.

"Stay calm," Nigel told her.

"But I've got the wrong papers. I wasn't expecting—"

"Oh, hell. Where are the others? In your bags?"

"I'm not an idiot—they're on my person. I just need a second and—"

"What's going on?" Jim said, growing alarmed. "Who—?"

But before he could complete that thought, one of the men in dark suits turned toward them, and he had a shock of recognition as he saw the heavy mustache and the red hair. It was Klaus Hossbach and a new assistant. Hossbach was thinner, his mustache less like a Bavarian farmer's and more like a government official's, and the red hair at his temples had sprouted a few gray hairs. His expression sharpened, and he nudged his companion, who handed Lula her papers before the two men strolled in their direction.

"I'm in trouble," Margaret whispered. "God help me, if they ask—"

"Still together," Hossbach said in English, his voice carrying over the huffing engine. "I never would have guessed it. I expected Herr Burnside, at least, would be in London by now. But alas, it seems the war has taken an eastward turn."

Nigel held out his hand. "Hossbach. Good to see you, old fellow. And new blood in the ministry, I see." His eyes trailed to Hossbach's companion.

"Ah, this is Wulf Katterman, my associate."

Katterman stood with his hands behind his back. He was a tall, slender man, handsome and with a strong bearing and a sharp eye. Jim would have cast him in a play as a right and proper Junker landlord who regularly considers scientific improvements to increase the yield on his estate.

"How has the tour gone since autumn?" Hossbach said. "I've heard gossip of course, but you must tell me everything yourself. Ah, but first, formalities."

Katterman held out one hand. "Your papers, please." His accent was almost flawless.

There was a split second of silence. It was like that moment on the stage in Amsterdam, where Jim sent up his lines as the lights came up. A jolt that threw the actors from the script, that's what did it. In Jim's case, it had been a green tie on the Irish ambassador. In Nigel and Margaret's, the wrong papers. And now the script was gone and in an instant the fourth wall would break apart and the audience would recognize that they were only actors on the stage.

"Our papers?" Nigel said with a laugh. "But Hossbach, old fellow, you don't know who we are by now?"

Step away from these two. Lift your finger and accuse them.

It was Jim's chance. Whatever crime he'd committed, fleeing the company in Amsterdam, even sending a message to Gordon Gaughran to enlist his help in defecting to Ireland, he'd earn forgiveness in one instant. Whatever these two were about, they were terrified of Hossbach and Katterman, which meant they were on the wrong side of the regime. All Jim had to do was make sure he was on the *right* side and he'd be safe. And during that long pause, when he thought about their treachery, the way Margaret hit him and Nigel threatened, he thought it would only serve them right.

And yet. Something tugged at him. His stage instincts.

Telling him to improvise.

A frown tugged at Katterman's lips, and his eyes flicked to Jim and then Margaret. A moment longer and he would voice the suspicion now spreading across his face.

Jim made a sudden decision. "May I speak to you first?" he asked Hossbach. The words tumbled out, clumsy in delivery. He hesitated, gathered himself. "Privately. Just me and the two of you?"

"Are you sure that's a good idea?" Nigel said. "Should we —?"

"No, I insist, it must be private. Herr Hossbach? Please?"

"Why yes, of course," Hossbach said. "Stay there, both of you."

Jim didn't have a plan, only knew he had to get away from Nigel and Margaret. He led the two Germans down the platform, and then hesitated, as if he couldn't decide if he'd taken them far enough. After a moment's consideration, he gestured for them to follow another dozen feet or so. "Here, this is good."

"What is this about, anyway?" Hossbach asked.

Improv. That's all this was, a improvisation onstage, thinking on your feet, getting out of a jam. And what was the first rule of improv? When someone gave you a prompt, you never said 'no,' you always said 'yes, but...'

Jim switched to German. "There's a spy on our train."

Hossbach's eyebrows went up and Katterman leaned in.

"We took the Col de Tende crossing through the mountains. The washroom at the Italian border was in awful shape, and they don't let you use the one on the train while you're in the station, because everything falls onto the track and soon the whole station will stink to high heaven, although I can't see how it could have been worse than that washroom, I'll tell you."

"I'm well aware of the sanitary deficiencies of Italy," Hossbach said, his tone peevish. "Get to the point."

"I only want to explain why I was in the bushes when I saw the man taking photos of the train, of the members of our company."

Hossbach stiffened. "What kind of man?"

"Short, Italian. Gray fedora." He stepped in closer to force Katterman to pay attention to the story. The other man's attention was drifting back to the others on the platform.

"He didn't see me," Jim continued. "I'm sure of it. Must have taken ten or twenty photos in all. And just before we left, he jumped into the second-class car to ride with us a while."

"Where is he now?"

Jim shrugged. "He jumped out as the train slowed before coming into the station. Here in Florence. Nobody bothered to stop him. Did you see that black car? He got into it."

"I didn't see a black car," Hossbach said. "But I wasn't looking, either. Did you see one?" When Katterman shook his head, Hossbach added, "Sounds to me like OVRA — Italian secret police. Not a surprise. My advice, don't draw attention to yourself. You're under protection of the Reich. So long as you don't do anything stupid you'll be fine."

"Well, all right." Jim let disappointment seep into his voice. "You don't think you should look into this?"

"No, I don't," Hossbach said.

Katterman frowned. "Why did you tell us this in private?"

"I didn't want to worry the others. You know how actors are—it might throw off their performance if they thought they were being followed."

Hossbach snorted. "You're either naïve, Heydrich, or you're an idiot. Act on the assumption that you're always being followed."

"I'm sorry, Herr Hossbach."

"Never mind. Is that all? Come on, then."

By the time they got back, he could tell from the change in Margaret's posture that she had swapped out papers. And yet both she and Nigel still looked tense, no doubt worried about whether or not Jim had denounced them. He would soon put them at ease.

"I'm sorry," he said to the two Germans. "I suppose I was overreacting. Should I call you if I see the photographer again?"

"What's this about, then?" Nigel said.

"It's nothing," Hossbach said. "Where were we? Ah yes, your papers."

This time there was no hesitation as Margaret and Nigel already had them in hand.

CHAPTER ELEVEN

THEY TOOK OVER THE TEATRO Fiorentino in the heart of Florence. It was a gorgeous, if dilapidated, old building with white marble pillars, carved luxury boxes, and frescoes of Roman mythology painted on the ceiling. Nigel set the crew to building the thrust for the drawing room scene in act 3, as well as installing the hardware for the flippable painted bookshelves/country estate windows. It was all hands on deck, and Jim climbed the ladder to move stage lights, even as he watched for an opportunity to slip away. The only people he couldn't see were Kyle Dunleavy and Károly Weil, the newcomer to the cast, who were supposedly working on lines. Jim had his suspicions and needed to locate the two men before making his way back to the dressing rooms. When the chance came, he slipped a pair of screwdrivers into his pocket and stepped behind the curtain and backstage.

Jim found the two men in the cast lounge, and they were, in fact, running lines, with Dunleavy reading from book. Weil paced the room as he delivered lines, periodically calling for a prompt. The Hungarian was a tall, strongly built man, middle aged and balding, with a stentorian voice that could become tremulous with false outrage about his son's idle lifestyle. He was, to Jim's surprise, a better Lord Caversham than Kristiann

Janssen, who had been passable, but was never accused of upstaging the stars. Weil was confident, yet flexible when Dunleavy stopped him to make a suggestion, and already making the part his own. In other words, a real stage actor.

Dunleavy caught Jim's eye and put down the book. "Want to run lines with the new chap?"

"No, I've got to get back to work. Came looking for that Dutch carpenter, what's his name?"

"Vandermeer? Haven't seen him."

"Never mind, then. I'll leave you to it."

Jim backtracked up the hallway, then took a turn toward the dressing rooms. This wing was bigger than what they were used to. In some cases, not even Lula and her leading lady reputation were enough to secure a private dressing room, but this was a world-class opera house — or had been, in more prosperous days — and there were enough dressing rooms for even the most bloated opera cast, stuffed full of prima donna warblers. Colorized photographs framed the walls of the hallway: Giacomo Puccini, Enrico Caruso with a black, upturned mustache and a feathered hat, and Rosina Storchio, dressed as Cio-Cio San from Madame Butterfly and holding a bouquet of roses. And stage actors too: Allan Aynesworth, Enrico Viarisio, and Maria Caserina as Lady Macbeth. And curiously, a signed photo of Charlie Chaplin standing on a boat with the Manhattan skyline to his rear.

It took three tries before he found the room that held Weil's steamer trunk. The trunk was battered metal painted in battleship gray, with brass handles. Passage stickers boasted that the trunk had been everywhere from Calcutta to Cairo. Jim eased the dressing room door closed behind him. The lights were on already. He tried the trunk, but it was locked. Like most of the cast, it seemed that Weil preferred to keep his personal belongings at the theater rather than in the hotel room, where it would be easier for maids, hotel staff, or Italian secret police to rifle through his belongings. Lula had traveled through Italy several times, and claimed the Italians would confiscate one's possessions for official investigation and then conveniently lose them. And forget the hotel safe — that was like gathering all your sheep into a single paddock, and then giving the keys to a wolf.

Jim wished he had a key now. He wanted to get inside that trunk and see what secrets Weil was carrying around with him. Nigel and Margaret hadn't broken poor Janssen's leg because Weil had better stage presence. Actor or no, Jim was certain he'd find something. He felt at the back of the trunk, to see if he could unscrew the hinges, but they sat on the inside. The trunk lid was, however, loose. These things were moved and battered around so much that if you didn't pay attention, you could lose handles or the entire top. In this case, Jim discovered he could slip the end of the large flat-head screwdriver beneath the lid. Work it back and forth and he might be able to pop the screws, especially if they were old and worn from travel, corroded by ocean air and tossed about by careless porters. He worked the screwdriver in and tried to decide if it would be worth it, knowing that his forced entry would be discovered and raise suspicions.

A voice sounded at his back. A foreign phrase.

He turned, heart in his throat. A man sat in the corner, partially concealed by a cloth rack, his own dark jacket blending among Weil's shirts and costumes. The man must have been there all along, motionless, while Jim came in, oblivious, his attention so drawn by the footlocker that he'd missed the more critical detail that someone was in the room already, waiting for him. And now Jim stood gaping and guilty, screwdriver wedged beneath the lid.

But the man didn't look at him. Instead, he studied a notebook, a pencil in one hand. It was Weil's man, his butler or servant, squat and dull-faced. Hungarian peasant stock. He frowned in concentration, like he was trying to compose a note and was unable to remember his letters. Jim twisted his wrist to remove the screwdriver, which made the hinges groan as it popped free. He slipped it back into his sleeve as Weil's servant looked up, seemed to notice him for the first time, and frowned.

"Sorry, I..." Jim's voice trailed off.

"Constant," the man said in heavily accented English. "What is constant?"

"Constant? As in continual?"

"Continual? What is continual? I do not understand this word."

"Like all the time, never-ending — that's what constant means."

"Yes, but what is constant?" He switched to German, with an equally heavy accent. *"Was ist konstant?"*

Jim tried to explain it in German, but this didn't work, either, in part because his own language skills weren't what they should be. He spelled it out in English. "C-O-N-S-T-A-N-T."

"What is constant?"

Something about the man's tone and continued insistence irritated him. "Maybe you should write the damn thing in your own language, have you thought about that?"

The man shook his head and returned to writing in his notebook. He said something in Hungarian, a burst of syllables that sounded like one long word. Jim didn't care to continue the conversation—he was relieved that Weil's inattentive servant was so preoccupied with struggling through the letter composition that he'd completely missed that Jim was trying to force open his master's footlocker.

Voices sounded in the hallway outside the dressing room. Jim opened the door to slip out and came face to face with Dunleavy and Weil.

"What are you doing in my room?" Weil's voice was heavy with suspicion.

Jim pushed open the door to show the strange little butler still puzzling over his notebook. "I heard a voice and I knew everyone was upstairs. I thought someone— well, your man is talking to himself. That's all."

"What did you say to him?" Weil asked.

"Nothing. Why would I say anything? He barely speaks English."

Both Dunleavy and Weil were big men—each of them must outweigh Jim by thirty or forty pounds. And with everything turned on end, he felt vulnerable down here, so far from the rest of the company, where nobody would hear him cry for help. And if they did hear his cries, would they come anyway? He should have taken his chances with Hossbach and Katterman at the train station.

Weil said something to his servant in Hungarian. A short answer came back. Another long question from Weil, and this time the servant looked up with a frown, spoke more at length. Whatever the man said, Weil didn't like it. His face darkened and his tone grew blunt and angry.

Jim glanced at Dunleavy, to see the Scotsman scowling. "Come on," Dunleavy said, and took his arm. "We're going back to help with the set." Once they were away from the two Hungarians, Dunleavy said, "I don't know what the devil you were doing in there, but you looked damned suspicious."

"I told you, I—"

"Oh, hang it all, I know what you said. But listen to me. Be careful with Károly Weil. Why, he only joined the cast two days ago."

"Nigel vouches for him."

"Yes, but who vouches for Nigel? He was in a pinch after Janssen's accident. In those circumstances, would you trust his judgment? I wouldn't."

"These days, I don't even trust my own judgment," Jim said.

Dunleavy's tone changed. "Come on, now, that's going too far. Trust yourself, at least do that. And the rest of us, too—by now you can be sure we're trustworthy."

This last part was so patently false that the only way Dunleavy would make the claim was if he didn't know about Nigel and Margaret, or at least, that he didn't know they'd already revealed to *Jim* that they were murderers and spies.

"I will. I mean, I do."

"And you'll be more careful."

"Right. I wasn't thinking."

"Good. That's what I want to hear." Dunleavy put a hand on his shoulder. "You know if anything happens, if you ever have doubts or suspicions or simply need a trustworthy man to unburden yourself on, don't hesitate to find me and we'll pour a glass of scotch and speak as candidly as we like."

"Thank you," Jim said. "I'll remember the offer."

That Dunleavy would propose such a conversation struck him as the most questionable thing the man could have said. Jim added Kyle Dunleavy to his list of suspicious characters. It was a long list already and its counterpart, the list of trusted characters, had dwindled to zero.

CHAPTER TWELVE

AN INSISTENT KNOCK WOKE JIM early the next morning. The curtain over the tiny window on the wall opposite his bed had turned a faint gray, indicating the hope of dawn, but it hadn't yet arrived. They'd assigned him the smallest, most cave-like room in the hotel, on the third floor, with a ten-inch window that overlooked a cobbled street, and a view of the stone wall of the church on the opposite side of a lane too narrow for automobiles.

Jim had slipped into his room last night, exhausted from a hard day of building the set, only to discover that someone had entered his room while he was gone. He had borrowed two books of Tuscan recipes from the hotel kitchen staff and propped them on the nightstand with a hair between them. He'd then turned one of his pillows just so, and turned the lamp so the switch faced the wall. When he returned, the pillow was in the right place and the books were where he'd left them, but the hair between them was gone. And the switch on the lamp now faced the bed. Had they broken in to rifle through his belongings, or had they entered to plant listening devices?

The knock started up again.

"Go away."

"Wake up, Jim." It was Margaret.

"Thank you, but you quite wore me out last night. I had no idea you were so athletic in bed."

"Don't be an ass. Come out here."

"I'll talk to you at breakfast, unless you want to bash down the door with that thick skull of yours."

He rolled over and put the other pillow over his head. Incredibly, she didn't knock again. He was drifting back to sleep when hooves clomped in the street below his window with the rattle of cart wheels. The bed in the room next to his creaked and someone coughed. Damn thin walls. And then he needed to pee. One moment he wasn't even aware of his bladder and the next it felt like it would burst like a toad beneath a panzer tread. He threw back the blankets, shivered at the cold, and unchained and unlocked the door on his way to the water closet. He stepped into the hallway and came face to face with Margaret. She was dressed, her hair brushed, her wool coat draped over one arm.

"Oh, hell," Jim said.

"Nigel is gone. I need to go to the piazza and you're coming with me."

He was still worried about listening devices, and so he stepped into the hall and pulled the door shut behind him. "You can't brave the streets by yourself? What are you afraid of?"

"Of leaving you alone, you idiot."

"Margaret, I was asleep. I'm not going to run off. I'm going down the hall to empty my bladder, and then I'm going to crawl back in bed and forget that my body is aching from swinging a hammer and bending over all day with a screwdriver."

"I don't care if you're tired and lazy, you have to come with me."

"Or what?"

She glared at him.

"That's what I thought," Jim said. "You don't have any leverage over me other than threats of violence, and I'm getting sick of those. Maybe if you asked nicely."

"What is that supposed to mean?"

"You know, manners. The sort of thing they teach nice young ladies in England."

Margaret clenched her jaw. "I am sorry I disturbed you. Please come with me."

It sounded so forced, so painful, that he laughed. "You say you're going to the piazza?"

"That's right. Don't you want to see the Duomo?"

"You're going sightseeing at this hour? It can't be seven yet."

She put her hands on her hips. "Jim, I said please. What more do you want? You want me to come back to your room and show you a good time? Is that what it will take? We have twenty minutes. Can you be quick?"

His eyebrows went up. "You'd do that? All to get me down to the piazza?"

"I would loathe you afterward more than any woman has ever loathed any man, but yes. I need to get down there, don't you see? Nigel is gone, I have no idea why he didn't come back, and I can't leave you alone. Now do you want me to spread my legs, or will you be a gentleman and come with me?"

"Women who expect men to behave as gentlemen don't usually chloroform them, threaten to slit their throats, and hit them in the face."

"I am sorry about that." She sounded sincere this time. "The stakes are high. I will do whatever is necessary, no matter how unpleasant."

He stared for a long moment. "I wouldn't make you do that." He sighed. "Okay. Give me fifteen minutes to wash up and get dressed. I'll meet you in the lobby."

She looked relieved. "No games, right?"

"No games."

It was more like ten minutes before Jim met Margaret in the lobby. He was still yawning and cranky, but Margaret looked grateful and he felt a twinge of guilt that she'd offered her body as the price for his cooperation. What the hell was so important in the piazza?

"I roused the kitchen staff," she said, and held out a cup of steaming coffee, which he took gratefully.

It was ersatz coffee, alas, the chicory root slop they drank in Europe these days, but it was hot, and the bitter flavor gave him the illusion of alertness after he'd singed his tongue gulping it down. They stepped out of the hotel and into the chill streets. The light was improving and there were men on the street in worn jackets and unwashed trousers. They carried buckets or pushed carts, or simply strode in groups of two and three as they hurried off to some factory or workshop. On the main boulevard, women joined them, with bundles of reeds propped on their heads or carrying sacks of rags.

"You knew I wasn't going anywhere, right?" Jim said. "I meant what I said. I was going back to sleep."

"I have my orders."

"So Nigel would be mad you left me alone. Big deal. Surely your brother would understand that I was being stubborn, and that you had no choice but to go out for... well, whatever it is you need to do."

"Nigel is not my brother."

Jim stopped and stared. "Huh?"

"Huh?" she mocked. "Canadians speak English, right? Words like 'not' and 'brother' mean the same thing in North America that they do in the United Kingdom, correct?"

"You act like brother and sister."

"*Act*, Jim. That's the key word. *Act*."

"And you look so much alike."

"I met him two hours before I met you. He's not even English, he's Welsh."

"But he has that *veddy, veddy* upper-class accent."

Suddenly, Margaret was speaking with a Brooklyn accent. "Whaddya think, the accent makes the person?"

"Wait, you're an American?"

"No, I'm not," she said, tone icy and English again. "My father is a member of the peerage and his father served in the House of Lords. It's called acting, Jim—that's all this is. We're actors playing actors. Like your stunt on the platform with Hossbach and Katterman. What was that about, anyway?"

"You had the wrong papers. I don't know why you're traveling with various documents and why you'd want to use one set in German-controlled territory and another in Italy, but I could tell that if Hossbach caught you out you'd be in trouble. So I improvised."

"But why? You could have denounced us."

"I don't know why. My head is spinning and I have no idea what's real. I'm trying to stay alive and so I'm changing my bets to suit the circumstances."

"That's your problem right there."

"Trying to stay alive here, Margaret. That's a problem for you?"

"A man cannot serve two masters." She fixed him with a hard look. "Courtesy of my *mother's* side of the family. *Her* father was a missionary in China."

They lapsed into silence as they continued toward the piazza. Brunilleschi's dome rose above the buildings to the left, a towering brick mosaic, but they continued on until he suddenly found himself face to face with a wide piazza and the most famous statue in the world. "Is that the...is it the original?"

Michelangelo's *David* sat in front of the palace on the far side of the piazza, a seventeen-foot masterpiece of the human body. White marble and beautiful, an image no photograph could capture, not really.

"No, it isn't. They moved the real one inside twenty, thirty years ago."

"Oh," he said, disappointed. "It looks real enough."

"Did the church bells chime yet?"

"Not yet, no."

"Come on, then, I'll show you. But walk past it—don't look like a tourist if you can help it."

The statue lost its glory as they drew closer. Pigeon droppings mucked up its face and shoulders, staining the marble. A boy stood behind the statue, urinating against the wall, even as foot and bicycle traffic picked up, fighting with carts and the occasional truck or automobile that crossed the square with no regard for traffic patterns. Vegetable booths and roadside apothecaries lined the sides of the street, the proprietors unloading and arranging their wares, sweeping away the rainwater that collected in glistening puddles in and around their stalls. Children in ragged clothes—pickpockets? beggars?— darted among the crowd. An attractive woman walked by in a mink coat and a ridiculous hat topped with flowers and glass fruit. Two Italian soldiers strolled behind her, either protecting her from the riff-raff or admiring her backside, or perhaps both. Nobody paid the *David* or any of the other statues in front of the palace and around the square any attention. The scene was like a slum plopped into the middle of a glorious outdoor art museum.

"You see," Margaret said. "It isn't real."

"Or maybe it is real and nobody cares."

He started to say something else, but then the church bells chimed and she stiffened and gestured for him to turn around and walk back the way they'd come.

"Where are we going?" he asked.

"Back to the hotel. Let's take a look at the Duomo on our way back, shall we?"

"What, that's it?"

"I made my rendezvous. I have everything I need."

Jim started to question her, but then he remembered Gaughran and the green tie. She must have been looking for a similar clue. Whatever it was, she was calm and relaxed. Or maybe that was more acting.

"In that case," he said, "you can check out the dome on your own time. I'm going back to my room to get some sleep."

"You're not interested in seeing the greatest engineering marvel of the Renaissance?"

"No, not today."

It wasn't strictly true. But he needed time to think. Time to figure out the next course of action.

What about that toss-off line from her grandfather, the missionary in China? Serving two masters and all that. What did Margaret expect? Jim grew up in Canada, yes, but in a German family with loyalty to the Fatherland. Either way you looked at it, he was a traitor to someone.

And he wasn't serving *any* master, he was trying to stay alive in a time when thousands, maybe millions of men his age were dying. Could she blame him for that?

Listen to yourself, he thought. *Stop whining and make your choice.*

CHAPTER THIRTEEN

NIGEL WAS LATE FOR REHEARSAL. He had a cue-to-cue that afternoon to get used to the new stage. By now, they'd performed so many times that most nights — barring the nights SS-Obergruppenführer Reinhard Heydrich sat in the front row on a night you planned to flee the continent — Jim could sleepwalk through an entire show. The problem was hitting light and sound cues, making sure the stagehands knew how to get props on- and offstage in the new space, and in general, growing comfortable with the new venue.

Lula showed up five minutes late, her heels clicking a drumbeat across the stage as she came around the curtain and hurried into place. "Sorry, everyone, sorry." She looked around in confusion. "What's wrong? Why aren't we working?"

"Our fearless leader is a no show," Jim called from out front of the stage. He sat in the second row, arms propped over the seat back in front of him. Crew and cast who didn't appear at the beginning of act 1 lounged around him, smoking or thumbing through notes. A few heads lolled back, actors who dozed with collars pulled up around their ears to ward against the damp chill in the unheated theater. "Margaret, are you back there?" Jim said. "Where's Nigel?"

She popped her head around the curtain. "He'll be here. I fancy he's arguing with the printer over the playbill."

"I was having a Stracotto for lunch with a nice Chianti," Lula said. "I wish I'd known, I wouldn't have rushed back."

"We finished eating an hour ago," another woman called. "I wouldn't say we were rushed."

"I was enjoying my wine."

The actors onstage settled into groups, fiddling with the placement of props or chatting. Dunleavy insisted the fireplace was half a meter upstage of its rightful position, while Weil said that the chaise lounge looked out of place, more Georgian than late Victorian. It had served them fine for two hundred shows, the stage manager snapped, so unless Weil had brought more-appropriate furniture with him from Hungary, he should keep suggested improvements to himself until he had, oh, maybe a single performance under his belt. The new girl in the light booth brought the lights up and down, which blinded the actors onstage and then plunged them into darkness again. They yelled at her to knock it off.

Meanwhile, Jim grew worried. Nigel was never late. Say the printer was difficult, Nigel would look at his watch, realize he needed to get back, and then issue a decision. No arguments. Jim was rising to go backstage and ask Margaret what was wrong, when Nigel staggered in from the lobby. He wore his coat buttoned tight and winced in pain. His face was pale, drained of blood. The man looked like he should be in the hospital, not rehearsal. Cast and crew alike turned to stare.

"What the bloody hell happened to you?" Dunleavy asked.

"Undercooked shellfish," Nigel said. "Food poisoning. I feel wretched." He leaned against one of the seats halfway down the aisle. "I only came in to tell you..." He stopped, took a few deep breaths. "...to tell you to carry on without me. I'll be in bed, waiting for the doctor, if one can be bothered." Another deep breath. "Jim, stand in, won't you, old fellow?"

He turned and made his way back up the aisle, his right hand gripping seat backs to steady himself. Margaret came down offstage and hurried up the aisle. She caught Nigel as he reached the lobby, and the two of them disappeared together. She came back a few minutes later with a worried expression.

"Margaret?" Lula said in a worried tone.

"He's fine, he feels better already. Needs a few hours in bed until it passes. Let's run the show. No time to waste."

Margaret knocked on Jim's hotel room door that evening, called for him with her voice muffled by the wooden door.

He was on his hands and knees when she knocked, checking the baseboard for signs of tampering. Already, he'd unscrewed the light bulb on the lamp, inspected the bed frame, and run his hands along every inch of the credenza and the armoire, and then lifted the rug to look for listening devices. Nothing.

"Jim, are you in there?"

"Hold on." He rose, dusted himself off, and unlatched the door.

Margaret pushed in, face flushed, chewing on her lip.

"He was shot."

"My God. What happened?"

"Never mind the circumstances. Bullet missed vital organs—he'll live. And it didn't happen in the city, so they cannot track him here. That's all that matters. But Nigel won't be onstage tomorrow. Probably not the next night, either. You have his part learned?"

"Theoretically."

"Good. We'll find someone else for the Phipps part. Maybe Higgins knows the lines. We'll throw a fake mustache on the fellow, pad his belly or something, and hopefully nobody will recognize that he's the viscount from act 1 by the time act 3 rolls around and he goes onstage again."

The implications sank in. "So I'm playing Lord Goring? Did you tell the rest of the cast? Are we going back to the theater to run the show tonight?"

"No time for rehearsal. I've got to get to the fish market before it closes, and I need you with me. Nigel is in no shape."

"That again? You still don't think I can be trusted not to run off?"

"Whether I think so or not doesn't matter. The man at the vegetable stall saw two people today, a man and a woman. That means the fishmonger will be expecting a man and a woman, too. I thought Nigel would be back, but he's not. So I need you to stiffen your upper lip and act like a man who cares about king and country. Can you do that?"

"Do you have to speak to me like that? Would a little civility kill you?"

"There are men searching the city. Carabinieri— military police. Maybe even Italian secret police."

"I thought you said—"

"Will you listen? If these men catch us alive, they'll work us over. The Italian methods of torture are not so organized as the NKVD's, or as brutally improvisational as the Gestapo's, but you'll find them effective enough."

"And again, you're not doing a very good job selling me on this. Don't they have charm lessons at that spy school of yours?"

Desperation washed over her face. "Hang it all, I don't have time to sell it. Please, for God's sake."

"I'll come, you don't have to throw yourself on me again." He reached into the armoire to get his coat and hat.

She gave him a world-weary look, and then ducked her head into the hall. A moment later, she waved for him to follow.

They slipped downstairs and into the dark street. The air was damp and cool, with a fine mist that drizzled from the sky. Jim and Margaret picked their way through foot traffic and reached the market a few minutes later. It stretched from a small piazza outside a neighborhood church, spilled into and choked off two side streets, and then split off pieces that huddled beneath the awnings of shop fronts. Vendors sold belts and shoes and used utensils and cookware. Women weaved through the crowd with baskets on their shoulders, from which they hawked fava beans and roasted nuts. Two rabbits turned on spits over a charcoal fire, and a woman stirred an enormous pot of broth, which she ladled into tin cups for working-class men, who handed over a few coins, sipped the broth while leaning against the building, and then handed back the cups to be rinsed and refilled for the next customer. A man pushed a cart that held an oak barrel with a spigot. When Margaret and Jim passed, he said, "*Vino rosso?*"

Two height-stunted children, who must have been five or six but looked even younger, sidled up to Jim on either side. He put his hands in his pockets and glared at each of them in turn to let them know he was watching for pickpockets. A filthy girl tugged on Margaret's sleeve and tried to hand her a daisy. They declined all these offers and distractions and ducked beneath the awnings to penetrate deeper into the market. The crowds grew thicker.

Jim took in the leather sellers with their belts and wallets laid out on tables, the wheels of cheese and jugs of table wine, the butchers selling mysterious cuts of meat — none of which appeared to be beef — and the men who haggled over resharpened and repaired garden tools.

"More goods for sale than in Holland," he said.

"The privilege of the invaders over the invaded. Still, do these people look rich to you?"

"They don't," he admitted. "But your average Italian wasn't rich before the war, either."

"And he's poorer now. The national wealth goes into bullets and bombs." She cocked her head and squinted against the light of candles and lanterns, the glow of cook fires. "I smell overripe fish. We must be close."

His nose caught it too, the stink of seafood that grew until it smothered the smell of cook fires and charred meat. They rounded a corner, past barrels of pig feet in brine and baskets of spices piled in green, red, and yellow powders to be weighed by the gram, and came upon the fish market. Crabs swam in buckets, together with catfish packed into bins until there was more fish than water. The fish lifted their heads to gasp at the air.

Larger, dead fish lay on top of a table. A man haggled with a frail little woman bundled in so many clothes that Jim wondered if you started removing coats and scarves and gloves whether you would find anything underneath or if she was nothing but layers of clothing all the way down. The woman seemed disgusted by the fish she was trying to purchase. Near as Jim could tell, she was complaining that it smelled, that it wasn't fresh. The fishmonger protested.

Midway through this exchange, the man glanced up, did a double take when he saw Jim and Margaret, and then called his assistant over. The assistant was a slender, dark-skinned man, perhaps a Libyan or half-Ethiopian.

"*Lei parla tedesco?*" Margaret asked. *Do you speak German?*

The assistant said that he did, a little, and then Margaret asked him in German about one medium-sized, suspicious-looking fish. The head was something like a large trout, but the body seemed off. Too broad and scaly. Whatever it was, it sat up top and didn't look particularly fresh or desirable, even by the low standards of the market.

"I wouldn't buy that, if I were you," he told her. "How about that flounder? That looks marginally fresh. Might have come out of the water some time since the start of the war."

"Quiet," Margaret said, then turned back to argue with the assistant fishmonger, who wanted thirty lire. She offered ten, which still seemed high, given that the frail woman was buying a much larger, more palatable-looking fish for fifteen. They eventually settled on twelve, and the man wrapped it deftly in newspaper, doubled over so none of the fish was visible. Money and fish traded hands. Moments later, Margaret and Jim were fighting their way back out of the market.

"Your fish head doesn't belong with its body," he said. "Bet if you took it out, the head would fall right off. Looks like a trout head with the body of some bottom feeder pulled out of the canal. Probably a carp."

"That's why I bought it. Nobody else was going to."

"Another secret message?"

She handed him the fish. It stank, even through the paper and with all the other smells that competed for his attention.

"What am I supposed to do with it?" he said.

"They're looking for us. I need to be able to get at my gun."

"Are you serious?"

"Quite. Carabinieri at three o'clock."

He glanced in that direction and spotted two men in olive uniforms with carbines over their shoulders. Unlike the police or carabinieri he'd spotted on the street, these two wore lean, purposeful expressions. Their uniforms were clean and their eyes sharp. They scanned the crowd, and Jim hunched over before they turned in his direction. He stood a full head above the other men around him, a tan fedora on his head out of place among the blacks and dark browns.

Margaret found a break in the crowd, took his arm, and pulled him left. "Take off your hat."

He pulled off the fedora and the fish in the newspaper slipped from beneath his arm and almost fell to the ground. Margaret hissed at him to be careful. A few minutes later they broke out of the market and onto a crowded boulevard that took them north. Margaret stopped and looked down a side street. "More police.

Are they all looking for us?"

"How would I know?"

She pulled him against a mason wall that enclosed a gated patio in front of one of the houses. "Do you know the city?"

"Only what I saw on the map," he said. "You want to get back to the hotel without passing through the piazzas?"

"That's right."

"The Ponte Vecchio is ahead of us, I think. We'll cross the Arno."

She shook her head. "Too busy."

"But if we get over the river, we're out of the commercial center, right? A few minutes on the bridge and then we're safe."

"And how do we get back?"

"There have to be more bridges over the river or it wouldn't be called 'the old bridge,'" he said. "We follow the riverbank until we find one and then we double back. Get back to the hotel without passing through the center of town."

"All right," Margaret said after a moment's hesitation. "You lead. My sense of direction is rubbish."

He followed the crowds, stopped once when they didn't see any police or carabinieri and asked an elderly woman how to cross the river: *Dove il Ponte Vecchio?* She responded through a mouth missing half its teeth, and he didn't understand a word of it. He asked her to repeat herself. She tried again, her answer one long sibilant phrase that was impossible to parse. At last she made a sound of disgust and pointed a crooked finger down and over.

They followed her directions, and found it a few

minutes later, the lit houses and shops stretching along the top of the arched bridge like a sepia-toned postcard come to life. Lanterns winked in windows and moonlight gleamed off the roofs and reflected from the sluggish river current. Lovers lined the wall above the river as it approached the bridge, with couples even curled around the pillars that supported the arches of the bridge, and more on a barge attached to a pillar in the middle of the river itself. Margaret and Jim joined the press of foot, bicycle, and cart traffic that passed through the choke point across the bridge.

Margaret stopped. "Turn around. Quickly, get off the bridge."

Jim's stomach lurched as he saw what had spooked her. Traffic snarled the Ponte Vecchio because three police officers were questioning every person who tried to reach the far side. He turned around, but a foot patrol of carabinieri with guns slung over their shoulders emerged from the pair of alleys at their back and an officer on a horse trotted along the road that ran parallel to the river.

Margaret urged Jim forward and onto the bridge. They glanced up and down the block of buildings that lined the street on either side as it crossed the Arno. A red light glimmered in one window, and a sleazy-looking bar occupied the building next to it, where working-class types smoked and drank, and sang what was either a drinking song or the most guttural opera ever. Behind them, the carabinieri had crossed the street and would soon enter the bridge from the near side as well. Jim and Margaret would find themselves pincered between forces on either side of the river; it would be a simple matter to sweep the bridge until Italians found the pair of foreigners.

"Should I toss the fish?" Jim asked.

"We can't," she said in an anguished tone. "The note..."

He looked up the bridge, terrified to be holding the contraband, and yet not ready to defy her and jettison the fish. More men reinforced the carabinieri asking for papers on the far side of the bridge. On the near side, the men crossed the street and started a second inspection. The carabinieri had sealed the bridge with Margaret and Jim on it.

CHAPTER FOURTEEN

KATTERMAN ORDERED THE DRIVER TO stop the car. It squealed to a halt with the sound of worn brake pads and bald tires on slick cobblestone. Hossbach and Katterman stepped out and into the night air. Italian military police, most of them poorly dressed and slouching, milled along the banks of the Arno or strolled up and down the old bridge itself. Women with children crossed without inspection, but the carabinieri challenged anyone else attempting to enter or leave the bridge. A few produced papers, but most people didn't seem to have any and faced questioning instead.

Katterman watched with dismay. "Who came up with such a system?"

"It would appear that Italy is a foreign country," Hossbach said in a dry tone. He pointed to a knot of officers. "Over here."

They made their way to where Captain Rosario stood among his men, gesturing with his hands like a Roman consul. They didn't teach those gestures in the language books, Katterman noted. Rosario spotted the two Germans and strutted over to meet them. "They were seen on the bridge," the captain said in Italian. "It's only a matter of time."

"Search the bridge," Katterman said. The Italian felt

sluggish as it came out of his mouth.

"What do you think we're doing?"

Nothing, you incompetent, preening man. Now get in there and find them.

Katterman understood the words perfectly well, but his tongue had turned to rubber. Again, that damnable disconnect between the Italian learned from books, records, and his language *professore,* and actual communication in the language. The correct words were in there, somewhere, but for a moment all he could remember of the language was the vinyl record with its scratch and hiss. "I went to the bakery yesterday," a man's voice said. A pause and then a woman translated in clear, melodious, and perfectly pronounced Italian: "*Ieri, io sono andato dal fornaio.*"

He bit his tongue to clear this unwanted intrusion from his head and forced the correct words from his mouth. "The longer you wait, the greater the chance that something goes wrong."

"There's no rush — let them sweat a little."

Anger clarified Katterman's Italian. "We'll sweat them in the holding cell."

"But they'll be more agitated the longer we wait. That will work to our advantage when we have them."

"Perhaps so agitated they try something foolish."

Hossbach demanded a translation, and then sputtered when he got it. "Tell them we need them alive and unharmed."

Katterman repeated this in Italian.

Rosario scraped the mud from his boot onto the curb above the cobblestone street. "Germans are not a patient race, are they? Always rushing about, always worrying."

"You have two dangerous criminals at large,"

Katterman said. "I want them in custody."

"Yes, and you shall have them."

"What's he saying?" Hossbach asked. When Katterman explained, the other German's face turned a deeper shade of crimson. "Damn it, we don't have time for this. You find them and find them now. *Trovare! Via!*"

Katterman mentally corrected his associate's Italian, but kept the corrections to himself. To Rosario he said, "My superior is not a patient man, captain. Men have died after defying him."

"Maybe in Germany," Rosario said. "This is Italy and you have no standing here."

"And how would our official complaint look in your record?"

Rosario scowled. "Don't threaten me. You have no authority here, do you understand?" Nevertheless, he turned and shouted at his men to begin the sweep. They saluted and marched onto the bridge, pushing people aside with the butts of their carbines. Rosario followed after them, shouting and waving his arms.

"Bloody Italians," Hossbach said.

"So I was right," Katterman said. "Heydrich's nephew and Burnside's sister."

"I wouldn't have guessed the girl. She's so silly and I've never heard her say anything political."

"They are actors. You see what they want you to see."

"Well, now you've flushed out suspicious behavior," Hossbach said. "The only question I have is whether Burnside himself is the leader or whether it's Heydrich."

The *only* question? Certainly not. Katterman had several. The who was one thing — and he wasn't convinced he was to the bottom of it — but the what and why were more important for the security of the Reich. Margaret and Heydrich had purchased a fish in the market. The Italians didn't know from whom, although the dozen or so vendors in the area would get worked over in the search. He guessed that some message or documents had passed between them. Or perhaps contraband, but he hoped not. It was a long, tedious trip from Germany to discover James Heydrich illegally buying black market stockings for his girlfriend, or sugar without a ration card. No doubt Hossbach had his suspicions, though he didn't see fit to reveal them to Katterman. Which was unfortunate. The lack of knowledge was a handicap, like going into battle with a musket when your enemy is armed with a machine gun.

Rosario came back twenty minutes later, his mouth twitching. He didn't look so smug anymore, but rubbed his hands together and wouldn't meet their gaze. "I don't understand it. Several people reported seeing the foreigners enter the bridge. One of them was my own man, damn him. Somehow, he lost track when they entered the crowd."

"You can't find them," Katterman said.

"There's nowhere to hide. They have to come out eventually, but I'll be buggered if I can figure out where they're hiding at the moment."

"Could they have jumped into the river?"

"Impossible. We are watching the river."

"What is it?" Hossbach said in German. "Tell me."

He reacted poorly when Katterman shared the news, grumbling about Italian incompetence, but at last he took on a philosophical tone, as he said. "I suppose we can go back to the hotel and arrest them when they return."

"No," Katterman said. "That doesn't fit my plan. Either the Italians are liars, or these two are still on the bridge somewhere. I want them found."

"You're right," Margaret said. "Do it. Throw the fish in the water."

"Hold it," Jim said. "I have an idea."

He thought about the couples he'd spotted lining the riverbank and hiding in the shadows at the base of the columns that supported the arches of the bridge, where they could steal kisses and grope each other in the shadows. And what about that barge beneath the bridge? Fish still tucked under one arm, he grabbed Margaret's hand and they squeezed into the gap between two buildings, an alley no more than eighteen inches wide. They wriggled their way to the end of the buildings and up to the water's edge.

He glanced down at the barge. Empty crates lay stacked on one side of the wide, flat boat lashed to the stone arch that emerged from the river. On the other side of the boat stood two couples, locked in embraces. Jim handed Margaret the fish, so he could lower himself down to the boat. When he'd dropped onto its swaying surface, the Italians pulled away with instinctive movements, not bothering to interrupt their kissing and amorous whispers.

He held up his hand for Margaret, who leaned over him, a silhouette against the sky. "Hurry!" he said. "Pass it down."

"One second."

She fumbled with something, and then handed him the fish and swung her legs over the side. He helped her down, she picked up the fish, and to his surprise let it slip out of the newspaper to slide noiselessly beneath the black, oily surface of the Arno. She crumpled the newspaper and tossed it out separately into the water.

"What did you do that for?"

"Quiet," she whispered. She stood in the shadows where the barge was lashed to the stone arch that emerged from the river. "Come here!"

She wrapped her arms around him and pulled him close, and then rested her cold cheek against his neck. A breeze lifted her hair and she shivered and drew tighter. Jim fell into the part, becoming the character he was playing, a young man in love with his Italian girlfriend, seeking warmth and solitude beneath the bridge. Her small, firm breasts pressed into his chest and her breath warmed his neck. She smelled like apple blossoms.

"Not so tight," she whispered in his ear.

"Sorry," he whispered back.

"It was a good idea. Maybe your first."

"Was that necessary?" he asked.

"What?"

"The gratuitous insult."

"It wasn't gratuitous."

"Why do you hate me?" he asked.

"I don't hate you, I *despise* you."

"But why? What did I ever do to you?"

"You're a worm."

"No, I'm not. I treat people with respect. I don't use position or money to take advantage."

"So you're a polite worm. Personally, you're likable enough. But everything you stand for chafes everything that I value. Understand now?"

"Margaret, what are you talking about? What did I ever do to you?"

"Where were you on June 3, 1940?"

"I don't know. Halle an der Saale, I suppose. In Saxony."

"I know where it is. I was there, remember? A pleasant little town. An old clock tower, charming church. Bet there's a Saturday market next to the river. Timber houses with flower boxes in every window. Beer gardens where old men in lederhosen and with kaiser mustaches sip their beers and talk about the good old days. Women lean over the fence to gossip or share recipes. Children wear school uniforms and walk in orderly lines on their way to school. When they get out, they play football in the street."

"What, England doesn't have towns like that, too?"

The noise picked up on the bridge above them. A man shouted in Italian, a woman screamed. Voices climbed in volume and pitch. Margaret's pulse beat a rapid, anxious cadence from her neck to his, but her low, whispered voice remained calm and withering.

"On June 3, 1940, while you were relaxing in Halle, my twin brother Harold was on a navy cruiser in the English Channel off the port of Dunkirk. Thousands of soldiers crowded the beaches, trying to get onto fishing boats, navy ships, anything they could. The Germans attacked with tanks, artillery, airplanes. One of Harold's mates told me that the sky was so black with smoke that it smelled like a foundry and looked like nightfall. Men bobbing in the water, screaming. The guns firing and firing. Junker bombers screaming down from the sky. One of them came in for a dive, took shrapnel, and caught on fire. It rammed my brother's ship. Harold went below deck to fight the fire. Burned horribly. They sent me a telegram. I caught the first train from London to visit him in the hospital in Southampton. But he died before I arrived."

"I'm sorry," Jim said.

"I'd just completed my training. Ten days later they infiltrated me into Europe. A week after that I was in the peaceful village of Halle. A smile on my face, cheer in my voice. Not a care in the world, but a black, hollow spot in my heart."

"So you met me and thought about your brother. And it wasn't fair."

Margaret pulled back and pounded his chest with her fist. "It *isn't* fair, you heartless — "

He clamped a hand over her mouth. "Shh. Don't."

She didn't struggle and he removed his hand. She was quiet for a few minutes, and when she spoke again her voice had regained its calm, though somehow the loathing came through even in a whisper. "Hundreds of Canadians at Dunkirk, too," she said. "Maybe thousands. A lot of them died. Doing their duty. So what's your problem?"

"I'm not Canadian, remember."

"That's a weak excuse."

"My German relatives don't understand, either. They think I should be fighting for the Fatherland."

"You make it sound ambiguous. Germany or Canada, Nazi bastards or freedom. Who can possibly make that choice?"

It *was* a weak excuse. Jim had known it the very day Hans von Steidle recruited him at the beer garden. He'd known it when he'd skipped out of town ahead of his uncle's efforts to get him into the SS, when he'd planned to flee to Ireland with Gordon Gaughran. What was it Margaret said? A man cannot serve two masters. That wasn't his problem. Jim's mistake was trying to escape the war by serving *no* master.

"How did you join the — what is it? — the British spy service?" Jim asked.

"Recruited for my language ability and acting talents. They came to my home one day, showed me papers, and whisked me off to London."

"They're recruiting girls now?"

"Girls?" she scoffed. "What do you think women are doing for the war effort? Giving out awards for who bottles the most peaches? No, we're digging bloody tank traps and learning how to shoot rifles. We know what will happen if you Germans overrun us. Rape and starvation."

"Oh, so now I'm German? I wish you'd make up your mind."

"And I wish you'd make up yours."

"Go to hell."

They fell silent. He regretted this last bit. Yes, her accusation was unfair, but he'd worked her up, tried to defend himself after she told him about her brother. In spite of her venom, he understood her better now. And with understanding came sympathy.

"What if we started over," he said at last.

"How so?"

"Pretend none of it happened. I had the wrong impression of you when we met. I thought you were... well, you know what. The role you rehearsed before you left London. Of course I would hate that person — that was the point."

"Go on," she said.

"Tell you what. I'll forget that. And I'll forget how you threatened me and bullied me, because I understand now why you did those things. In return, you'll forget what you know about me, or think you know. I'll help you in whatever you and Nigel are trying to do and you will help keep me out of the hands of the Gestapo, the carabinieri, and other unpleasant sorts. You don't even have to share the details of your mission."

Margaret was quiet again for a long moment before she said, "No, Jim, it wouldn't work. I'm more loyal than you, I don't change like that."

"Loyal to your prejudice, you mean."

"You don't understand and you never will."

Jim felt hurt, and angry too, both with himself and with Margaret. What did he think was going to happen? They'd broken Janssen's leg without pity, murdered Gaughran and dumped him in a Dutch canal. What did he expect from people like that? So why did he try?

It was Margaret's body, he decided. He was responding to her touch, her warm, tender embrace.

Acting, you idiot. She's pretending she doesn't want to cut your throat, that's all.

The commotion died down on the bridge and, looking up, he spotted foot traffic exiting the bridge at last. He pulled away from Margaret, relieved on several levels.

"I think that's it," he said. "I'll climb up first and then help you up." He stopped. "Wait, what about the fish? Did you take something out of it before you dumped it?"

"Jim, look," she said. "They've turned around and are coming back over the bridge."

"Oh, hell."

It was true. Lanterns multiplied along the shoreline and more bobbed up and down on the Ponte Vecchio. They hadn't given up, they'd reorganized to do a second, more thorough search. Soon enough they'd press some shop keeper, some prostitute, who would ask the carabinieri if they'd checked the dark, hidden spaces where lovers gathered to enjoy privacy.

"What are they going to do if they catch us?" he said.

"Torture, most likely."

Margaret sounded so calm she might as well have been talking about what kind of bread she wanted with her pasta. But at the word *torture*, Jim's knees went weak and his calves trembled.

"Can you swim?" she asked.

"Of course."

Margaret kicked off her shoes, stripped out of her skirt until she stood in a bra and white underwear that went halfway to her knees. She wrapped her shoes and outer clothes in her jacket, which she formed into a bundle. The other two couples stopped kissing and stared. Jim pulled off his jacket and his trousers, which he bundled the same way Margaret had.

"Let the current carry us past the next bridge," she said, "then come to shore the first place you can climb out of the water. Go!"

She pinned the bundle of clothes under her arm, turned, and jumped into the water. He followed.

CHAPTER FIFTEEN

THE WATER WAS LIKE ICE. Jim came up sputtering, gasping against the chill of the river that knifed into his body and sapped his energy. Margaret's head appeared above the water to his left, twenty or thirty feet downstream already. The Arno was a sluggish, barely flowing current, and he kicked his feet to get moving. He gasped and puffed, already chilled and his limbs growing numb. The next bridge was a dark shadow a few hundred yards distant still. No more than a minute or two downstream, if he could keep moving, but it seemed impossibly, discouragingly far.

His clothes soaked with water until the bundle felt like a weight in his arms. He thought about letting them go, but then he'd come up on shore in his underwear, practically naked and easy to spot. They'd be freezing in the wet clothes, but if they could keep to the shadows, they had a chance of making it back to the hotel, depending on how far through Florence the search had spread.

Gradually, he caught up with Margaret. Her head bobbed up and down, huffing steam. Jim's arms and legs were like lead, numb and heavy, and it was all he could do to propel them through the water, but as he drew next to her, he saw that she couldn't even manage that. She barely kept her head above the surface.

"Keep going," he urged.

"Can't. Must reach shore."

"No. Too soon." He turned his head to see dark shapes searching the shore to their left with lanterns and flashlights. No sign of pursuit on the opposite bank, but that was too far to fight the current in the icy waters. "Give me your clothes."

"No."

"Come on. I'll take them both. You can swim more easily."

"You'll drop the gun. It's in the clothes."

"Forget the gun," he said. "We're not going to shoot it out."

"No."

"Dammit Margaret. Listen to me."

"Shut up, you're not in charge. I am."

Her anger seemed to give her strength. She kicked her feet and pushed downstream. The bridge loomed, and he thought they'd outpaced the search on the shore. The current grew swift as it swept over the shallows by the bridge. Rocks battered at his legs. He tucked them, slammed into a boulder that didn't break the surface, and then passed into the darker shadows beneath the bridge, before the current flushed them out the far side. As he came up sputtering into calmer water, his pants and jacket floated past, lost somehow in the rapids. He flailed for them, but they were gone. Margaret drifted past, bobbing up and down and barely moving toward shore. Whatever reserves she'd drawn on were apparently gone.

Jim kicked to her side, swung his arm over her shoulder, and grabbed her under the chin. She didn't struggle, but flopped onto her back with her clothes clutched to her chest. He scissor kicked toward shore. It inched closer, and with relief he saw it was a grassy slope and not a rock wall as it had been upstream. He gave one final, ferocious kick, and then his feet sank into cold mud that congealed around his toes. He heaved Margaret into the shallows, pulled himself onto shore, and then dragged her up after him.

The cold clung to him in dripping, freezing water. The wind fluttered his wet shirt. Margaret lay next to him on her back, gasping, with mud on her face. Her bundle of clothing was a wet, muddy mess. A dog barked, and flashlights waved along the riverbank upstream, drawing nearer. Jim had to get them up the slope, across the road, and into the tangle of narrow alleys on the other side. Maybe someone would help them, some anti-fascist who would recognize their plight and drag them indoors to hide until the carabinieri and police gave up the search.

"Get up," he told her. "We've got to go."

"You go. Wrap my coat around your legs."

"Not a chance."

He rose to his knees and dug his hands under her armpits. She resisted and he couldn't get her up. She pawed through her clothes and came out with a pistol, dripping water, but clear of mud. Two dogs now, barking. The lights were almost above them.

"Margaret!"

"Don't be an ass. I can't make it. Tell Nigel…" She stopped and coughed. "Tell him what happened. The fish — what I did —"

But before she could complete this thought, the dogs started to howl. Dark shapes poured down the hillside. Lights flashed on their position. Margaret rolled onto her belly and lifted the Mauser, sighted down a trembling arm. He grabbed her wrist.

"Let me go."

He wrestled away the gun, pulled from her flailing grasp, and chucked the weapon at the river. It fell with a plop. Margaret let out an anguished cry.

And then came triumphant shouts in Italian. Men surrounded them with lights and snarling dogs and carbines pointed at their heads. Jim sat on his backside and lifted his hands in surrender.

They separated Jim from Margaret, kicked him in the ribs and beat his shoulders with truncheons while he cowered on the grass, and then pushed and kneed him up the hillside to a waiting car, where they shoved him into the back seat. The driver barreled down the road, sweeping aside people on foot and bicycle, and forcing carts and other vehicles from the road, while the two uniformed men on either side of Jim in the back seat spat abuse and jabbed him in the forehead with pistols. They were asking him questions, too, but his head pounded from the cold and the beating and it was so rapid fire and unrelenting that he could scarcely pick out one word from the next.

As soon as they got out of town and onto a dirt road through the countryside, they pulled him out of the car, dragged him in front of the hood and forced him to his knees. The headlamps glared in his eyes. One of the men pressed the barrel of his pistol to the back of Jim's head, and he closed his eyes, terrified, to wait for the shock of pain. And then nothing. But then another car pulled up and two men got out. One of them pulled a hood over

Jim's head, while the other bound his hands behind his back. They yanked him to his feet and dragged him to one of the cars, shoved him in the back seat and took off again.

The car stopped about ten minutes later and they pulled him out for a second time. He heard voices and boots on stone, smelled something like an oily cook fire and the stench of human waste. They marched him through what sounded like a creaking metal gate. Down a hallway, and then the hood came off as they opened a metal door and shoved him into a dark cell. It slammed shut behind him.

There was no light in the cell. The floor was stone beneath his bare feet. The odor of piss and human sweat hung in the air. He stood gasping against his fear, his cold, and his relief.

I'm alive. Thank God, I'm alive.

After a few minutes, when his heart stopped hammering and the sour taste of fear relaxed in his gut and throat, he groped through the darkness for the wall. It was stone, too.

"Is anyone in here?"

No answer.

"Am I alone?"

He felt his way along the wall until he got to the corner, only a few feet away. He felt along that wall, too, which passed for no more than eight feet before it hit the next wall. Here was a straw mat, and a wool blanket, for which he was grateful, even if it stank of urine and human sweat, and had holes torn or gnawed in it. He wrapped himself and resumed his search. He found an empty chamber pot, and then, on the second pass, found an iron ring on each wall, presumably for chaining up prisoners.

Exploration complete, Jim curled in a ball on the straw mat and shivered. His body ached all over, but nothing felt broken. A dark feeling settled over him as he thought about Margaret. A woman had her own special fears in the hands of animals like these. He shouldn't have taken the Mauser. Should have let her shoot it out. It would have been kinder. Quicker.

"I *am* a worm, that's why. A coward."

A coward about to face interrogation at the hands of brutal fascists.

Exhaustion won the battle with cold and pain, and Jim fell asleep. Of all things to dream about, he had a theater nightmare. He stood backstage in the dream with a script in his hand, all the pages loose. A red pencil underlined random lines. Who had marked this up? And wasn't this the first rehearsal, the read through? That's what they told him, but the lights were up onstage, the actors in front of the curtain, delivering lines to a live audience.

The stage manager tapped his shoulder. "Get ready to go onstage. Your cue is when the king says, 'But now, my cousin Hamlet, and my son.'"

"Wait, this is *Hamlet? I'm* Hamlet? I don't know my lines!"

He dropped the script and the pages scattered across the floor backstage. The stage manager bent to help him, but the man only mixed the script up more. The pages came together upside down, and sideways. Mixed in were pages from their other show, *An Ideal Husband.*

Jim woke with a twinge of relief as he realized it

was a dream, but then remembered where he was, and why. The fading, heart-pounding stage fright vanished, replaced by a dread that radiated from his gut until it penetrated his bones.

A dim light filtered in through a barred window some eight feet overhead. In addition to the rings he'd discovered by feel last night, there were two more on the ceiling overhead. If he jumped, he could grab them, but he guessed they were not for performing pull-ups to keep in good form. Prisoners had scratched graffiti on the walls: days marked in lines, a woman's face drawn in half a dozen delicate lines, the names of prisoners — Fabricio Ansaldo, Lucio Ignazi, Achille Orlando.

A key rattled in the lock. It was this, not the light that had awakened him. A clank, keys falling, then another attempt. This time the door swung open with a groan. A man stepped into the room, tall, in a pressed uniform. An officer. Another man stood behind his left shoulder and said something in Italian. The officer moved to one side to let two others enter the room. They flanked the officer, truncheons in hand. Jim swung his feet around and put them on the floor. He stared straight ahead.

I will not betray them.

They wouldn't kill Jim, right? No, they might turn him over to the Gestapo, but they wouldn't dare assault Reinhard Heydrich's nephew. But Nigel and Margaret and even the innocent members of the company would have no such protection. There was only one choice. He had to sacrifice himself.

"*Parlai gli Italiano?*" the officer asked.

Jim shook his head. "*Solo picolo.* Do you speak English? *Deutch?*"

"*Français?*" the man asked.

"*Pas parfaitment, mais oui.*"

"Very good," the man continued in French. "Then we can understand each other. I spent several years in France in the last war. That was before the English and French betrayed us. Stand up when I'm speaking to you."

Jim obeyed. He let the blanket drop from his shoulders. He stood in his shirt and underwear.

"My name is Capitano Emilio Rosario."

"I'm James Heydrich. My uncle is SS-Obergruppenführer Reinhard Heydrich. Military governor of Moravia."

"I see. And you think this will protect you from your criminal behavior?"

"Please call the German consulate. I would like to speak with a representative of my government. They will vouch for my innocence."

Rosario laughed. He said something to the other men, and they laughed, too. Two more men came into the room, carrying manacles fixed to ropes. They fitted the manacles around Jim's wrists, and then someone got a chair, pulled the ropes through the iron rings on the ceiling and dragged him up by the arms until his toes brushed the ground. They tied the ropes to the iron rings on the wall and stood back. Jim swayed back and forth, the pressure unpleasant on his shoulders, but not yet painful. He forced himself to breath slowly and carefully.

"Please. I am innocent."

"You are not innocent. You are a criminal."

"Don't hurt me."

"You will talk. You will tell us everything. If you do, we will turn you over to the Germans for punishment. If not, you will die here. Most painfully. Do you understand."

Jim didn't answer. Not yet. Too quickly and they

wouldn't believe anything he claimed. They had to force it out of him. His mind struggled to put together a narrative. A story. It had to be coherent.

One of the men struck him across the buttocks with a truncheon. A sharp pain. He drew in his breath. The blow left him spinning. The rope cut into his wrists, and his shoulders ached already.

He clenched his teeth. "What do you want to know?"

"Why did you buy a fish?"

"I like seafood. It tastes good with garlic and butter."

Another blow, this one across the back of his thighs. He gasped and his eyes watered.

"Please, stop."

"Was it your idea?" Rosario asked. "Or the girl's?"

He laughed bitterly. "Margaret? Ideas? Have you spoken with her? She has no ideas, she is a pretty face and an empty head."

"Then why did you bring her to the market?"

"We're lovers. She'll screw all night long. Who cares what goes on inside her head?"

One of the soldiers snickered at this and translated it for his mates, who laughed. Rosario withered their laughter with a look.

"Listen," Jim said, "if you must know, I was trying to buy her perfume on the black market. That's why she came with me. Margaret likes pretty things. She's a pleasant girl, really. I shouldn't have said those nasty things about her. But she's innocent."

He could tell from the look on Rosario's face that he'd taken a wrong path. He'd been trying to deepen the story, make it sound more plausible. Instead, the cunning expression on the captain's face told Jim the man sensed an opening.

"Let's talk about your girl," Rosario said. "Wouldn't you know, she's not talking either. I left her with a pair of Sardinians—rough sorts from the mountains—to see what they could get out of her. I told them to use whatever methods they could improvise. You know how these village types are, and they've never seen hair that blond before."

Jim thought about bluffing, telling them he was working for his uncle and they'd better let him down if they knew what was good for them. But these Italians were prickly, and apparently unconcerned with his family privilege. They could kill him, make it look like his throat was cut by bandits. His only hope was if they turned him over to the Germans and let Margaret go.

"Leave her alone, she's innocent. They're all innocent."

"Innocent of what?"

Jim closed his eyes, as if struggling. He opened them and said, "I'm a smuggler."

"A what?"

"I work on the black market, using the theater company to smuggle coffee and Scotch into the Reich. It is a lucrative operation. Or it was. Before."

"And you expect me to believe you're working alone?" Rosario asked. "That none of your companions are complicit in your behavior?"

"The ones you see know nothing, but I did have one confederate. A Dane named Kristiann Janssen. Someone set us up in Amsterdam—robbed us. Janssen broke his leg chasing him. The company manager dropped him because he couldn't act his part anymore. You can check that, I'm telling the truth. So I've lost most of my contacts." Jim struggled for breath. "That's what I was doing last night, trying to make contact with someone in the Florentine...how do you say?"

"The underground?"

"Yes, the underground. He sold me a fish. It had instructions on a note in the gut, but I had to throw the fish in the water when I swam away."

"And who was this contact?" Rosario asked. "We would like to question the man."

"I don't remember."

This time a soldier gave him three blows across the buttocks. Jim cried out. When they finished, he swung back and forth, his backside throbbing, his shoulders on fire. He couldn't catch his breath.

His eyes fixed on the wall opposite his straw mat and the names scratched into the stone. "His name was Lucio. Let me think. Lucio Ansaldo. A Sicilian."

He waited for a sneer from Rosario, for the man to point out that this was a combination of two names from former prisoners, but Rosario merely looked thoughtful. He said something to the soldiers, who untied the rope from the rings. Jim trembled with relief when his feet touched the ground.

They took off his manacles, and then backed out of the room. Rosario was last. "You'll have your Germans," he said. "Assuming your girlfriend doesn't contradict your confession."

Jim fell back on the straw mat, scarcely able to believe his fortune. Turned over to the Germans — he might escape from that. He could soften his story. What could he say? Something embarrassing that no man would invent. He'd claim he'd only been trying to buy medicine for gonorrhea he'd picked up from a Dutch whore. That was it, yes. True, he'd confessed to running a smuggling ring, but that was only to get out of this stinking Italian prison. The Germans would believe him. Maybe word would get back to his uncle, and Reinhard would order him to Prague at once, to get him away from the decadent theater lifestyle.

He eased onto the straw mat with a wince, then reached for the blanket. But he'd scarcely settled into place to wait out the morning while they contacted the consulate, when the lock turned again. A familiar redheaded face poked into the room. Klaus Hossbach, from the ministry.

Hossbach tossed him a pair of pants. "Put these on and come with me."

Jim fumbled with the pants. His mind was reeling, initial relief gone as he put the facts together.

Hossbach had appeared at once. He must have been waiting outside. Did that mean the man was complicit with the interrogation? Maybe he'd even ordered it.

CHAPTER SIXTEEN

K ATTERMAN DROVE THROUGH THE OPEN gates and into the prison courtyard. Women and children filed past the guard towers on foot to bring food or clothing to the male inmates, who wore black-and-white striped clothing. Other women cooked soup or rice over open fires, and one woman held a pair of live chickens upside down by their feet.

As he rolled forward, prisoners and visitors alike shrank back as soon as they fixed on the car. It was a black Mercedes on loan from the consulate, and flew a pair of swastika flags above the headlights. One woman crossed herself. Another made a warding sign with her thumb and middle two fingers forming a ring and the index and little finger upright like a pair of horns.

The prison spread to the right and left in a pair of wings, three stories high, on either side of the courtyard. The two wings were dull cement, speckled with lichen, atop a sagging, cracked foundation, but the main building at the far end of the courtyard was a handsome stone structure with twenty-foot columns, balconies, and a broad staircase that led up to the front doors. It reminded Katterman of a Bavarian health sanatorium.

Klaus Hossbach stood with Jim Heydrich in front of the stairs, and he trotted into the driveway when

Katterman pulled up. The young man gave a fearful glimpse over his shoulder, then hobbled down the stairs after Hossbach, moving as if his legs were stiff or injured. He was barefoot, wore a pair of filthy trousers that were torn and too short for his legs, and his white shirt was wrinkled and dirty. Hossbach told him to sit in the back, then motioned for Katterman to get out. He shut the door on the young man.

The two men stepped away from the car, where Hossbach told Katterman what Jim confessed under interrogation.

"Did Rosario believe him?" Katterman asked.

"Yes, except for the part about working alone. He thinks Heydrich is protecting his girlfriend." Hossbach glanced back at the car. "Let's see what else we can get. Come on."

The two men climbed into the front seat of the car and Katterman drove away. Once they'd fought their way out of the prison courtyard, Jim said, "Where are you taking me?"

"Don't you have a show tonight?" Hossbach asked.

"You mean you're taking me to the theater?"

"Would you rather we drop you at the hotel?"

"No, no the theater is fine." He cleared his throat as if he were going to say something else, but fell silent.

"You've had an unpleasant night," Katterman said.

"Yes, it was terrible."

Katterman waited. You could get a lot of information by simply exploiting the tendency people had to fill silences, to succumb to the urge to explain. But Jim looked out the window without elaborating, so he gave another nudge. "You look troubled."

"I'm worried about Margaret."

Katterman glanced into the rearview mirror. "She is already at the hotel."

Jim whipped his head around. "She is? Thank God. When I came out and saw you alone in the car, I thought they'd kept her."

"Why would you think that?" Katterman asked. "She was innocent, right? Wouldn't you expect her to be released first?"

"True, I hadn't thought about that." Again, he fell silent.

Katterman gave Hossbach a look and the man returned a barely perceptible nod.

"We have our information from the Italians," Hossbach said, "but they are unreliable historians. We are required to file an official report with both the consulate and the ministry. Tell us what happened last night so we can get it straight."

"Well, all right. After they took me to the prison, they put me in that cell. I was alone and cold, and I—"

"Back up," Hossbach interrupted. "Why did you leave the hotel? Start there."

Jim admitted at once that he'd gone out last night to buy goods on the black market, but the story was softer than what he'd confessed to Rosario. He wanted to get stockings for Margaret, gave American cigarettes he'd acquired illegally in Amsterdam to a man who claimed to have some, but came away with nothing except for a smelly fish. He seemed confused as to the details of the swindle. The story had enough detail, enough self-deprecating wit that it sounded plausible. And yet...

"And you jumped into the water because of a rotting fish?" Katterman said. "I find myself wondering about that."

"There is, ah…there is something else."

"Go on." When Jim hesitated, Katterman added, "We shall find out everything, you understand. It will go better for you if you do not dissemble."

Jim nodded. "I seem to have picked up something in Holland. I don't want Margaret to find out."

"What kind of something?"

The young man explained. There was a girl in Amsterdam. He didn't understand at first that she was a prostitute, not until he'd slept with her twice and she started asking for food and cigarettes and what she called "pocket money."

"And then it started to burn down there. You know, ah, below the belt."

Katterman pulled the car to a stop to wait for a donkey cart to cross. He turned to look at the young man. "You developed an infection in your penis?"

Jim blushed. "I want to clear it up—I don't want Margaret to find out. Or anyone else, for that matter."

"It's funny," Hossbach said. "I seem to remember that you disliked Margaret in Berlin."

"Things changed. You spend a lot of time with someone backstage, on trains, and…well, it's on again, off again. Lately on again and I don't want to tell her about the Dutch girl."

"What does her brother think about you seeing his sister?" Hossbach asked.

"He likes it. He hopes I'll settle Margaret down."

"Introducing her to the black market seems a strange way to accomplish that," Katterman said. "Not to mention infecting her with a venereal disease."

"It was all a mistake and won't happen again. And I haven't infected her. I won't." Jim hesitated. "You won't tell my uncle, will you? I mean, you can word the report so it sounds like a mistake, right?"

"That's right," Hossbach said. "You're joining him in Prague in another week. That might be...awkward."

They continued in silence. Katterman dodged animals, farm trucks, and bicyclists, and was shortly crossing the Arno—the same bridge, in fact, where the carabinieri had arrested Margaret and Jim last night. He fought his way into the center of Florence. At last, he pulled the car in front of the old opera house and they told Jim that he was free to go, but that he should consider himself on curfew until he left Italy, confined to either the hotel or the theater at all times. Jim was effusive in his gratitude.

"He sounded convincing," Katterman said as they watched the young man hurry up the front stairs and disappear into the opera house.

Hossbach lit a cigarette. "I expect no less from a professional actor. Do you want to interrogate the girl?"

"No. Let her think she got away with it."

"Like Nigel."

"Right."

Word had come through the consulate yesterday that the Italians had shot and killed a British agent at Livorno, on the coast. But the body, they claimed, had washed out to sea. Later that same day, Nigel was spotted getting off the train from Livorno. And now, word at the theater was that the man was ill and would be a couple of nights off, with Jim stepping into the part as understudy. Katterman wanted to see if Nigel's illness wasn't a gunshot wound instead. Hossbach, for some reason, wanted to wait before confronting the man.

"What about Kristiann Janssen?" Hossbach asked. "Was that a story of convenience, or is there something else there?"

"Where is Janssen now?"

"Copenhagen."

"Have him taken into custody," Katterman said. "Quietly, so word doesn't reach the theater company."

"I'll use the Danish police. No need to bring in the Gestapo."

Again, the reluctance to use the Gestapo. Was Hossbach afraid that the news would get back to Reinhard Heydrich and the SS-Obergruppenführer would take revenge on an underling who dared investigate his nephew? Or was it something else?

"Very well," Katterman said. "But if we suspect Janssen, we have to suspect the Hungarian as well."

"You think Weil is dirty?"

"If Janssen is part of the conspiracy, then it's almost certain the Hungarian is as well. Otherwise, how convenient that he joined the troupe at just the right time. That would give us five conspirators — Burnside and his sister, Heydrich, Janssen, and Weil."

"That we know about." Hossbach finished his cigarette, rolled down the window a crack, and flicked the butt out to the street. "One is in Denmark, another is wounded, and a third is under curfew. Let's see what else we can flush out."

Katterman thought about Hossbach's unusual methods as he pulled away from the theater. The Gestapo, for all its policy of "night and fog," preferred the blunt instrument to subtleties. So why this careful detective work? Katterman had objections to torture, not only on moral grounds, but because torture was notoriously ineffective. People under torture confessed what they thought their interrogators wanted to hear, not the truth.

But that wasn't how the Gestapo thought.

And aggressive interrogation might even work in this case, with so many people under suspicion. Hossbach held the rank of Obersturmbannführer in the SS — colonel. Who would object if he detained any of the conspirators, with the exception, perhaps, of Heydrich's nephew, and subjected them, one after another, to the most brutal methods until one of them talked?

Katterman didn't know the answer to these questions about Hossbach's motives and methods, but he decided to find out.

CHAPTER SEVENTEEN

JIM STEPPED INTO HIS DRESSING room and let out a deep breath. He sat on the chair in front of the makeup table and buried his head in his hands. When he looked up again, he caught a glimpse in the mirror of what he would look like as an old man. Eyes droopy and bloodshot. Bags underneath. The pain and exhaustion visible in his grimace. He looked down at his hands, shaking, and imagined them with blue veins and wrinkles.

A knock at the door. He watched Margaret through the mirror as she entered. She wore a trim dress with a cheery floral pattern. She looked rested, bathed, and wore a touch of rouge on her cheeks. He turned, surprised.

She winced when she met his gaze. "My God, you look awful."

"Rough night of sleep." He shrugged. "You look... not bad, really. I thought about you. Wondered what you were going through."

"I went through nothing. The captain who took me in was a perfect gentleman who spoke excellent French."

"Rosario? Yes, I met him, too." Jim rubbed his wrists, still raw from where the rope had dragged him from his feet. "We had a lovely chat."

"He wrapped me in his coat and drove me back to the hotel personally. Told me that I kept bad company and should be more careful or I would get myself in trouble."

"I've heard worse advice."

She took a deep breath. "I have something to tell you."

"Go on."

"I am a proud woman, you know that. This is hard for me to say. Please don't make it difficult with sarcastic jibes or whatnot."

"No worries. The fascists beat the sarcasm out of me."

Margaret pulled up a chair. She met his gaze. "I am sorry. I was wrong about you."

"Not as wrong as you think. Most of what you said was true. I *am* a coward and my loyalties *are* suspect. I think mostly of myself. How I can get myself out of the army, out of danger, out of Europe. And last night, how I could keep myself from getting tortured."

"You didn't talk or I wouldn't be here."

"They didn't try hard enough. I'm sure I would have eventually."

"Never mind that. You kept me alive. You helped me when I was drowning and then kept me from getting shot when I took out the gun."

"Self-interest. I didn't want to be caught in the crossfire."

She frowned as she looked down at his wrists where he'd been rubbing them, then turned his face to look into her eyes. "I mean it, Jim. I owe you my life and more. Thank you."

Looking into Margaret's eyes, separated by only a few inches, he felt his guard slipping, the anger disappearing. She was haughty, judgmental, treacherous. She was also beautiful, and with the mask stripped away, her expression vulnerable, it was hard to remember everything he disliked about her. He looked away.

"It's nothing," he said. "I'm glad we're both okay. Now, I'm exhausted, so I want to lie down and get a few hours sleep before it's time to dress for the show."

She rolled her chair back. "You can't do that. We have to rehearse."

"Rehearse?" And then he remembered. "Oh, God. Nigel? He's not—?"

"He's alive. But it's a bad injury. We got a surgeon to come stitch up the wound, but he won't be onstage any time soon. You've got to play Lord Goring. Where's your script?"

He went to the edge of the makeup table and swept away old copies of *Das Reich* until he found his understudy script. He thumbed through with dismay, looking at page after page after page of red underlined passages. Some were practically monologues, they went on so long.

"You know the lines?" she asked.

"No, not really. I mean, yes, as well as you can know something without, you know, having it memorized. It's passive knowledge, like how you can repeat a song if it's playing, but..." His voice trailed off. "I'm in trouble. We have to cancel the show."

"We can't cancel."

"Why not? The lead actor is sick in bed. We'll run a matinee on Saturday. Double up shows."

"Because we need Hossbach and Katterman looking at us, not at Nigel, not at...*other* people in the cast. You understand?"

"You mean the Hungarian? Who is he, anyway?"

"Someone important to the war effort. That's all that matters. Now let's figure out how to make this work."

"I don't have the lines. My God, I don't think I can

learn them in time. Maybe if I were rested, if I'd started yesterday. Why didn't I do that?"

"Don't panic," she said. "I'm here, I'll help you. Let's break it down. You can do act 3 already, because you're either onstage or you're backstage waiting for your cue. You've heard it a hundred times."

"I suppose so."

She thumbed through the script. "Let's be sure. All right, here is one. Your father says 'That is a paradox, sir. I hate paradoxes.'"

Jim closed his eyes. "So do I, Father. Everybody... ah...everybody one meets is a paradox nowadays. It is a great bore. It makes society so obvious."

"Do you always really understand what you say, sir?"

"Yes, Father, if I listen attentively."

"Good," Margaret said. "Let's try another. Don't forget your accent. You still sound like Phipps. A bit more arrogance for Goring, as well. No, that's the wrong word. *Insouciance*." She looked down at the script. "Lady Cheveley says, 'Arthur, you loved me once.'"

"Yes."

"And you asked me to be your wife."

"That was the natural result of my loving you."

"And you threw me over because you saw, or said you saw, poor old Lord Mortlake trying to have a violent flirtation with me in the conservatory at Tenby."

"I am under the impression that my lawyer settled that matter with you on certain terms...dictated by yourself."

Margaret gave an encouraging nod and continued, "At the time I was poor. You were rich."

"Quite so. That is why you pretended to love me."

Margaret smiled and put down the script. "Perfect, Jim. We'll run the whole thing, but it seems you've got act 3 cold. Act 1 is easy. You're almost entirely reacting, and Oscar Wilde's script does all the work setting up your lines. Act 4 is easy, too. I'll be with you onstage and I can rescue you if you stumble. Act 2 is the problem."

"Right," Jim said. "Long speeches. I'm feeding Dunleavy his lines instead of vice versa."

"So we'll focus our attention on that. Once we're sure, we can run the easy stuff."

"Higgins is playing my old part?" he asked.

"No, I tried him. He doesn't have the lines. I mean, really doesn't have them, not like you. Instead, we're going with Vilmos Kovács."

"Who the devil is that?"

"You remember Weil's servant?"

Jim thought about the short, funny little man who had been muttering to himself in Hungarian from the corner of Weil's dressing room. "He's not an actor."

"No, but Weil says he has a photographic memory. Once through and he's got it."

"He doesn't even speak English."

"Kovács can perfectly mimic an accent, even an inflexion."

"Didn't sound that way to me. He had a hell of an accent."

"That's because he wasn't making the attempt. Trust me."

Kovács didn't look the part, he didn't sound the part. But Margaret was claiming he had some strange, parrot-like ability. Jim couldn't understand it.

"Isn't there someone else?" he asked. "One of the crew with stage experience, maybe, who has been secretly learning lines."

"Trust me. The role of Phipps is dry, wooden. Your

replacement doesn't need to act it, he needs to do it."

"Hmm, what does that say about my own role in this company?"

"It says that Nigel wanted you onstage because your family connection greased the wheels. But you already knew that. And you're a fine actor. Maybe not Dunleavy or Lula caliber, but you're as good as me, and you can pull off Lord Goring, I know it."

"Can you answer me something that has been bugging me since Holland?" he asked.

"Perhaps."

"How did you find me beneath that bridge in Haarlem? I got away at the theater, and I know you weren't following me because I crossed open fields and was hiding with a group of derelicts on the edge of the square. But you got there first."

"We followed Gaughran," Margaret said. "By the time he set out from his apartment next to Herengracht, we were in a government car with official papers to let us break curfew. We tracked him to Haarlem and followed him down to the bridge."

"But how did you know in the first place?"

"We've known about Gaughran for years. London had a full dossier on you and your contacts before von Steidle recruited you in Saxony. We knew already that you'd sent a note to the Irish legation. When you disappeared, Nigel put two and two together."

"That man was trying to help me. He didn't need to be caught up in your schemes."

"First of all, no, he wasn't helping. You don't think the Nazis would let the Irish legation operate in Amsterdam if it wasn't corrupted with anti-British sentiment, do you? He's a known fascist."

"So were you. So was Nigel. Except you weren't."

"In this case it's true." She shook her head. "I don't know what game Gordon Gaughran was playing, but equal chances you'd have ended up back in German custody."

"That doesn't mean you had to kill him."

Margaret gave him a look. "Is that what you think? We didn't kill the man. He was already dead when we got there. We spotted two men running away, Gaughran's pockets turned inside out, his coat gone. What you saw was how we found him."

"I'm not sure I believe that."

"Believe it or not, it's the truth."

Jim thought about it for a moment. "No, too much of a coincidence. Haarlem is quiet — that's why I chose it. And it was early dawn, not exactly a time for strong-armed robbery. There were German foot patrols through town, for God's sake. And you're telling me that with Gaughran, you and Nigel, and me all converging on the same bridge underpass there happened to be two desperate criminals down there, too?"

"I don't know, a crime of opportunity. Some local thugs saw him climb down. We didn't stick around to make our inquiries or file a report with the police."

"If you're telling the truth, and you didn't kill Gaughran, then it wasn't criminals. Had to be someone else. Gestapo, maybe."

"Or members of the Dutch resistance," Margaret said, "who knew Gaughran was an enemy and saw their chance to have him killed. Yes, Nigel and I have been over all of that. The fact is, we made it to the train station and escaped Holland without being implicated in the crime. Let's stay focused on the task at hand."

"Which is what, exactly? Smuggling Weil out of

the Reich?"

"No, you idiot, it's running your lines so you don't humiliate yourself tonight and get us all arrested." She flipped to the front of the script. "Ready?"

CHAPTER EIGHTEEN

MARGARET KEPT JIM AT HIS lines until deep in the afternoon, when she took him back to the hotel. He was exhausted, his mind churning with dialogue, words all tumbled on top of each other. He still needed prompts in the big speech with Lady Chiltern in the final act, and then fumbled over the romantic part with Margaret at the end, not because the lines were difficult, so much as the embrace between Lord Goring and Miss Mable. Nigel and Margaret — supposedly brother and sister — didn't actually kiss, as the script called for. Instead, they'd always sealed their engagement with a chaste embrace. Prudish types in the ministry had frowned at any kissing on the theater stage anyway.

"But if you find it easier in the moment," Margaret had said, "follow the script. The Italians won't care if we kiss onstage. Whatever gets you through the lines."

Nevertheless, they didn't rehearse it.

He went upstairs to change his clothes and wash up. He felt a little better by the time he met her in the hotel restaurant.

They took a table near the window. It was drizzling outside, and men walked by with newspapers held overhead. Two carabinieri trudged past, their boots caked in mud, their faces damp and miserable. A donkey struggled down the cobblestone street, pulling a cart overloaded with barrels, its head drooped. The cart driver looked similarly bent and forlorn. Inside the restaurant, smartly dressed men in suits or wearing uniforms decorated with medals joined handsome women in fine dresses with elegantly coiffed hair.

Jim and Margaret ordered linguine with clams. A waiter in a white jacket looked at their ration coupons before taking the order back to the kitchen. He returned with a bottle of Chianti. The first glass slid down on an empty stomach and went straight to Jim's head. His tongue loosened. "I don't hate you anymore."

"Is that so?"

"I'm trying. I want to hold onto it. But I was worried about you. In the river. And when they took you away. I was sure they'd take you into a back room and...you know."

"And what? Insult my honor? Well, isn't that gallant of you?"

"I want to help," he said.

"You already are, believe me. And if Nigel can't carry out his duties, I might have to lean on you some more."

"Does that mean we've started over?"

Margaret ran a finger around the rim of her wine glass for a moment before she looked up and met his gaze. "Yes, I suppose we have." She held out her hand. "Partners? No, scratch that. Friends?"

He took her hand. Her hand was petite, but she took his in a firm grip.

"About that stuff on the barge," he said. "When I was holding you in my arms. I—"

"Jim, maybe you should stop there. Before you say something you'll regret later."

"Is that what you think I'm saying?"

"Isn't it?"

"You have an awfully high opinion of yourself." He poured more wine. "I'd need something harder than wine to come on to you, believe me. No, that isn't what I was going to say — I was going to apologize for being insensitive about your brother, that's all."

"I understand the temptation," she said, as if she either hadn't heard his denial or didn't believe it. "I'm not judging you. If you take two attractive people of the opposite sex, throw them into close proximity, add danger, stress, it's natural for certain feelings to stir. There's nothing real about those feelings, that's the key. You have to remind yourself that until it sinks in."

"Is that what they taught you in London? Don't let yourself get seduced by the enemy? Oh, for God's sake, never mind. Look, here's our food."

The waiter delivered the steaming plates of pasta with a flourish, and then grated pepper and Parmesan cheese over the food. *"Buon appetito."*

Jim was still irritated as he took his first bite, but the food soon made him forget his anger. The butter and garlic rolled across his taste buds, and the clams added the perfect flavor to the linguine, which was soft without being overcooked. He was so hungry that his hand trembled as it brought the fork to his mouth. By the time he was halfway done he decided that Margaret was absolutely correct, even if she'd misinterpreted his words. Friendship only — no romantic feelings. Let this be his reminder.

A figure hobbled into the restaurant from the hotel lobby, leaning heavily on a cane. It was Nigel, gray and frail as an old man. He spotted them and made his way slowly over, face rigid and expressionless. He took a chair from an empty table and eased himself next to Jim and Margaret.

"Where have you been?" he asked Margaret.

"Helping Jim with his lines. We still have a show tonight, remember? Anyway, why aren't you in bed?"

"Never mind that. I'm worried about the fish."

"He knows about the note," she said.

Nigel looked pointedly at Jim. "Are you almost finished?"

"Let him stay," Margaret said.

"It's safer if —"

"No. You're a wreck. I can't do this alone, not if I have to go to the coast."

"What about Weil?" Nigel said.

"He's a courier, that's all. He knows less than Jim, and frankly, I trust him less, too."

"Wait a minute," Jim said. "The Hungarian isn't in on this? Then what about the business with Janssen's leg?"

"You're both right and wrong," Margaret said. "This is about the Hungarian, but not the one you mean."

"Oh."

Kovács. He thought about that strange conversation in Weil's dressing room, and the bit about his photographic memory and his perfect ear for accents.

"Very well," Nigel said. "Jim stays. Let's talk about the note from the fishmonger."

"I'm guessing it's at the bottom of the river," Jim said. "We had to throw it away."

Margaret twisted noodles onto her fork. "That is not entirely accurate. I retrieved the note while I was above you on the bridge. I scraped out a bit of broken mortar and tucked it between two stones on the Ponte Vecchio before I came down to the barge."

"You should have looked at the note," Nigel said. "Memorized it, and *then* tossed the damn thing."

"Did you miss the part where the carabinieri were chasing us through the darkened streets of Florence?" Margaret said. "Anyway, I caught a glimpse and it was a big string of numbers. Code. I don't have Kovács's memory."

"Code," Nigel said. "Lovely. Never mind. So here's the problem. The rendezvous might be tonight, for all we know. It's certainly no later than the day after tomorrow, but until we retrieve the note, we have no way of knowing."

"This rendezvous you're talking about," Jim said. "Why didn't the fishmonger give the information to Margaret directly?"

"He's a smuggler, that's all," Margaret said. "And he got the note from another smuggler—a man with a fishing boat in Livorno."

"Which is why we have to go back for the note," Nigel said. He winced and put a hand to his side, and then smoothed out his face before he spoke again. "I'll go to the bridge during the show."

"You?" Margaret said. "After the way you staggered in here just now?"

"I'll manage."

"You'll manage to get yourself killed," Jim said. "Let someone else do it."

"No other choice because nobody else will be alone long enough to get it done. It's opening night—the instant the show ends, they'll whisk the cast off to Count d'Angelo's villa for the party. Our German minders will be following you, especially after what happened last night."

"I'll pretend I'm not feeling well," Margaret said. "They'll follow Jim to the party, leaving me to get the note. You can stay in bed."

"Too suspicious," Nigel said. "And you may have charmed your way into Rosario's good graces, but Katterman and Hossbach might not be so easily fooled." Nigel shook his head. "It has to be me. I'll slip out of the hotel a few minutes after the lights go up onstage."

Jim had his doubts. The man shouldn't be in the restaurant, let alone wandering the streets. If Nigel couldn't handle the rigors of the stage, how could he manage to sneak out of the hotel, walk or drive to the Ponte Vecchio, search for the note, and make it backstage by the intermission? His mind turned over various alternatives, but he didn't see a solution. No way to get out of the post-show celebration, not with half the dignitaries of Florence in the audience, expecting Lord Goring to make a triumphal entry (assuming Jim didn't humiliate himself onstage) and two government minders following his every move. And the note had to be retrieved tonight?

Margaret frowned and tapped her finger against the side of the wine bottle. "What about Weil?" Margaret tried again.

The waiter approached, but Nigel waved him away. "Weil is out of the question," he said when the waiter was out of earshot again. "And I'm not walking away now, not after two years of creeping around Europe, planting seeds. This is it. This is why I came. I'll will myself to retrieve that note. Even if it kills me."

She shook her head. "You can't do it."

"I bloody well can."

"Shh," Jim said, alarmed at the raised voices. "We have an objective, right? That's what's important, not your part in it. If we could find another way, you wouldn't throw away your life and wreck the mission out of stubbornness. Right?"

Nigel scowled. "What do you know about it?"

"Listen to him," Margaret said.

"Don't forget," Jim continued, "I'm your understudy. I'm not the real Lord Goring."

"And?"

"They're not expecting James Heydrich at the party, they're expecting Lord Goring."

"But you'll be Lord Goring to these people," Nigel said. "It's the same thing."

Margaret leaned forward. "Wait, I understand. Nigel, you're a typical actor. You're proud and jealous. They'll understand that. They may not be happy, but will they be surprised that the head of our company is a prima donna who cannot stand the thought of his understudy stealing his glory on opening night? With your injuries you'll have an easier time navigating the party than the streets of Florence. You can stay long enough to deflect attention, and then make your excuses and go back to the hotel."

"That gets Jim out of the party," Nigel said. "But what about our friends from the ministry? They'll still be watching him."

Jim smiled. "How about the old switcheroo?"

"Could you speak the king's English, please?"

"You'll be waiting backstage. As soon as I get to my dressing room you'll put on the jacket, bottonhole, cummerbund — even Goring's top hat and cane. Margaret will get a car around back, distract the Germans, if necessary, and send you off to the party. By the time Hossbach and Katterman reach the villa, realize that we've swapped places, I'll have the note."

Nigel was quiet for a long moment. "And when the Germans interrogate you again?"

"They won't. Because I'll have a second car. As soon as I have the note I'll meet you at the villa, dressed in my old, boring costume as Phipps, the butler. I'll only be a few minutes late. If questioned, I'll claim I was sulking and almost went back to the hotel in a huff."

"Brilliant," Margaret said. "I'll take Kovács with me and stick him in a back room at the villa where he can't say or do something that will get us in trouble."

"Very well, I'll meet you backstage the moment the show ends." Nigel pushed away from the table. He fixed Jim with a penetrating gaze. "The stakes are higher than you can imagine, Heydrich. Don't fail us."

CHAPTER NINETEEN

I NSPECTOR KATTERMAN DIDN'T GO TO the German consulate
to make his call, even though that would have been
the easiest way to telephone Saxony. Instead, he drove
to the headquarters of Captain Rosario of the carabinieri.
The man ushered him into an office that overlooked
the Arno, not five hundred meters from where they'd
arrested the trembling, half-frozen fugitives last night.
The drizzle was ending, the clouds parting, and the late
afternoon sun illuminated the salmon and tan buildings
that stretched along the river, their tiled roofs glinting
with speckles of reflected raindrops. Rosario sat at a
heavy oak desk with feet carved in the shape of lions.
Two pretty young women sat on opposite sides of
another desk in the corner, one working a typewriter and
the other clanking at a telex machine.

Rosario looked up from his papers and removed a
pince-nez, which he tucked into a desk drawer. He stood
up and saluted. Katterman didn't wear a uniform and
responded with some reluctance. "I regret disturbing
your work."

"It is nothing."

The captain offered him a glass of port, which
Katterman declined, and a cigarette, which he accepted.

"I've been meaning to compliment you on your

Italian," Rosario said as he lit his own cigarette. "Not only is it grammatically perfect, your accent is excellent, not the Piedmontese nonsense, or the vulgar Roman dialect. How long have you been in Tuscany?"

"Four days."

"Yes, but when were you here before?"

"This is my first trip out of Germany, although my wife and I did visit Vienna once, when it was a separate country. I am a student of languages. It is a hobby."

"Curious hobby." Rosario cleared his throat, bent to straighten his papers. "Did you come for the report? One of my girls is typing it now."

"No. Send it to Hossbach when it's ready. What I need is a telephone."

Rosario raised an eyebrow. "A telephone?"

Katterman gave his story, sprinkling in a little truth to season the lie. The Germans, he said, were inclined to believe that James Heydrich was a petty black marketeer who worked alone. The young man was politically connected and likely to get away with his crimes, so long as they remained minor. However, a hint of suspicion remained that he might be concealing something larger, or that others, less protected — the English brother and sister, for example — might be involved.

"I don't know about the brother," Rosario said, "but certainly not the young lady. She was perfectly charming."

Katterman bit back his first response. "Nevertheless, we must be sure. You would hate to discover later that your report had missed critical details, and that you allowed a major criminal enterprise to flourish under your nose."

"I suppose so. And I would prefer not to anger the German consulate and have them complain bitterly to Rome."

"Of course not. My reputation is on the line as well—
it makes sense for both of us to be prudent. That is why
I would like to use your telephone. I would rather keep
this quiet from the consulate, avoid whoever might be
listening at their switchboard. I have a discrete inquiry
to make in Germany."

"Very well." Rosario fished keys out of his desk and
handed them to one of the girls, who rose to her feet as
he approached. "This is Velia. She will show you to the
telephone room."

The girl gave Katterman a charming smile. She had
big brown eyes, a tiny waist and breasts that swelled to
fill her blouse. "This way, *signore*."

He followed the girl down the hall, surprised at how
easily Rosario had agreed. He'd been prepared to explain
to Rosario why he was alone, instead of in the company
of his superior. To Katterman's knowledge, Hossbach
remained in his hotel room, sleeping. It had been a
long night, and tonight would be a late one, too. The
villa of Count d'Angelo was twenty kilometers outside
of Florence, in the Tuscan hills, and the party would
no doubt continue until tediously late in the evening.
Hossbach would expect his partner to be sleeping as
well—with any luck Katterman would return to the hotel
before the man noticed his absence.

Velia unlocked a door and ushered him into a room,
empty except for a chair, a table, and a telephone. The
room had no windows, but was decorated with black
velvet drapes. The phone was a newer model, brass
and black resin, with a dial. She gestured. "Will that be
all, *signore*?"

"I don't know your Italian system. Do you know how

to use the phone?"

"Yes, *signore.*"

"And do you speak German?"

"No, *signore.*"

"In that case, have the operators patch me through to Berlin. As soon as the switchboard operator answers in German, hand me the phone and I shall complete the call. When that happens, please leave the room until I am done."

"Yes, *signore.*"

She picked up the phone and dialed. A moment later, she asked to be patched through. More patching. On the third switchboard, she handed him the phone, nodded her head slightly, and backed out of the room. She shut the door behind her.

"Are you there?" a woman's voice said in German, sounding mildly annoyed. "This is Berlin exchange 321. Do you have a call?"

Katterman was reasonably sure that there would be no eavesdropping along the line, and if there were, it would be some bewildered member of the Italian secret police who spoke no more German than Rosario's secretary. Just in case, he affected a mushy-mouthed Palatinate accent, like his mother's family spoke in their home region of Pfalz. The operator in Berlin turned brusque when she heard his accent, but had no trouble understanding and patched him through. Moments later the line was chattering, and he imagined it ringing in the police station in Halle an der Saale.

Someone picked up. "Weipert," a man answered in a thin, crackly connection.

"Katterman," he said. "Give me Scholl."

"Who is this?" Weipert answered, tone cold.

"Katterman. Is the line that bad?" He realized, belatedly, that he was still using his peasant accent. No wonder Weipert sounded suspicious. He tried again, this time in his normal accent. "I said it's Katterman, you suspicious old goat. Get me Scholl and make it quick. I'm calling from Florence."

"Oh, Katterman. I'll get him."

He waited for what seemed like minutes for Scholl to appear on the other end. He was afraid the line would go dead while he waited, or an operator would break into the line to warn him that he'd run up a bill of so many thousand lire or so many hundred reichmarks and did he want to speak to his banker about a small loan so he could continue the conversation? With any luck nobody would send a bill to the German consulate on his behalf.

"Scholl here."

"It's Katterman. Say, has anyone moved into Fritz Wenck's villa?" An answer mumbled back. "Speak up, man, I can't hear you."

"No, I said it's sealed off." Scholl's voice sounded pinched, nervous even across several switchboards and hundreds of kilometers of static-filled telephone wire.

"And his possessions, all those tapestries and fine art. Confiscated by the regime, or turned over to his estate?"

The line went dead. Katterman waited, and a few seconds later, Scholl was back. "What is that you say?"

Katterman repeated himself.

"One moment." Scholl shouted something, voice muffled. Boots. A door slamming. "There," the man said a moment later. "I sent them out. I was afraid to speak frankly."

The line went dead again. "Scholl, are you there? Scholl?"

"Yes, yes, I'm here."

"Well, what about Wenk's villa?"

"As far as I know, nothing has been touched. The investigation continues."

"What investigation?" Katterman said.

"The Gestapo. They're turning Halle upside down, looking for Wenck's killer. Meanwhile, the villa is off limits to anyone without proper SS credentials."

Katterman fell silent. His theory dissolved. After driving back from the opera house with Hossbach, he'd retreated to his room, turning over his growing suspicions in his mind, wondering why they'd come all the way to Florence to investigate what seemed to be a simple black market operation. As he kicked off his shoes and lay back on his bed, he thought about how Hossbach had manipulated the situation that night in Saxony, when Katterman shot Wenck dead. And he thought about Wenck's opulent possessions, Hossbach's dismissal of their acquisition as "vulgar." And he wondered if maybe Wenck had been at the heart of some larger smuggling operation that led to SS-Obergruppenführer Reinhard Heydrich's nephew.

His working theory dissolved.

"Are you there?" Scholl said. "Hello? Damn this line."

Katterman recovered. "Yes, I'm here. Tell me, hasn't the Gestapo questioned you about the disappearance?"

"Interrogated me for more than an hour, yes. I admitted nothing. I said what they told me to say."

"Who told you? And what?"

"A man in a suit arrived at my house the morning after we went to Wenck's villa. He said he was from the Gestapo, showed me his death's head ring. He told me other men would be arriving in Halle to inquire about

Wenck's disappearance—other Gestapo—but I must not tell them anything. The man helped me rehearse a story. He said if I failed, if I told them the truth, I would disappear and never be seen again."

"You did the right thing."

Katterman considered. So Wenck's death was a secret, even within the Gestapo. Could the smuggling conspiracy go all the way up, from James Heydrich, to Fritz Wenck, to the SS-Obergruppenführer Reinhard Heydrich himself? No, that was impossible. Reinhard Heydrich had no need to subvert the law—his word *was* the law. His looting and manipulation of the system were all sanctioned, even enforced, by the regime. If he wanted something, all he had to do was take it and nobody, not Himmler, not even the Führer, would tell him no.

"They've torn the town apart," Scholl said. "At least a dozen men have disappeared in town—mostly peasants, former criminals, you know the type we round up whenever there's a burglary or arson. Nobody knows where they are."

"Suffering interrogation somewhere, no doubt. Nothing will come of that."

"Not nothing. They've found a few Jews, at least. And a former communist deputy in the Reichstag who has been hiding in a crawl space under his sister's house since 1937. Can you believe that?" Both men fell silent and then Scholl added, "They believed your story, at least. Someone in the Navy vouched for it."

Story? Navy? He didn't know what this meant, except that it was additional evidence that Hossbach was not working alone, but had allies within the government. Was this a power struggle within the Gestapo? But then why involve Katterman in the investigation?

"Am I doing the right thing?" Scholl asked.

"Yes, absolutely. Follow the plan, stick with the story the first Gestapo agent told you. The investigation is all for show. Soon the regime will leave Halle alone— as much as they ever do, that is."

Katterman hung up the phone, more confused and conflicted than ever, but with a plan starting to come together in his head.

He opened the door to find Rosario's secretary waiting in a chair a few meters down the hallway, hands held primly on her lap. She rose to her feet. "Are you finished, *signore*?"

"Almost, Velia. I need you to help me make on more phone call."

"To Germany again, *signore*?"

"Yes, that's right."

Only this time he wouldn't be calling Saxony. He would be calling the Reich Ministry of Public Enlightenment and Propaganda, his and Hossbach's supposed employer while they were in Italy. It was time to pry away another layer of Hossbach's lies.

CHAPTER TWENTY

"THE FIRST LINE IS THE hardest," Margaret said. She straightened Jim's cravat, fiddled with his buttonhole, as if the position of the carnation on his lapel somehow mattered when he'd be lucky not to trip and collapse as he came down the stairs, maybe even stumble off the stage and land in the lap of some Italian contessa.

"It's much easier to recover from a mid-scene stumble," she continued, "but if you send up the first line, you'll stand gaping like a fish with nobody to rescue you. Want to run it one more time?"

"No worries, I've got it," Jim said.

Truth was, he'd been running that first line again and again in his head. *I did not think you would remember me, Mrs. Cheveley. I did not think you would remember me, Mrs. Cheveley.* He may collapse into a quivering heap onstage, but he'd be damned if it happened on line one.

Where had the day gone? Could it really be time, already, time to step around the backdrop and into the nineteenth-century drawing room of the Chilterns, his tongue dripping with clever wordplay and flirtatious repartee? Thousands of words piled up in his brain, ready to spill out, and hopefully in the proper order. Or at least proper enough order that he wouldn't be booed, chased off the stage with empty bottles of Chianti and fistfuls of fettuccine.

The light dimmed backstage to a single, orange bulb, and the audience chatter dulled, and then disappeared, replaced by an expectant hush and a few scattered coughs.

"Break a leg," Margaret whispered.

"You don't mean that literally, do you? Like with poor Janssen?"

"Shh," Dunleavy said as he came up behind them. Cast members now milled about them in the dim light behind the curtain. Several filed past to take their places on the stage. Others waited next to Jim. Lula Larouche came up in her elegant green dress. She leaned in, he thought to whisper another curse against his leg, but instead said, "Your big debut. Don't botch it." And then she kissed him on the cheek and waited in position for her cue.

The show began. onstage, Mrs. Marchmont and Lady Basildon opened the silly prater that marked the beginning of the show. Mason, the Chiltern's butler, announced party guests as they arrived onstage: the Barfords, Lord Caversham, Lady Markby, Mrs. Cheveley, who would become the villain of the show. *An Ideal Husband* started innocently enough, an Oscar Wilde comedy not much more serious than The *Importance of Being Earnest,* but by the end of the first act, the audience would see the sting in the tail.

For months now, Jim had spent most of the show in the green room with the other bit players. Waiting for act 3, in his case, a wait that dragged and dragged. Now, of course, with the largest part in the show, the other characters galloped through their lines, a rapid-fire burst of words that would soon bring him onstage. The audience laughed, maybe not as vigorously as they would have in London or Toronto, but enough. More than any other time, Anglophones filled the theater on opening night—it was that, he realized, that made Nigel's theater troupe the perfect front for recruiting spies. These were people who had studied at Oxford or Cambridge, had done business in New York and London, were veterans of embassies and consulates in Ottawa and Capetown. English nannies and summers spent in Newport cottages and country estates in Kent. In short, not just Anglophones, but Anglo*philes*. At an opening party like the one at the Count d'Angelo's villa, it would be a simple matter to approach the most valuable, most vulnerable foreigners, and recruit them to British intelligence. Nigel and Margaret probably had to turn people away it was so easy.

And then it came.

Onstage, the butler announced him in a loud voice, "Lord Goring!"

Jim swallowed hard, put a devil-may-care expression on his face and in his posture, the air of a rich, idle young man of the English upper crust, and stepped through the curtains and into the blinding light of the stage. The audience was a dim, washed-out shadow behind the lights, but he could feel five hundred pairs of eyes turn in his direction.

Introductions, opening salvos, and then his line: "I did not think you would remember me, Mrs. Cheveley," Goring said with a disingenuous hint to his tone.

The next few lines buzzed past, as he bantered and flirted with one character after another. And then he was alone upstage with Margaret—make that Miss Mable. She wore, perfectly, as if she'd been born with the look on her face, the beautiful, slightly empty-headed expression that was so charming on the stage, but wore thin so quickly when encountered in real life.

It was this look she had worn in private these past twenty months. Margaret offstage was the same as Miss Mable onstage. She had essentially played the same role. And done it so well that Jim had believed every second of it until the moment he caught Nigel and Margaret breaking Janssen's leg on top of the theater in Amsterdam.

"You are very late!" she said.

"Have you missed me?"

"Awfully!"

"Then I am sorry I did not stay away longer. I like being missed."

He felt it, that perfect moment onstage when you are no longer acting, when you *become* the character. He was Lord Goring, he always had been. And this charming, beautiful young lady bantering with him was Miss Mable, the young sister of Goring's best friend. He would make love to her with wit and charisma.

Minutes later, she met him backstage. Her face was shining. "That was good. Very good."

He nodded, feeling flushed. "You were...I never saw it before. Miss Mable's charm. It's the same part you play offstage."

Her smile faltered. "What do you mean?"

The Miss Mable persona was a woman who was lazy in her beauty. A woman who could toss her head, make eyes at a man and melt him to her will. A pout on her lips, a touch to the arm, a giggle at a stupid joke—all could be played so easily and so effectively that the possessor of such power could grow careless, even cruel in her treatment of others. Except now he'd seen behind the mask, caught moments like Margaret's terror in the river, her pain telling the story of her brother's death in the Channel, and her guilt that she'd flirted her way out of Rosario's clutches while they beat Jim with batons.

Margaret wasn't an arrogant beauty, she was a tangle of insecurities, fears, hopes, and aspirations. Like anyone else.

"I don't know," he said, unable to explain in a way that didn't sound like an insult. "But I like the real Margaret better than the stage Margaret."

She stared at him and then blinked. "Never mind that. I have to talk to you in your dressing room. Quickly."

"What is it?"

"An emergency. Hurry!" She grabbed his wrist and pulled.

He let her pull him along, confused. What on earth sort of emergency could have happened between the time when the first act started and now? Something backstage during those few moments when they weren't out there together? Someone spotted in the audience? Something whispered in her ear while Miss Mable was supposedly flirting with the Vicomte in a different part of the party?

Within seconds she had him in his dressing room, the door locked. She had a strange, manic look on her face.

"You're scaring me," he said. "Is Nigel okay?"

She looked at the clock over his makeup mirror. "Seventeen minutes until you go back onstage."

"What? No, I open act 2."

"Seventeen minutes," she said. "Eight forty-nine on that clock. I've timed it many times."

"It's a new theater, how can you be sure?"

"Many times and many locations," Margaret insisted. "Nigel comes backstage, uses that seventeen-minute delay to pass a note, have a secret meeting, even leave the theater for some purpose or other. There are several minutes between Chiltern and Cheveley onstage, then the curtain comes down, applause, scene change. Places. Lights come up." She glanced back at the clock. "Sixteen minutes now."

"Okay, I'm convinced we have a few minutes. But what's this about? Wait, you're not thinking we'll rush out to the bridge and get the note now, are you? We'll never make it. We—"

Margaret threw her arms around his neck. Before Jim had a chance to let out a startled squawk, her mouth was on his and she was pushing him against the makeup table, scattering bottles, combs, makeup, and compacts. A brush clattered to the floor.

"Margaret, I—are you sure?"

"Stop talking, you fool."

She tore off his cravat, his jacket, unbuttoned his shirt. His own hands worked at the strings on the back of her dress. The underwear was a blouse/corset combination meant to facilitate quick dress changes but with no exact counterpart in the real world, and it took both of them to get it off. Moments later she stood naked in front of him. God, she was beautiful. Smooth, perfect skin, a trim waist, beautiful breasts that filled him with hunger. She pushed him to the ground, got his pants unclasped and around his ankles, his drawers down.

"I want you so badly," she whispered, voice husky. "Do you want me, too?" He managed a dumb nod and she laughed. "That's your answer?"

He said, "I want to say something witty, but the blood has rushed from my head."

"Oh? Where did it go? Down here, I think."

Margaret straddled him and reached between his legs

to guide him in. He gasped and she arched her back. She took his hands and put them on her breasts. It was frantic, anxious lovemaking, but all the stress, all the fear and anger disappeared and he was nowhere else but in her arms as they rocked and moaned together. It took only minutes, and then they were lying in a heap, gasping for air, kissing, as their spent bodies relaxed.

Margaret put one hand against his cheek. "Thank you."

He smiled. "Thank you?"

"Do you know how long it has been?" She let out a little laugh. "Not since I left London. My fiance and I had a terrible row. He thought I should stay home, wait for him. He's an RAF pilot. Somehow that is noble, but this was foolhardy."

"You're engaged?"

"No, not any more. It's long over. How about you? Has it been a while?"

"I'm a European virgin. In fact, I wasn't much of a playboy in Ottawa, either. One furtive encounter in the boathouse of the college yacht club, and something — not quite this — with a girl in one of my shows."

"Oh, so you regularly seduce girls in your theater productions?"

"I wouldn't use the word seduce. In either case."

"And did this measure up?" she asked.

"I don't think we're even using the same scale."

Margaret propped herself on one elbow. "I know what you must think of me," she said.

"I'm not thinking anything. The moment you touched me, the top of my skull popped off and my brain sprouted wings and flew away."

"You were helpless to resist?"

"Helpless enough." He rolled onto his side. "Does

this mean anything? Or were you—I mean, were we both, you know...?"

A serious look passed over her face. "Jim, I have to tell you the truth..." Her voice trailed off and she took a deep breath.

He'd known. What was it? Oh, yes, two attractive people thrown together. A little danger, etc. Still, his heart sank. Why did he ask? He should have left it alone, let things fall where they may.

"Never mind," he said. "Forget I said anything."

"Jim, you have to understand. Sometimes we have to—" she started again, and then looked up at the clock. "Oh, my God. Eight forty-six. You have three minutes until the lights come up on act 2."

He leaped to his feet, stumbling into his pants. Margaret sprang up and scooped up his clothes. She got his shirt on him, then furiously smoothed at his hair while he buttoned his shirt. Still naked, she got his cravat straightened while he fastened the cummerbund. He looked at the clock. Eight forty-eight.

Someone pounded on the door. "Jim?"

"One second!"

It was Lula. "The lights are down! Dunleavy's onstage. Jim! For God's sake."

He threw open the door. She stood with a frightened, angry look on her face. "My God, you forgot about Goring, didn't you. You thought you weren't on again until—" Lula stopped as she looked over his shoulder. "Margaret? Good lord. You didn't, you wouldn't."

"Jim, I'm so sorry," Margaret said. She held her dress against her chest. "I shouldn't have, I'm sorry!"

"What in hell's name were you thinking?" Lula asked her. She kept yelling at Margaret as Jim raced up the stairs. People parted for him backstage. He rushed around the curtain, almost tripped on the stairs as he clunked to his spot on the divan, where Goring opened the scene opposite his friend Robert Chiltern. Dunleavy let out a hiss, though whether it was anger or relief, Jim couldn't say. The audience rustled, a vast, indifferent crowd. Most of them expected skill and professionalism, but many would be delighted to see him fail.

"My dear Robert," Dunleavy whispered.

"What?" It made no sense.

"Your opening line, you fool. I'm feeding you your line."

Oh, yes. Dear Robert, something about an awkward business. A big speech to open the act. What was it? What were his lines? It was as if his mind had been washed clean, all those months spent as Nigel's understudy, all those hours that afternoon working with Margaret to fix them in his head. All of it gone.

My God. It's my nightmare turned real.

And then the lights came up.

CHAPTER TWENTY-ONE

THE AUDIENCE LEANED FORWARD AS the lights came up.
Jim found himself onstage, opposite Dunleavy — no,
make that Robert Chiltern, the title character of *An Ideal
Husband*. Chiltern was an honorable man who owed
his wealth, his power, and his position to a single,
dishonorable act in his youth. And now his friend Lord
Goring, calm, rational and goodhearted beneath his
outwardly flippant appearance, would help him salvage
his life in the face of a ruthless blackmailer.

But only if Jim could remember his lines.

My dear Robert...

My dear Robert, it's a very...awkward?

Awkward what? Situation? No, that wasn't it.

One curious thing about the stage was how time
changed. Early in rehearsals, when you were trying to
nail your lines to the spongy shape a scene held in your
mind, time accelerated, cues jumped you like a back-
alley thug to demand your lines. *Snap, snap! What's your
line? Quickly, now. Too late!*

Later, when the words fixed in your head, as solid
and permanent as Egyptian hieroglyphs chiseled into
stone, time slowed, stretched. There was time for stage
business: significant looks, to tap your foot or make eye
contact with someone across the stage, to mess around

with props. Time to work on the proper inflection of your lines. Time to do all of the above and still plan ahead or react when another actor fumbled.

And if you forgot your lines? Then somehow, both things happened at once. Somehow, the stage and everything on it warped like some Einsteinian nightmare of space and time, both shrinking and expanding at once. And that was the position in which Jim found himself. Simultaneously dead, dying, and terrifyingly alive. Like that moment in Amsterdam when he saw Gaughran's green tie, only this one would never end.

Dunleavy, operating from an alternate universe, saved him. "I suppose it's an awkward business."

"Yes, a very awkward business. Very awkward indeed." Jim stopped, blocked again. But this time, the words piled up behind the dam, searching for a way to break through. And then they came. "You should have told your wife the whole thing. Secrets from other people's wives are a necessary luxury in modern life. So, at least, I am always told at the club by people who are bald enough to know better. But no man should have a secret from his own wife. She invariably finds out. Women have a wonderful instinct about things. They can discover everything except the obvious."

And then they were off and running. By the time Robert Chiltern finished his next line, Jim Heydrich was gone, replaced onstage by Lord Goring. Alive, breathing, and with time ticking along at its normal pace. The prompts helped; most of the heavy lifting was Chiltern's, with Goring responding with clever plays on words. It went well all the way until Margaret — Miss Mable — came back onstage. She looked perfectly composed, but then again she would, wouldn't she? Ten, fifteen additional minutes to get her head in the right place.

Miss Mable and Lord Goring flirted a little, and then some back and forth with Lady Chiltern, and then Jim stepped offstage. Safe again, until act 3. And he knew act 3, didn't he, because he'd been onstage many times in the role of the butler, or backstage waiting for his cue. If he could only get through the opening bit of act 4, until Margaret came on again, he'd survive the entire show.

Kyle Dunleavy dragged him back to the green room. Minor members of the cast and stage crew sat smoking or playing cards. "Everyone out," Dunleavy said.

"What the devil is your problem?" Jim said when Dunleavy shut the door behind them.

"What the devil is *yours*?"

"I found out last night I'd be Goring. Considering the circumstances, I feel pretty good about how it's gone so far. And what are you trying to do, anyway, ice me? I've still got to go back there, so I'd appreciate it if you didn't get me worked up about one little mistake."

"You know bloody well that's not what I'm talking about. Where the hell were you?"

"Dressing room. I...I lost track of the time."

"And how did you do that?"

"Why are you hassling me about this? Don't you have an entrance?"

"Not yet, I don't," Dunleavy said. "And I want to know what you were doing. Where did you go? Did you leave the theater?"

Jim tightened his lips. He wasn't about to admit he'd been in his dressing room in a naked tangle with Margaret Burnside. Let Margaret confess that, if she wanted. Lula might yell at him, but she wouldn't talk. He didn't know what Dunleavy was after—Nigel must have told the man to keep him under observation. He was about to tell Dunleavy to take it up with Nigel, when the man let him go and paced across the room.

"Nigel isn't ill, is he? That was a lie. Something else is going on, and he put you up onstage for a reason. Why?"

"Excuse me?"

"What is it? Does it have anything to do with the commotion in town last night? Those two from the ministry?"

"Hossbach and Katterman?" Jim said. "What do you mean?"

"You know what I mean."

"No, really. I have no idea what you're talking about."

The hostile expression on Dunleavy's face made it clear exactly what he thought about Jim's claims. And so Dunleavy was not, in fact, working with Nigel and Margaret. But why was he so angry? Did he suspect something? Could he be working for Hossbach and Katterman and that last bit had been misdirection?

"I'll find out," Dunleavy said. "And when I do..." He glanced at the clock, gave Jim a black look, and then slipped from the green room.

Jim grabbed a script where it sat on the armrest of one of the chairs — Weil's Lord Caversham, from the lines underlined — and thumbed through until he got to act 4. He covered his lines with his hand and only looked at his prompts. Margaret opened the door and slipped inside.

"I heard it was rough," she said as she sat next to him.

"I survived." A smile played across his lips. "And it was worth it."

She blushed and stared down at her hands. When she looked up a moment later, the blush was gone. "Everything is ready. A black Fiat will pull up in the back alley five minutes after the last actor leaves the theater. There will be two men in the car. Neither speaks English, and they may be armed. Do not be alarmed."

"I'm alarmed already." He caught her look. "But it can't be more terrifying than sweating beneath the lights while five hundred businessmen, Italian nobles, and fascist government officials wonder if you'll ever remember your lines. I'll be okay. Who are these men in the car?"

"Hired thugs. They're ours for tonight only. Tomorrow, they may report us to the secret police for a few thousand lire more. Don't let them see the note, or even that it *is* a note."

"Got it. And where did you hide it?"

She explained in remarkably precise details—five stones up and three stones over, in a chink left by missing mortar.

Applause sounded from the audience. The second act was over.

"One other thing," Jim said. "Does Dunleavy work for you?"

"Jim, you know I shouldn't."

"He accosted me backstage. Demanded answers. I didn't give them, but I want to know."

Margaret hesitated. "No, he doesn't. In fact, none of them do, except for Weil, and he knows very little. You could say he's another hired thug."

"But not Dunleavy. You're certain."

"He's an actor, that's all."

"Maybe, maybe not." The applause died. It was intermission and he had to get this out before Dunleavy came back to interrogate him again. "He's on to something," Jim continued. "He dragged me back here and questioned me, and it wasn't about why I blanked my line. He wanted to know why I was late onstage, what was really wrong with Nigel. Maybe he's working for Hossbach and Katterman."

She chewed on her lip and frowned. "Let's hope not. If—"

Dunleavy pushed open the door. He took in the two actors and opened his mouth as if to say something.

Margaret didn't look at him, but grabbed the script from Jim's hand without missing a beat. "Very good. Now let's run the part where you come out of the conservatory to speak with Lady Chiltern."

Dunleavy backed out of the room.

Jim's biggest worry in the third act was not his own lines, but his old part, Goring's butler, Phipps. It was played by a real-life butler, Weil's funny little man Vilmos Kovács, who was apparently involved in Nigel and Margaret's schemes somehow. Before the lights came up on the same buttonhole scene that had bedeviled Jim in Amsterdam upon sight of the Irish diplomat's green tie, Jim had never heard Kovács speak in anything but a thick Hungarian accent. And not fluently, either. The man didn't know what the word 'constant' meant. How would he manage the very proper, very English accent of Phipps while trying to remember all his lines?

Perfectly, it turned out.

Kovács moved woodenly, a posture that would have been disastrous under other circumstances. But he was a butler, after all. And it wasn't only his timing and his accent that were perfect, but his inflexion, dry and with a hint of irony. It didn't sound like Jim's rendition of the same part. It sounded like Nigel, and Jim wondered if Weil and Margaret had brought the man into Nigel's hotel room and run lines there, where he'd picked up on the delivery exactly as Nigel had done it. Was that sort of mimicry possible? Who was this man?

The third act went well, but the fourth act was shaky. Jim was out there with his onstage father, Károly Weil, and neither man had a lot of experience in their respective roles, and none working with each other. They made it through, but it wasn't sharp. Hard to say if the audience would notice.

Later in the act, he was nervous in his proposal with Miss Mable. He and Margaret had never settled if they would kiss, as the script called for, or if they'd end it with a chaste embrace, as Nigel and Margaret had always done. And so Margaret tried to kiss, he tried to hug, and it ended up a fumbling mess. But the audience laughed — the good kind of laughter — and it was clear they thought the incident was intended as comedy. This was a fortunate turn of events; if not, the awkward exchange might have torn him out of the scene again. Instead, he made it through to the end, and then, blessedly, the curtain came down.

As Jim and Margaret came onstage for their curtain call, holding hands, she leaned up and whispered, "Not bad at all, considering. I only wish you'd get a chance to do it again. To get it perfect. You'd be great."

"Won't I?"

"No. Tonight is our last show."

But what about tomorrow night's show, and the shows into the weekend? Forget his pending summons to meet Uncle Reinhard in Prague, the company itself had bookings next week in Rome, and then in Venice, before they would circle into Austria, Hungary, and possibly even Kiev if the Wehrmacht could pacify the Ukraine by summer.

As for himself, he had several more days before his summons to Prague, and he'd thought, hoped, that Nigel and Margaret would find a way to get him out of it. Once they cleared up this business with the note, and the... and then he stopped thinking his way down that path. Whatever was going on here it was too big, it was going to end Nigel and Margaret's spying operation.

They left the stage, but the clapping and cries of "Bravo!" were so enthusiastic that the cast came back out for a second bow. One woman on the front row in an indigo-blue gown seemed especially enthralled. There were age lines at her eyes and mouth, but she had a patrician, almost Roman face, a slender figure, and thick black hair held up by a jeweled comb. Her eyes were shining, opened wide in that far-off look audiences wore when they'd been swept up in the story.

Margaret gave Jim a side glance and whispered. "Lady d'Angelo. Our hostess at the villa tonight."

"Nice to know we can count on at least one fan at the party."

"Or at least a fan of Oscar Wilde. I was watching her from behind the curtain stage right. She was mouthing Lady Chiltern's lines at one point."

After their final bows, Margaret came with him backstage, and then moved to intercept Dunleavy while Jim raced to his dressing room. He flipped the switch and locked the door. When he turned around, Nigel was standing in his underwear in front of the mirror. He had laid out clothing—hangars with a coat and tails and all the other items to complete Jim's transition to the butler Phipps for the party.

Nigel's left side was wrapped heavily below the ribs, and spots of blood worked through the bandages. He leaned against the chair, face pale. He should be in bed, not hauling himself out to a party in the Tuscan countryside.

"You have to hurry, too," Jim said as he stripped his clothes with practically the same urgency he'd done earlier that evening when Margaret was tearing them from his body. "Dunleavy suspects something. He—"

"I know. She told me."

Nigel took the clothes from Jim the instant they came off. He almost fell as he climbed into the pants, and Jim insisted that he sit down to finish the job. Jim helped the man with his shoes, the cummerbund, the cravat. By the end, Nigel stood leaning against the counter, face pale, but not shaking, while Jim fitted the top hat into place.

Jim looked him over doubtfully. "Can you manage?"

"I have to get to the car, that's all."

"Keep your head down, so nobody sees your face."

"Am I wrong, old fellow, or is this your first time doing this sort of thing?" Nigel said with an attempted smile.

"It's not spycraft, *old fellow*, it's acting advice."

"Very well. Tell me how to hit my mark."

"Forget the British upper crust, you need to walk with the slouch we've perfected in North America. Pretend you're walking into a Chicago speakeasy. Remember, you've got to be me, at least for the next few minutes. In case they're watching the alley when you climb in the car."

"Right." Nigel dropped his shoulders, pulled the hat low. When he spoke again his accent sounded like a Canadian's, or at least an American's. "Okay, pal, check the hall. Tell me if the coast is clear."

Jim cracked the door. One of the minor cast members stepped into her dressing room and shut the door, but the hallway was otherwise empty. Most of the cast would still be onstage or taking a post-show drink or a cigarette in the green room.

"You're good."

Nigel pushed past him and down the hall. Only when the man slipped out the back door did Jim return to his dressing room. He locked the door, got dressed, turned out the lights, and waited in the dark. Voices sounded in the hall, laughter, the sound of feet on concrete. Doors opened and shut. Margaret called for everyone to hurry or they'd miss the cars to the villa. And nobody would want to skip the count's party, and the chance to eat porchetta, olives, pecorino, and pane toscano, or to drain the count's wine cellar. The pace accelerated. The back door opened, banged shut, opened, banged shut.

Perhaps ten minutes later Margaret called in a loud voice. "Anyone else in here? I guess that's it, I'm the last one."

And then the door opened and closed one final time. Jim waited two or three minutes more before he groped his way to his dressing room door, hoping that Margaret had the car waiting in the street to pick him up, as promised. He reached for the handle.

And stopped, heart pounding.

Footsteps sounded in the hall outside his room. And then the clank of metal on metal, the sound of a key sliding into a lock.

Chapter Twenty-Two

KATTERMAN AND HOSSBACH STOOD IN the aisle as the actors retired from the stage and the audience filed out of the opera house, chatting in Italian with smatterings of English conversation here and there.

"That was not the disaster I was expecting," Hossbach said.

"There were a few fumbles," Katterman said, "but Heydrich managed."

Katterman had watched the show with interest. He was unfamiliar with Oscar Wilde except for the infamous details about the man's sodomy trial in Britain. One of his professors at Halle-Wittenberg used Wilde, together with Lewis Carroll and D.H. Lawrence, as an example of why the British Empire had fallen into decay. Moral turpitude. The feminization of society and government. The corruption of money and moneyed interests. According to Katterman's professor, much of this was the fault of outside forces, usually Jews, but in this case a homosexual Irishman.

And yet *An Ideal Husband* proved more subtle and refined than Katterman expected. Yes, there were the affectations of Lord Goring—played competently by James Heydrich filling in after Burnside's illness—that delighted the audience. But Katterman was more interested in Dunleavy's character, Robert Chiltern, the titular husband. He had transgressed the law for personal gain. And now, years later, via the delightfully wicked Mrs. Cheveley, he would pay for his crimes. Never mind that Chiltern had otherwise led an honorable life, he had committed a crime and crimes always came to light in the end. While Katterman thought it would have made a better story to have a police detective solve the crime, Sherlock Holmes-style, the important thing was to show thematically that no man was above the law.

But then the story fell apart. Somehow Chiltern weaseled out of his punishment and even managed to rise to greater heights. Public acclaim, private reconciliation with his honorable wife. The dastardly Mrs. Cheveley was defeated, her evidence burned to ash, and Chiltern safe. Katterman wanted to rush to the stage after the curtain call, push through the admiring crowds of Italian ladies and nobles, and argue his point.

Instead, he and Hossbach watched the departing crowd for irregularities. There were Italian secret police in the audience as well, plus a pair of SS officers from the consulate, but these two were functionaries, from the look of it. No suspicious behavior in the crowd. Nothing seemed amiss.

"Take the car to the villa," Hossbach said when the theater was almost empty. "Keep an eye on Heydrich and the girl until I arrive."

"Captain Rosario has four men on them already. They'll be following in the car."

"I don't trust the Italians, either their motives or their competence."

"Of course not," Katterman said. "But why aren't we going together?"

"Not this time, no. Quickly, now. You have your orders."

Yesterday, Katterman would have obeyed without a second thought, but he was still turning over the strange telephone conversations from earlier in the day, first that business with Scholl and the violent Gestapo response to Fritz Wenck's death, and then a call to Berlin that only raised more questions, when Katterman failed to confirm that Hossbach had any connection to the ministry, either. So who, exactly, authorized Hossbach's investigations?

And so he pushed.

"And where will you be going?"

"I have a few things to investigate backstage," Hossbach said. "Once the actors are gone, which will take some time. I want to keep it quiet. One person is better than two."

"Shouldn't I be the one to do it, then? I am the trained investigator with an eye for noticing important details."

"Ideally, yes. But we have no choice but to split up because I need your trained eye at that party, do you understand? We need to make sure Heydrich doesn't establish contact with a new liaison."

This was pure bluff and Katterman knew it. But he also knew that Hossbach was so desperate to get rid of him that pushing would only increase the level of mutual suspicion. Instead, Katterman came up with a better idea. He nodded. "Very well. Remember details — I shall have questions for you."

"Yes, of course. We'll see each other soon."

They shared Nazi salutes, and then the two men turned their separate ways, Hossbach going backstage and Katterman continuing into the lobby and out the front of the opera building, where women gathered their dresses above the dirty flagstones while their husbands and lovers opened the doors of private automobiles. Bands of soldiers blocked the street on either end and only let theater-related traffic pass. Katterman walked around the building to the mouth of the alley. Two long-nosed Fiat 1100s with shield-shaped front grilles pulled from the alley and onto the street. Actors crowded the seats, rushing off to the party. Soldiers stopped each car briefly, glanced inside rather than check papers, and then waived them on again.

Katterman glanced down the alley from which they'd come, saw no more cars, and slipped inside. He patted his breast pocket to verify he had his pistol, the same gun he'd used to kill that child murderer, Wenck. When he got to the end of the alley, about to round the corner into the back lot behind the opera house, a car turned from the street behind him and pulled into the alley. A final car for the stragglers from the theater company? Or someone who had spotted Katterman ducking into the alley and now came after him to work some mischief? Neither explanation would be good news, so he rounded the corner, into the closed-off back lot, filthy with the smell of night soil and oily rags. He pushed through the back door of the opera and into the long hallway that led past the dressing rooms. It was dark, but he heard footsteps coming from the other direction. Katterman eased the door shut behind him and stood motionless.

Metal clanked on metal. A key rattled into a lock and the door of one of the dressing rooms swung open. Light poured into the hallway and Katterman saw Hossbach for an instant before the man disappeared inside. Katterman crept down the hallway, more curious than alarmed. His mind turned over excuses if he were caught.

Two pistol shots rang out: b*ang! bang!*

Even muffled by the dressing room door and the thick stone walls of the opera house, they shattered the silence. Katterman took out his Mauser and ran the last few meters to where light bled from beneath the door of one of the dressing rooms. He threw open the door, expecting to see Hossbach dead and one of the actors — Burnside? Heydrich? — standing over him with a drawn pistol. Instead, it was Hossbach with the gun and a second man on the ground. The injured man grabbed at his chest. His hands found bloody wounds, and he groped as if he could plug the holes like a Dutch child holding back the North Sea by sticking his fingers in the dike. More blood gushed out his back in a rapidly spreading puddle on the ground that spread into clothes pulled down from hangers in the fall.

Hossbach whirled, gun outstretched.

"Stop!" Katterman said. His own gun was in his hand, his finger squeezing on the trigger of its own accord. He barely held back from gunning down his partner.

The two men lowered their guns, slowly, and then put them away. A vein throbbed on Hossbach's head and he took quick, shallow gulps. "I had to," he said. "He was going to…"

"Going to what?"

Katterman's eyes dropped to the dying man. He was unarmed. And he had turned in such a way as he fell that Katterman saw he'd been flinching from the gunshots, and not charging the shooter.

The man twitched his left leg twice and then was still. Blood dribbled from his mouth and his eyes turned glassy. It wasn't Heydrich and it wasn't Burnside or Weil, either, but Kyle Dunleavy, the Scotsman. Not long ago, no more than half an hour, Dunleavy had been onstage, basking in the applause of the crowd, bowing when they called "Bravo! Bravo!" And Katterman, watching with a frown, disappointed the Robert Chiltern character had escaped retribution for his crimes. He hadn't escaped them for long.

Except this was Dunleavy, not Chiltern. And wasn't that curious? Why the Scotsman? What made Hossbach seek the man out and murder him? And why was he now going to concoct a lie, as Katterman knew he would, to cover what he'd done, instead of telling the truth about his actions?

"He came at me," Hossbach said. "He was reaching for something. I thought it was a gun."

"Naturally." Katterman bent and reached into Dunleavy's jacket, ready to turn with a frown and point out there was no gun. But to his surprise he came out with a pistol, a Walther PPK, like Katterman's own weapon. He slid out the magazine. It was loaded.

"You see?" Hossbach said. "He *was* reaching for his gun."

Except the position of the body, lying on its side, said that he was not. And yet armed, and so not a bystander either. Katterman's mind reeled.

"What do we do with the body?" he asked, to buy himself time.

"I'll...ah...I'll call someone from the consulate to clean up the mess. We'll go to d'Angelo's villa — figure out what happened here later." Hossbach took out a cigarette, but it took three matches for his shaking hands to light it. "Put the man's gun back."

Katterman bent to return the gun to Dunleavy's pocket. His hand brushed something else in the pocket. Folded papers. With a glance at Hossbach, who puffed nervously while looking away from the dead body, he pulled out the papers and had them in his own jacket pocket before his partner turned around.

"Ready?" Katterman said.

"Yes, let's go."

A door shut somewhere nearby. Both men froze. Feet ran down the hallway.

Katterman reached the hall as the back door swung open and a figure ducked outside, hidden in shadow. He drew his gun, intending to give chase, but Hossbach grabbed his arm.

"No! Let him go."

"He heard the gunshots."

"But he didn't see who. Don't show him."

"But—"

"No," Hossbach said. "It doesn't matter. Listen to me. We can't hide Dunleavy's death—we have to come up with a story anyway. It was a failed robbery, that's what we'll say. We gave chase, but the murder got away. Let the consulate handle it, we're finished here."

Katterman put away his gun for a second time and stared down the dark hall to the gray shadow that marked the open door. A cold draft blew in from outside. A car engine revved and pulled out of the alley.

Behind him, Hossbach pulled Dunleavy's dressing room door shut. "Come on, we'll go out together. Through the front doors."

Katterman followed, wondering about the second witness to the shooting, and wondering what other criminal behavior this night would flush out. His hand went to the papers in his pocket, taken from Dunleavy's dead body, and he followed Hossbach, suspicions deepening.

CHAPTER TWENTY-THREE

J IM FOUGHT THE URGE TO duck low in the back seat as the car pulled out of the alley and onto the street. He expected gunfire at the back tires, or carabinieri to charge out of the front of the opera house with lowered weapons and screams for him to get out of the car. But nobody seemed to have heard the pistol shots in the theater because nobody on the street acted alarmed, not the last of the theater audience climbing into sleek Alfa Romeo Berlinettas and elegant Fiat Cabriolets, nor the soldiers who gave a perfunctory inspection to each car that drove past on the way to the main boulevard.

The driver said nothing to Jim, but queued behind the checkpoint. He had a thick neck and a head the shape of a block of marble, with more hair tufting from his ears than his bald, uncovered head. His hands were thick and short-fingered on the wheel. He rolled down the window while the soldiers glanced inside and shone a flashlight around the interior before waving them forward.

Jim now struggled with a fresh worry. Margaret said two men would pick him up — where was the second? Not that Jim was in a position to complain. What was he going to do, bail out of the car and return to the opera house to chat with the killers? The sound of gunfire was fresh in his mind, coming from the dressing room next to his. A body hitting the floor. Two men speaking in urgent tones. He couldn't pick out the words, or even the language, but it was German or English. Not Italian.

Who was it? Who did they kill?

One of the actors, maybe? One of the crew? Margaret hadn't come back, had she? It couldn't have been her, could it? His stomach gave a sick lurch at the thought. No, it couldn't have been. She'd been clear about her intentions.

After they had left the checkpoint well behind, the driver turned and said, "*Ho sentito spari dietro?*"

"Sorry, what?"

"*Pistole? Spari?*" He made a shooting motion with his hand.

"Gunfire? *Si, si.* Never mind, I'm okay. *Non importante.*"

The driver said something else, his tone saying, *No worries. It's all in a night's work, pal.*

Or maybe he was saying, *I'm not getting paid for this. Next street I'm throwing this idiot to the curb.* Or maybe even, *Poor fool, the fascists will flay his skin and clarify their wine with his blood. But what can I do? They pay so well. Don't worry, kid, I'll raise a glass of grappa in your memory.*

Apparently not, because the man kept driving, turning again and again as he threaded his way through the cramped streets of central Florence. At first Jim didn't recognize the streets, but then he saw the shadow of the Duomo to his left, and they came upon the Ponte Vecchio. The driver pulled onto the street that ran parallel to the Arno River. He stopped by the side of the road midway between the Ponte Vecchio and the bridge where Jim and Margaret had dragged themselves from the river. The bridges didn't look so far apart from up above.

"You'll wait for me, right?" Jim put his coat on

over the butler jacket with its tails. He buttoned it up. "*Attendez-vous?*" he tried in French, and then the Italian word came to him. "*Attendere. Attendere. Cinque minuti.*"

"*Si, spero che qui.*" A toss of the head for emphasis. "*Andiamo.*"

There was no curb and Jim couldn't fight his way across the street through the crush of bicycles, cars, and donkey carts, so he hugged the stone wall that kept one from simply tumbling over the bank and down to the river, and worked his way back up the road toward the bridge. He caught his breath when a pair of soldiers emerged from the bridge, but they'd unbuttoned their jackets and one of them had a girl on his arm. Not on duty, then.

But that didn't mean the bridge would be unwatched. Maybe someone had found Margaret's note and waited in the shadows or watched from the second floor of one of the apartments on the bridge, ready to pounce when someone came for the note. He thought about the torture in the prison, and how fortunate he had been to escape with nothing worse than sore wrists and a few blows across the buttocks. It could have been worse, much worse. He stepped onto the Ponte Vecchio.

A formation of priests marched across the bridge, three abreast and fifteen or twenty deep. They wore black cassocks that fell to their ankles, burgundy shoulder capes, circular-brimmed capellos, and carried ceremonial spears over their right shoulders. A flag adorned each spear, emblazoned with a cross in a shield. A man in red robes walked in front with a torch, and led the priests in a Latin chant. At first Jim thought it was a protest, a defiance of the regime as only the church would dare, but the people who crowded either side cheered and gave a variety of salutes: high and outstretched like the Nazis, lower but palm still flat, arm forming a square, and salutes to the brim of one's hat by two soldiers. Three youth dressed like altar boys followed the procession, beating a drum and starting a second chant, this one in Italian, that sounded like a football song, with a shout of "*Vincere! Vincere! Vincere!*"

The crowd picked it up in their wake and spread it backward along the bridge. "*Vincere! Vincere! Vincere!*"

Jim took advantage of the confusion and wormed his way between the crowd and the buildings until he reached the alley. It was narrower than he remembered, and harder to squeeze through, but fear had greased his passage the previous night. He made his way to the end of the building and glanced over the edge, down to the river. The barge was gone from the pillar below the bridge, leaving only cold, glimmering water that rippled in the reflected light.

He felt along the stone wall. It was uneven beneath his fingers, mismatched bricks and stones from different periods of time. The mortar was patched and repatched, some areas solid and others crumbling and rotten. His fingers smeared something wet and slimy like bird droppings, and he stopped to wipe them on the brick before continuing. His fingers passed the spot without finding the note. Had Rosario's men discovered it? A deep breath and he tried again, and this time he counted the stones with more care. And then he found it, a rolled-up piece of paper the size and shape of a cigarette.

Jim unrolled the paper and held it up to the light. It read Act IV, followed by a string of numbers, then ACT III, more numbers, Act I, more numbers, and ACT III again, followed by more numbers. He thought briefly about memorizing the numbers via a theater-style mnemonic, in case he lost the note, but he didn't dare take the time, not with the promise to the driver that he'd be back in *cinque minuti*. The man might leave him if he took too long. Instead, he rolled it back into its cigarette shape, removed his shoe and tucked it into the toe.

The priest-led fascist parade had passed by the time he squirmed back out of the alley, and just as quickly the fascist triumphalism dissipated from the air. It was replaced with slumped shoulders, pinched, hungry faces, children with sharp cheekbones and ribs visible through shirts that were too thin for the chill winter air. Even the donkeys pulling carts looked underfed and exhausted. Two men carried a pole between them with chickens upside down and bound by their feet. The animals were thin, with torn plumage, their eyes glassy and resigned to their fate, their wings barely flapping a protest. Several shops on the bridge sat dark, closed doors little more than repositories for fascist bills, not so different from the propaganda that hung everywhere in the Reich, but all the more frantic in comparison with the hunger around him. And this was Florence, fat and pampered, not Sicily or Sardinia, cut off by hostile Allied naval forces.

You fools. What do you think war means?

His disgust and hatred for the fascists only grew as the last chants of the priests faded down the street beyond the Ponte Vecchio. He imagined Canadian and American troops in Florence, the fingers that would point accusations at the fascists who would invariably try to fade into the population and claim that they, too, had been victims of Mussolini.

Jim felt a strange eagerness when he imagined the

Allies in Italy, and it was that, even more than his affair with Margaret, its parameters still undefined, but burning in the back of his mind, that gave him a critical insight.

I'm not a German anymore, he thought. *I'm Canadian.*

By the time he reached the car, he felt calmer than he had in months. He had finally, definitively chosen his side.

Chapter Twenty-Four

THE VILLA OF COMTE GIOVANNI d'Angelo overlooked hundreds of acres of vineyards and olive groves from atop a magnificent Tuscan hill. Some of the land at the base of the hill had been given over to plowed fields, with the stumps of olive trees still pocking the ground, but the upper reaches surrounding the villa didn't give Jim the illusion of poverty or decline. Electric lights lit the road as it snaked its way to the top, and illuminated the crushed stone driveway like the border between two hostile nations. Upon reaching the top, Jim's driver surrendered his car key to a valet with a scowl that only deepened when they sent him around the side to the servant entrance. Jim stepped out of the car and took in his surroundings.

The villa itself looked like a French chateau from a postcard—Chenanceaux or Chantilly. Smooth, elegant lines in marble, with statues of Roman gods and goddesses dotting the gardens that spread from either wing of the house. A pair of grand marble staircases wreathed the entrance to rise to a balcony patio, with doors that opened into a second-floor ballroom. Orchestral music mingled with the sounds of conversation to fill the night air.

At least thirty automobiles parked to the right of the villa, with more cars still arriving. Handsome women in evening dresses, pearls, and fur coats took the arms of men in evening jackets or dress uniforms. Above Jim's head, Klaus Hossbach leaned over the patio railing to watch him. Wulf Katterman stood to one side, speaking in what sounded like perfect Italian to a handsome officer with a tricolored sash, gold-threaded bullion cuffs, and a chest weighed down by row after row of crosses, medallions, stars, and other military honors. The man's hair was cropped short, but offset by a glorious upturned mustache with waxed tips that nearly reached his ears. Hossbach nudged Katterman, who said something that sounded like an apology to the Italian officer, and then came down the stairs while Hossbach waited above.

Jim met Katterman midway up. He expected questions about his tardy arrival, but the man brushed past and hurried after Jim's driver, who queued for inspection outside the ground-level servant entrance.

Jim gave a sideways glance, worried that Katterman would approach the driver and ferret out the reason for the delayed arrival, but then Hossbach called down, "You're late."

The music swelled as Jim reached the patio. He looked through the ten-foot-high windows to see men and women dancing in the ballroom. By the time he reached Hossbach's side, he'd had a chance to practice the lines he'd composed earlier. Specificity of detail — that was the key to a good lie.

"Did you see the woman in the lavender dress?" Jim asked.

"Who?"

"Rather tall, bad teeth." He glanced over Hossbach's shoulder into the ballroom. "With any luck she's not here."

"Who is this woman?"

"From the audience. A fan. She tracked me down in the green room after the curtain call and practically threw herself at me." He chuckled, as if at Hossbach's raised eyebrow. "Maybe if she weren't so homely...but when you've been onstage with the likes of beautiful women like Lula Larouche and Margaret Burnside you become rather picky."

"Strange. I didn't see anyone." Hossbach stubbed out his cigarette butt and looked around for somewhere to put it before dropping it into an urn. "You changed costumes."

"I'm Phipps again, I'm afraid. Nigel was jealous. He said Goring is his role. Always has been, and will be again, once he's recovered."

"I figured that out when I saw him. The fool should be in bed, if not the hospital under a doctor's watchful care. He looks altogether of poor health. But you didn't warn us, and nobody saw you leave the theater. I was going to send Rosario back to look for you."

"I'm sorry, I didn't think."

"We follow you for your own protection. Would hate to have further misunderstandings with the local authorities. I can't imagine you'd like to spend another night in an Italian prison."

Hossbach's words were casual, but sounded pinched, and his posture was stiffer than usual. For an instant, Jim saw a man playing his own theatrical role, but then it disappeared.

"No, of course not. But I'm here now, perfectly fine. Assuming," Jim added, "the homely Italian with the lovesick eyes didn't follow me here. In which case I'll ask Rosario to take me back into protective custody."

Hossbach didn't appear to find that very funny.

"Don't do it again. Ah, here are your fellow stars."

Nigel and Margaret made their way through the crowd, Nigel moving gingerly, as if he were merely tired or had already drunk too much wine, instead of nursing a serious wound.

"There he is," Margaret said in German, relief in her voice. "I told you, didn't I?" She took Jim's arm. "Bet you were sulking, weren't you?"

"Of course not," Jim said. "Well, maybe a little."

"Come on. The contessa wants to meet you. Insists you're the real Goring." She gave Nigel a smile and a raised eyebrow. "Better be careful, dear brother. You see where this is going, don't you?"

"Yes, well, I heard he did a fine job. I'm not jealous." Nevertheless, every word dripped with jealousy. These two were good, Jim thought. No wonder they'd hoodwinked him for so long.

"You'll excuse us?" she said to Hossbach.

"Yes, of course. Let us know before you leave the party. In fact, I want all the actors to leave together. There are only two of us, after all, and I don't want to chase you all over Tuscany to make sure you don't get in trouble."

Jim followed Margaret and Nigel past the windows into the ballroom.

"Don't you believe it," Margaret said in a low voice in English. "I've spotted two other Germans from the consulate. They're undoubtedly watching, plus the Italians. You got the note?"

"I did."

Nigel gave him a side look. "What's wrong? You look spooked."

Jim said, "Is anyone missing from the cast or crew?"

"Crew are at the servant party," Nigel said. "Except for lights, stage manager, and a couple of others. Kovács is here, but we've stashed him away so he doesn't draw attention to himself. I think everyone else has arrived."

"Dunleavy," Margaret said. "He's not here yet, but you know how he is. Probably waiting to make a grand entrance. Give him another half hour."

"The chap is probably back at the hotel," Nigel said. "Asleep."

"Or dead," Jim said.

The other two turned with sharp looks. "What the devil—?" Nigel began, but then the doors swung open and the contessa was upon them.

She had changed from her gown at the opera house to a satiny green dress with white gloves to her elbows, emerald earrings, diamond rings over her gloved fingers that made her hands look like glittering claws, and a diamond tiara on her head. Up closer she was rather striking, the same handsome, well-aged beauty as the marble house itself. In fact, she could have stepped comfortably onto the ballroom scene in their play, kept downstage, and nobody would have thought her out of place.

She introduced herself, held out her hand for the men to take and kiss with lips not touching the glove, continental style. "I adored the show," she said in English with a lilting Italian accent. "You do not know how wonderful it is to bring culture to our beloved Florence. Something cheery and modern." She looked like she was going to say something else, but then sighed and glanced over their shoulders. Jim resisted the urge to turn and check if one of their German minders was approaching.

"We're delighted you enjoyed the performance,"

Margaret said. "And so excited to be here. Florence is a beautiful city."

"It is a reminder, that is what it is," the contessa said. "A reminder that this horrid war will not last forever and then we shall open again to the world."

The contessa lifted a pair of lunettes on a gold chain and inspected the two men and their outfits. After a moment of contemplation, she said to Nigel, "And Lord Goring was my favorite character."

"Thank you, that's very kind," Nigel said. "But tonight it was Jim who —"

Margaret nudged Nigel and said with a laugh, "Listen to my brother feigning humility. Lady d'Angelo, that is the worst sort of flattery. It will make Nigel quite helpless to your command."

"Do you know that I am a true aficionado of Oscar Wilde? I once saw *Lady Windermere's Fan* right here in *Firenze*," the contessa said. "And I confess that I read that speech of Lady Chiltern's so many times I've almost committed it to memory. It reduces me to tears."

"I know what you mean," Nigel said. "But —"

"You must come and recite it with me. Do you remember Lady Chiltern's speech to her husband?" She put a hand on Nigel's arm. "Will you not say yes?"

"I think we could spare him for a few minutes, don't you, Jim?" Margaret put in before Nigel could resist again.

"So long as she doesn't keep him to herself the whole night," Jim said. "No doubt he has other admirers. None of them half so charming and beautiful, of course."

The contessa laughed. "Twenty minutes. I promise."

She led Nigel into the grand foyer, and then the conservatory opposite the ballroom. Jim followed

Margaret toward the ballroom.

"She needs a stronger prescription on those glasses if she thinks Nigel played Goring," Jim said.

Margaret turned with a raised eyebrow. "I do believe you're jealous."

"Maybe a tiny bit," he admitted. "I don't need to be fawned over, but would it hurt to be recognized? The d'Angelos had a box practically overhanging the stage."

"It's a compliment. You made it look effortless."

"I wouldn't say that. Not after I blanked at the beginning of act 2."

Margaret shrugged. "That was a hiccup. The audience doesn't notice that sort of thing. You made it look effortless, fooled the contessa completely."

"I suppose I did." He felt a pleasant glow that cut through his exhaustion.

"You've got it with you?"

"In my shoe."

"Good," she said. "Come with me. I did reconnaissance before you arrived."

She led him into the ballroom. A chamber orchestra of eight or ten string instruments played a waltz. Florentine high society mingled with men in uniforms, sashes, and medals. Banners with eagles and crosses decorated the room above paintings of saints, grisly crucifixion scenes, and later, more subtle classical tableaux: Greek gods, satyrs, bare-breasted nymphs feeding grapes to a fat man in a purple toga. Jim heard French, English, German, and even Latin from two cardinals dressed in red and white. A Japanese diplomat argued in Italian with a man who looked like he was from the German consulate. Servants bustled in and out of the room carrying silver platters with flutes of champagne and antipasti. Lula Larouche flirted shamelessly with a bald old general, and Károly Weil carried on in Hungarian with a tall, thin man with an ivory-handled cane and a finely waxed mustache. The Hungarian ambassador, perhaps.

People stopped Jim and Margaret to congratulate, chat, and even make thinly-veiled passes at Margaret, but the pair slipped away from one conversation after another until they left the ballroom on the far side and found themselves in a long couloir lined with busts of Roman senators and Caesars. A few people had pulled into the hallway for more intimate conversations away from the music and loud conversations, but Jim and Margaret were alone by the time they reached the far end.

She swung open a pair of French doors and they entered a huge library of dark wood that smelled of cigar smoke and musty books. A fire roared in the hearth. A young couple sat on a settee near the fire, the man leaning intimately toward a woman who tilted her head with a demure expression.

"It was empty a few minutes ago," Margaret said in a low voice. "I suppose we could go outside and risk running into Hossbach and Katterman."

"Let's wait a few minutes." He caught a glance from the young man, who frowned and looked back to his lady friend. "These two want to be alone. We'll get rid of them quickly enough."

Margaret took him over to the bookshelf and pulled out a leather-bound tome that turned out to be Petrarch's *Canzoniere*. She flipped it open. "What's this about Dunleavy? Please tell me that was a metaphor, that he's not dead, not really."

Jim told her what he'd heard: shots, a body falling, voices in German. She stiffened as he relayed how he'd run to the car, stopped him to clarify that there had only been one man in the car, her face darkening at this new detail, and then had him continue to the retrieval of the note. Worry pinched her face and she chewed on her lower lip.

"So they shot him," she said when he finished. "You're sure it was Dunleavy?"

"I didn't see the body. But who else could it have been? Down in the dressing room. All the other actors are here. And it came from next door, Dunleavy's dressing room."

"How awful. He was alive not two hours ago, standing next to me on the stage."

"I know. He bailed me out when I sent up my lines. In his typical, arrogant fashion, of course. But he was part of our company, no matter what else. Who was it? Hossbach and Katterman, do you think?"

"It must be," she said. "They arrived at the party not long before you. Hossbach seemed shaken. I guess we know why. But then again...Dunleavy? Why him?"

"What part was he playing in your operation?"

"I already told you, he had no part, I swear it. London suggested recruiting him at one point—this was last summer, in Paris. You remember the night we ate at that little French restaurant with the Negro jazz band and there was that incident with the serving girl?"

"Sure," Jim said. "Le Coq Rouge. In the 4th Arrondissement."

"Yes, that's the place. After you, Lula, and Janssen left, Nigel got a few drinks down Dunleavy and tested his patriotism to the old country. Dunleavy seemed a little too...how would I put it? Too free with his opinions. We decided to leave him in the cold."

"Isn't that why you got Dunleavy drunk? To pry out

his loyalties?"

"Perhaps. But our number one requirement is discretion. I suppose Dunleavy might have figured he could trust us after so many months on the road, but Nigel didn't like it."

"Or maybe he was trying to recruit you, too."

"How do you mean?"

Jim turned it over in his mind. "If you were in the pay of the Germans and you were trying to find British spies, how would you do it? I guess you'd wait until you were trusted, drink a little, and let loose your tongue. See if they follow suit."

"That occurred to me, but at the time I dismissed it." She shook her head. "If that were the case, if he were working for the Gestapo or the ministry, why would they kill him now?"

He had no answer. The shooting had no good explanation. Perhaps it was all a coincidence — though he couldn't really believe that — or perhaps Dunleavy would come strolling into the library at any moment, holding a snifter of Scotch and complaining about the quality of the antipasti. Margaret stared at the open book in her hands, but her eyes didn't move across the page. He took it from her and put it back on the shelf.

"What are you and Nigel about, anyway?" he asked at last. "What's the note for?" He gave voice to a suspicion rising in him since he'd attempted to break into Weil's footlocker. "You said something about Kovács, right?"

"He's important to the war effort. That's all I know."

"How important?"

"Important enough that London told us to drop everything to exfiltrate him from Europe. Important enough that Janssen broke his leg to get the Hungarians into the company." She glanced over at the young couple, a good distance away and thoroughly engrossed in each other. "That's what the note gives us, the time and place to smuggle Kovács out of Europe."

A servant came into the room and pulled away the metal screen from the fireplace, turned over the logs with an iron poker, and then heaped more wood onto the fire. It crackled and hissed as the bark went up in gouts of flame. Apparently deciding there would be no privacy for their lovemaking, the young couple rose from the settee near the fire and moved off toward a door on the far side of the room. The young man shot a disgruntled look over his shoulder as they exited. Moments later, the servant replaced the grille and disappeared through the doors that led back to the couloir.

"About bloody time," Margaret said. "Quickly, the note."

CHAPTER TWENTY-FIVE

J IM UNLACED HIS SHOE, TOOK it off, and removed the rolled-up note he'd retrieved from the bridge. The light was too dim by the bookshelves, so they made their way to the hearth, which cast off great waves of heat and light as the freshly placed logs sent flames up the chimney. Margaret took the note, unrolled it, and read the contents aloud.

"Acts four, three, one, and three. And a bunch of numbers" She looked up with a grimace. "Didn't try to hide it, did they?"

"What does it mean?"

"We use one of three texts for our code key. One is the play script itself, but usually they disguise it better than this."

"But that's good," Jim said. "If it's the play it should be easy enough to break."

"Sure, if I had my script with me."

He smiled. "If you don't know your lines by now..."

"It's not that simple. The numbers are an offset to a code, but I need to calculate it while looking at the written text. I guess we could reconstruct the play and write it out, but it would be faster to go back to the hotel."

"Except for the part where Hossback and Katterman see us slipping away and challenge us," Jim said. "Or the carabinieri send someone to arrest us at the hotel."

"Yeah, that." She chewed her lip. "We need Nigel. He can help. How long has it been, do you suppose, since we turned him over to the contessa?"

"Ten minutes? Maybe a little bit less. We'll give him a few more and then rescue him."

She told him to put the note away, and he slipped it into his pocket. They stood in front of the fireplace, an uncomfortable pause growing until it felt like something physical that would need to be broken by more than small talk. Margaret stared into the flames, reflected firelight illuminating a troubled expression on her face.

"What's wrong?" he said at last. "Are you still thinking about Dunleavy?"

"Yes and no. I suppose not as much as I should. I'm too damn selfish, worrying about my own problems."

"Is it the other thing?" he said. "What happened in the dressing room?"

Margaret looked away. "I told you I'm not very good at apologies."

"I don't need an apology. I wasn't pushing you away."

"But I messed up your performance. You scratched the opening. I know you recovered, you did a great job, but it was no thanks to me. I shouldn't have put you in that position, and I don't know what came over me. I'm not like that, I promise."

"Not like what? Lonely?" He turned her around. "The only thing I need to know is if that's all it is. Loneliness? The need for a few minutes in someone's arms to forget the war, the danger, the Nazis, and all the rest?"

"I don't know, maybe." Margaret looked up at him and held his gaze. "But I think I made a mistake. A very big, awful mistake."

"You do? I'm not so sure."

"We hate each other. That's well established."

"We *hated* each other. Past tense. We started over, remember?"

"And what has changed?" she said. "Nothing. We had a...a *moment*. It's over. Now we're back to where we started."

"I can only speak for one of us," Jim said slowly. "But for my part, it's not true. What I hated didn't exist, it was a character with a mask, playing a part on a stage. The play is over now." He took her hands. "And I find I like the actress under the mask."

"Jim, stop that." She pulled her hands away. "It's not helping me get to where I need to be."

"And where is that? Why are you trying to talk yourself into despising me?"

"Because it is easier. I do hate you, don't you see? Everything you are, everything you stand for."

"What in God's name are you talking about, Margaret?"

"Your uncle, do you know what he's doing in Berlin, why he didn't have time for you in Amsterdam, why he rushed off like that? I'll tell you. Your beloved Führer has called a conference of his top deputies. The ruthless, the insane, the criminal, the paranoid, the delusional. That is to say, the masters of Europe—the SS, the Gestapo.

"That's what we were about in Amsterdam," she continued. "Passing along information about this conference to our contacts. London is very interested, but nobody knows what will come of it. What we do know is that Heinrich Himmler and Reinhard Heydrich are said to be presenting a final solution to the Jewish problem. Heydrich, they say, is the architect of the plan. Your uncle. A final solution, did you hear that? *Final.*"

Jim's mouth felt dry. "Heart of iron."

"What?"

"That's what Hitler said about my uncle. No compassion, no ability to look at the suffering of other people with anything more than curiosity. Hitler himself said that." He took a deep breath. "Uncle Reinhard hates Jews—I don't think he'll advocate sending them to Palestine for resettlement."

"So what do you think this final solution will entail? Ten, twelve million Jews in Europe, many of them rounded up already, working as labor in factories and mines to further the war effort. But that's not good enough for your uncle. So will he work them to death building munitions and ball bearings? Build a road to Moscow out of their skulls like a modern-day Genghis Khan?"

Jim's own heart felt, not like iron perhaps, but lead. Uncle Reinhard was a man who played the violin, quoted Goethe, and loved nature and beautiful art, but was, in his soul, a black, twisted monster of a human.

"It's awful," he said. "He should be killed—I should have done it myself. But I'm ready to enlist as his enemy, I'm on your side."

"My name isn't Margaret Burnside."

"I figured that out when I realized you weren't Nigel's sister. But what does that have to do with anything?"

"Let me share a few things. My real family history. I told you about my brother already."

"Shot down over the Channel. It was terrible, I know, but Margaret—"

"My only brother, the only one who could have carried on the family name, which my father thinks is important. My great-grandfather on that side immigrated to Britain in the 1850s when his banking firm in Amsterdam opened a branch in London. He did well, supported the Tories, and his son — that would be my grandfather — was elevated to the peerage in the 1890s."

He stared at her. What did this have to do with anything, except to contrast her wonderful family with his terrible one? But he sensed that any response he gave would be the wrong one.

"Grandpa was a moral crusader," she continued. "He even mentioned Oscar Wilde in a particularly reactionary speech from the House of Lords. Something about moral degeneracy. The Nazis would have approved of the message, if not the source."

"Margaret..."

"My mother is from Manchester. Missionary family. Anglicans. The Higgins are very proper, very middle class. My grandparents on that side of the family were not pleased when she married my father, in spite of his wealth and status. Do you know why?"

"No, why?"

Margaret looked into his eyes and held his gaze. "Because my real name, and the family name that died when my brother's Spitfire went down in flames off the coast of France, is Gold. My proper name is Margaret Gold."

He blinked, mind taking a moment to catch up. "Oh. So you're half..."

"Non-practicing, not observant in any way. But yes. That is who I am. *What* I am." She turned away. "So you see why I could never be with you."

"My blood is tainted. That's it."

"Don't trivialize this," she said, voice quiet. "It isn't you, it's what you represent. How could I ever look at you without thinking about the Jews, murdered every minute of every day? Lined up in the Ukraine and shot as partisans. Packed like rats into a filthy ghetto in Warsaw. Driven from their homes, arrested at night, deported to work as slave labor in camps. You understand? Those are my people."

"Your *half* people you mean."

She stared at him, gaping. "Take that back," she said at last, voice poisonous.

"After all, I'm German only by birth, Canadian by upbringing. Half-German, you could say. But the German half tainted me, apparently, just like your money-loving, banking half corrupted you. Your people are the root of Europe's evils, crushing the Nordic races with unbridled moneylenders on one side, and rapacious Bolsheviks on the other. The war is all your fault, people like you. Or *half* you, anyway. No wonder they want a 'final solution.'"

"You bastard."

She swung for his face. He caught her wrist this time and pulled her to his chest. "Listen to me!" He grappled with her flailing arms. "Listen! You think that's me? You think that's what I believe? Margaret, look at me!"

She stopped struggling and looked up at him with her breast heaving, her eyes like hot cinders, burning through his face.

"I'm not *half* anything. That's what I'm telling you. I'm not half-German or half-Canadian, or half-Nazi. I'm not anything, I'm just me, just James Heydrich, can't you see that? And James Heydrich is on your side. He wants the same things you do. He wants the British to win, the Americans to win. He wants to overthrow the Nazis and see men like Hitler and Himmler and my own uncle dead or imprisoned. To stop the war, to end the killing. He wants...I mean, what I want is..."

"What?"

"I want to be with you." He didn't look away. "And not just one half of you, either. The actress, the spy, the

Brit, the Jew. All of me wants all of you."

Jim let her go. She stepped away, to the far side of the crackling fireplace, hands at her face. She looked for a moment as though she were going to break down and sob, her shoulders slumped, her hair falling around her face. A shudder worked through her body. But then she straightened and dropped her hands to her side, and when she turned to him, she'd smoothed all emotions from her face.

"Enough of that. We're finished here."

"Margaret."

"We have work to do. Let's find Nigel and see if we can reconstruct the text to the play. Oh, I wish we'd got this note last night. We were staring at a script all day trying to get your lines down."

Some bit of machinery clicked, as if Jim's subconscious had been down in the boiler room, shoveling coal into the furnace of his mind while he struggled with Margaret's prejudice. He fetched the message from his pocket and stared at the numbers for moment. And then a smile broke out on his face.

"We have it already. Lady d'Angelo is downstairs reciting lines with Nigel. Remember how she was mouthing the words at the theater? She's got a script lying around somewhere."

"Of course!" Margaret laughed. "How could I be so stupid?" She clapped her hands. "You're a genius!"

She stretched and kissed him on the cheek, and then turned and hurried from the room back in the direction of the party.

Jim put a hand to his face where she'd kissed it. He stared after her for a long moment, more confused than ever, and then set off in pursuit.

CHAPTER TWENTY-SIX

JIM AND MARGARET FOUGHT THEIR way through the ballroom and found Nigel still with Lady d'Angelo in the garden conservatory. She sat next to him on a divan, closer, more intimately than Lady Chiltern would sit with Lord Goring in the play. The characters were close friends and confidants, but not lovers. But Jim could see as he crossed the tiled, palm-and-orange-tree-lined floor that the contessa hoped for much more out of the young Englishman. They cut a handsome pair, even though she was at least fifteen years his senior.

The two sat on a divan that had been turned away from its natural position facing an oversized harpsichord. Nigel leaned awkwardly against the back of the settee, with one hand pressed to his side. Jim wondered if the shirt below the Lord Goring jacket was splotched with blood from a leaking bandage. The contessa seemed oblivious to Nigel's physical distress.

Nigel looked up as they crossed and stopped midway through a line. "It seems that you have it down cold, my dear Contessa, and my friends have arrived to spirit me away."

The contessa put a hand on his arm to keep him from rising. "You think so?"

Margaret grabbed Jim's arm and squeezed. There,

in the contessa's lap, sat a script. And not a book, but laid out in aged sheets of paper, scribbled with stage directions. It was exactly what they needed.

Lady d'Angelo smiled at Margaret and Jim as they approached. "I have been onstage myself, you know. Many times, although I'm afraid not since I was a young girl."

"So, ten years ago?" Nigel asked. "Or was it longer?"

She let out a laugh that sounded like the call of a songbird. "You are such a flatterer."

"Sounds like you've got stage experience," Jim said, "and you've already been practicing. I'll bet it's perfect. How about one more time?"

"Oh, I don't know," she said, suddenly blushing and modest.

Nigel frowned and gave a tiny shake of the head, but Jim ignored him.

Margaret put her hands on her hips and a mock stern look on her face. "Hand over the script, Contessa. That's the only way to prove you've got it."

"I'm not sure..." the woman began, voice faltering.

"We'll prompt you," Jim said. "You'll do fine."

He took the script before she could protest further and handed it to Margaret, slipping her the rolled up note from the bridge at the same time. Nigel glanced between Margaret and Jim with a frown, but said nothing to contradict them.

"Now," Jim said. "How about we start it with Lord Goring's line: 'Lady Chiltern, I have a certain amount of very good news to tell you.'"

Nigel hesitated, but then he started in from the prompt. The contessa faltered when it was her turn, perhaps suffering a bit of stage fright, but with encouragement she was able to continue.

Meanwhile, Margaret stepped behind the divan, as if to watch from a different angle, but when she was out of the contessa's line of sight, she opened the script across the harpsichord and unrolled the note on top of it. She used her finger to count through the words, while Jim tried not to stare.

"Jim?" Nigel said.

He looked down to see the contessa chewing anxiously at her lip. "I'm sorry," she said. "I am so silly, I can not keep the words in my head."

"You're doing great," Jim said as he rewound the lines in his head to the last thing he'd heard. "Well, what use..." he prompted. So easy now that he wasn't the one onstage.

The contessa stumbled through the rest of the scene, looking ever more distraught with herself. When she finished, Margaret was still working.

"Not bad at all," Jim said. "A good start, Contessa. How about one more time, now that you've worked out the stage fright?"

She played with her string of pearls. "You have been so kind, I should not like to impose."

"Not at all," Nigel said. He wasn't facing Margaret, furiously thumbing through the script laid out on top of the harpsichord, but he seemed to have picked up on the ruse. "You're the one who is kind, welcoming us to your home and country. And Jim is right, it was excellent. You should be on the stage."

"I suppose I could give it one more try."

It may have been flattery, but apart from the Italian accent, which lent the lines a continental charm, she wasn't bad, now that she'd warmed to the role. This time she only needed a single prompt to get through the exchange. Jim wondered how many times she'd read this part before their arrival, perhaps daydreaming of jumping in from the audience when the real Lady Chiltern fell ill. Margaret was still working, and Jim tried to think of an excuse for running it a third time, but suddenly Margaret swept the pages together and stepped away from the harpsichord with a triumphant expression.

"That was wonderful, Contessa," she said. "Do you mind if we take my brother away now? I do say he looks rather famished."

"No, of course not. Thank you so much, this has been wonderful." She put her hand on Nigel's arm as they rose from the settee. "Come find me later, dear, and I'll show you my Faberge collection."

"Show you her Faberge?" Jim said as he left the conservatory in the company of Margaret and Nigel, while the contessa stayed behind, running her finger along her ostrich-plume fan, caught up in some private thought. "Is that Italian slang for 'naked parts'?"

"Under other circumstances, I might take the private tour," Nigel said. "But the dear contessa is so energetic, it would be the death of me in my present condition." He offered a wan smile. "I suppose there are worse ways to go. You got the note?"

"Have it, translated it," Margaret said. She slipped it to Nigel, who tucked it into a pocket. She waited until a servant carrying a silver platter of food brushed past, then said, "Meet at port Thursday morning at four."

"Thursday is tomorrow," Jim said. "Which port?"

Nigel groaned. "Livorno, on the coast. Why Thursday? Why not Saturday to give us more time to get the note, get settled into Florence, and the like?"

"Perhaps no other reason than the word Saturday doesn't appear in the script and Thursday does," Margaret said.

"They could have spelled out the bloody letters."

"Never mind, we have no choice," Jim said. "That's five hours from now. How are we going to get there?"

"We have to leave now," Nigel said. "To account for delays getting through Florence, the possibility of bombed roads, delays, and the like."

"Can we break curfew?" Margaret said.

"It's a soft curfew, not like Amsterdam. Chances are we can bluff and bribe our way to the coast."

"And what about our German friends?" she asked.

"No doubt they're lurking around here somewhere," Jim said. "Katterman went around to the servant quarters to question my driver."

"Hopefully the fool knows to keep his mouth shut," Nigel said. "What about the other Italian chap? Weren't there two men in the car at the theater?"

He frowned when Jim explained how there had only been one man in the car, but then nodded when Jim described what the driver looked like. "That's our man," Nigel said. "Or one of them. Never mind the mix-up, you got here. Here's what we'll do. Jim, go find Kovács. He was supposed to stay in the gallery, but he was muttering again—you know how he gets. Could be anywhere. When you find him, send him out the back doors that lead into the gardens. Margaret, get your driver, what's his name?"

"Gatti."

"Right, tell Gatti to bring the car around as soon as he sees me leave, then go down and wait for Jim to bring you Kovács."

"Where are you going?" she asked Nigel.

"I'm heading for my car with the intention of drawing the Italians away. If Section Six is right, Rosario will have me followed. I'll try to lose them. If I can, we'll meet up again outside Vinci, assuming we can rely on these smugglers to get it done. If I don't show, take Kovács through to Livorno on your own. You know what to do, right?"

Margaret gave a curt nod and set her lips in a thin line.

"What about Hossbach and Katterman?" Jim said.

"That incident on the bridge may be a blessing in disguise. They'll follow you, not me, I think. To be sure, as soon as you pass off Kovács, go back to the ballroom and find the count and get him onto the balcony if you can. Make a show of it. Keep the Germans looking at you, not at Margaret."

"You got it."

Nigel held out his hand to Jim. "I hope you'll forgive me for that business in Amsterdam."

"I understand now."

"I hope so. I wouldn't have killed you. I mean, unless you...but you weren't. You didn't. But I'm sorry about all of this."

"We'll talk about it later," Jim said.

"No, we won't."

"You're not coming back?"

Nigel shook his head. "I'm afraid not, old fellow."

They were leaving him to the wolves, he knew. Heydrich's nephew or not, there would be some hard questions at the end of the night. Margaret and Nigel gone, Dunleavy dead. Kovács missing. No way to hide it.

But of course they were taking an awful chance, too, going out after curfew, possibly followed by members of the Italian secret police. Any or all three of them might be dead or worse by morning, so Jim wasn't about to shirk his small role in the drama.

But he did wonder. Who the hell was Kovács, to be worth such a risk?

Jim looked at Margaret. She stared back, eyes deep and sad. She put a hand on his shoulder. "Goodbye, Jim. And good luck in Prague. Don't turn into your uncle."

"I won't."

He wanted to say something else, but Nigel tugged on her arm and they broke up, moving in different directions down the hallway. And then Margaret was out of sight and he worried he would never speak to her again.

Jim began his search for Kovács in the ballroom, but the short Hungarian wasn't in the crowd. Lula spotted Jim across the room and tried to wave him over, but he pretended he didn't see her and slipped away, afraid he'd find himself roped into conversation with some puffed-up fascist minister. Or worse, waltzing with said minister's wife.

He wandered down the hallways on the main floor, past fading tapestries, frescoes of cherubs and satyrs, paintings of battles, and a life-size statue of a naked girl carrying an urn and a statue of a second girl armed with a bow and wearing a helmet, but otherwise nude. He searched the entire first floor, even looking in the cloakroom, where he surprised the same pair of young lovers from the library. He excused himself and made his way to the base of a sprawling marble staircase. Here he paused and looked doubtfully up to the mezzanine.

It was one thing to wander through the main level, and another to sneak around upstairs. He'd run into a servant and then how would he explain? Meanwhile, it had been several minutes since he'd left Margaret and Nigel and he was growing anxious.

"*Scusi, signore*, are you lost?"

He turned, alarmed. It was the contessa. Her face brightened when she saw him. "Oh, it's you," she said in English. "Goring's understudy. What did you think? Be honest."

Think about what? His mind was so distracted that it took a moment before he understood what she meant.

"You were good."

"So many years since I set foot on the stage, but my memory is still good. And sometimes I wonder. Hypothetically, of course. I'm in no position..." Her voice trailed off and a frown shadowed her face.

"You have a presence," he answered honestly. "We'd need to do something about your accent."

"I could work on that. My English is good, but I have never had a voice coach, to perfect my accent. There are not many native English speakers in Florence these days."

"I guess not."

"I don't like it, you know. It used to be so different."

"How do you mean?" he asked.

"Did you know I once hosted a ball attended by Cornelius Vanderbilt IV, the Duke of Marlborough, and Baron Maurice de Rothschild? Russian counts and Prussian junkers." She shook her head. "Look at us now. Deranged, unhinged. Bolsheviks killed our Russian friends in Minsk, Nazis drove the Rothschilds from Europe. The Vanderbilts are our enemies. We spent two lovely summers in Newport."

"Yes, I see. Excuse me, Contessa, I am looking for someone."

She took his arm. "We have suffered, too. You can see that, right?"

Jim turned to her, blinking his astonishment that she could claim such a thing. "You've suffered? Because the price of lobster has doubled? Because you can't pass a summer yachting and entertaining in America? Give me a break."

"My brother was an officer with the Tenth Army in North Africa."

"Living like a sultan in Tripoli, no doubt."

"He drove over a mine," she said in a quiet voice.

Jim was taken aback and suddenly noticed the arrogance in his own tone. "Oh, I'm sorry, I didn't mean...is he okay?"

"I don't know. He is in a prison hospital in Cairo. The Red Cross says he lost one leg and is blind in one eye, but that was three months ago. I pray to God that he is still alive."

"I didn't understand. I shouldn't have said that."

"My sister fled Italy when they arrested her husband. They brought my husband in for questioning, and while he was in Rome, the fascists searched my house. One of the officers would not leave me alone. I finally —" She stopped, swallowed. " — finally gave in so he would stop bothering me. If my husband found out he would revenge himself on my honor. The fascists would kill him."

Jim felt like a rat. Did he think she wasn't a person, because she was rich?

When she looked up, the expression on her face begged him to understand. "You think me vain and silly, don't you? Well, maybe I am. Maybe that is why I dream about being on the stage. It is an escape."

"I don't think that at all."

"You wouldn't tell anyone what I said, would you? It was a mistake, I should have stayed quiet. I am so lonely. And isolated. Entire weeks pass when I see no one but servants and government ministers. I needed to talk to someone. Anyone." She opened her mouth to say something else and then fell silent, her mouth downturned. She ran a gloved finger over the edge of her ostrich-feather fan.

"I won't tell anyone," he assured her. "But Contessa, could I ask you a favor?"

"Yes, of course."

"Do you remember Goring's butler in the play?"

"Phipps, wasn't it? Yes, of course. Played by a short little man, very stiff."

"Our actor is...unusual. Not particularly gregarious, and I think he wandered off to find some privacy." Jim nodded up the stairs. "He might be up there, but I don't want to stumble around in your private quarters, looking for him. Would you mind terribly..."

She studied his face, and he saw gears shifting in her mind, machinery left idle and creaky through disuse, but perfectly functional once it started into motion.

"What is this?" she asked.

"I'm sorry, it was an imposition. I shouldn't have asked."

But she placed a hand on his wrist when he turned to go. "Who is your funny little man? And what was happening in the conservatory? You were passing a look to the English girl. I thought you were lovers, but now I think it was something else."

"Excuse me, Contessa. I should return to the ballroom.

Someone might see us and misunderstand. You know how gossip starts."

"Follow me."

The contessa picked up her skirts and climbed the stairs, revealing shapely calves. Jim hesitated a moment, then followed her up. She glanced back down when they reached the second-floor landing, but nobody had followed. She moved swiftly down the hall, opening doors, looking in bedrooms and bathrooms. They even checked her boudoir, together with its sitting room, with its portraits of women in diamond tiaras and square-jawed men with uniforms and medals and big, bushy mustaches. Nobody inside. It was only when they were passing around the back hallways to the children's nursery that they found him.

Kovács stood at a child's blackboard, propped on an easel. He held a piece of chalk in his hand, and its dust powdered his knuckles and the cuffs of his jacket. He had covered the blackboard from one side to the other in numbers, Greek letters, and algebraic equations. He didn't turn when they came in, but scribbled out a formula.

The contessa drew short. "Here he is, working like a mad scientist. What is this?"

Jim stared as Kovács worked madly at his figures without turning around. "I have no idea."

She cocked her head, and a frown crossed her face. "Someone coming. Maybe a servant, maybe my husband. Follow this corridor and you can come down the servant staircase. Less obvious that way."

The contessa backed out of the room, gathered her dress, and hurried down the hallway with her shoes clacking.

Jim turned back to the Hungarian. "Kovács, what the devil are you doing up here?"

"One moment. Almost there."

There was no fire in the hearth and the room was cold. Kovács blew on his hands, before rubbing out a number with the side of his fist and writing something else in its place. He turned to Jim. "I think I have it. Or close."

"How did you know there was a chalkboard up here? No, never mind. We have to go now."

"One moment."

He scratched something else on the board. "Two and a half neutrons per fission. That is my guess." He tapped his chalk against one of the equations. "Constant is not right, but is, how do you say? In vicinity."

Constant. What is constant? Jim almost laughed as he understood. Kovács had been talking about a mathematical constant when Jim found him muttering to himself in Weil's dressing room.

"Is this astronomy? Math about the universe or something?"

"No, is much, much smaller."

"You mean like atoms? No, never mind." Jim grabbed the man's arm. "Listen to me. I don't know what you're messing around with here, but we've got to get you out of here. Margaret and Nigel sent me to get you. They're leaving tonight. Now. And you're going with them."

The man pulled away and made for the blackboard.

"Damn you, Kovács. I said now."

"Yes, yes. But equation more important. Must remember." He stared at the scribblings.

Jim didn't know what this was about, but looking at the man's mathematical work, and thinking about his strange personality and abilities, he was suddenly certain that whatever Kovács was doing was the key to this whole business, and why he was so important. Perhaps it was some new radio wave or navigation work, or a death ray like from a men's adventure magazine where spacemen battled strange creatures in the deserts of Mars.

"Kovács, for God's sake. We have to get out of here."

The Hungarian turned and looked at Jim as if noticing him for the first time. "I remember all. Now we erase, yes? Help me."

Jim joined the man in rubbing out the equations with their hands. But when they'd smudged it out, many of the equations were still legible.

"Why did you do this now, here, where it would be seen and where it would raise questions?"

"Yes, timing is bad. But I have thought." Kovács tapped a chalky finger to the side of his head. "I must write out. You understand?"

Jim demanded the chalk, then placed it flat against the blackboard and rubbed it back and forth to cover the entire surface until he'd eroded the chalk to a sliver and covered the surface in white. When he'd finished, he took the velvet covering off a table and used it to erase the new markings, but even then he could see numbers, perhaps not enough to decipher Kovács's work, but enough to figure out what the man had been about, perhaps. Only when he'd doused the board with water from a pitcher and dried it was he satisfied. He put it back on the easel, turned the velvet covering around to hide the chalk and water, and then hauled Kovács out of the nursery and into the hallway.

They were halfway to the back staircase when Jim heard a car sounding its horn outside the house. He drew back the curtains on the window and looked down into the courtyard. A car spit gravel as it pulled down the driveway and carbinieri crowded into two more long, black Fiats very much like the first and took off in pursuit. One of the men, Jim saw, was Captain Rosario. Whatever Nigel had done as he'd left the party, he'd attracted the attention of their Italian hosts. He'd bought Margaret and Jim a few moments of distraction.

"Kovács, run!"

Chapter Twenty-Seven

Katterman watched the cars race away down the hillside with growing suspicion. Too obvious, too staged.

First the black Fiat came around from the gravel lot between the villa and the surrounding olive groves, moving quickly, tires spitting up stones. A few carabinieri milled around smoking, and they jumped back in alarm. Someone peered inside, shouted, and this brought Captain Rosario running. Withing moments Rosario and his men were squeezing into a pair of Fiats and tearing after the first car in pursuit.

Hossbach ran around from the back, out of breath, jacket flapping. He had his luger in hand. "That was Burnside, damn him. Too sick to step onstage, but well enough to come to the party dressed in his Goring costume. I knew it was suspicious." He stopped to pant for breath. "I sent for our car."

"But where is Burnside going?"

"The devil only knows, but he sure took off in a hurry." He looked over his shoulder. "Where's our driver?"

Yes, such a hurry that even a fool would expect immediate pursuit. So what was it that spooked him? A jealous husband on his heels? Italian secret service? Or perhaps it was another Gestapo agent, working independently. And yet nobody came out of the villa to look for him. It didn't make sense.

Katterman thought about the note in his pocket, the one he'd retrieved from Dunleavy's jacket as the man lay dying on the floor. He had to phone Rome, to find out what it meant.

"We've got to follow him," Hossbach continued, his back turned. "And I want him before the Italians have a chance to work him over. Damn that driver."

The man kept talking with his back turned as Katterman left his side to step into the shadows cast by the stone stairs that climbed to the terrace. People came out of the ballroom to lean over the edge, their conversation animated, hands gesturing, people peering into the darkness at the car lights circling down the hill to reach the road below. The lead car — that would be Nigel Burnside's — turned northeast, in the direction away from Florence. Katterman hugged the shadows and moved around the side of the villa. His hand slipped into his jacket and felt for the comforting weight of his pistol.

A diversion. He'd seen this kind of behavior before. One man runs while a half dozen others slip away.

Servants, butlers, and maids lingered around the back door, smoking, gossiping in loud voices in a fashion not much different than their masters and mistresses on the terrace out front, except their language and gestures were coarse, their accents difficult to decipher. Katterman was about to turn around and go back around front when the back door swung open, a head popped out, and someone met his gaze with an alarmed expression before ducking back in. It was Nigel's sister. Margaret Burnside.

That look on her face was unmistakable. A scout. Checking for the all clear.

He drew his gun and shoved through the crowd of servants. They fell back with hisses of alarm or warnings about the gun. Katterman pushed his way inside to find himself in a service porch, with metal bins for delivering bread, eggs, and produce, cubicles for mail or messages, and buzzers to ring various parts of the servant wing. Not one, but three figures were running through the far door, into the kitchens. His eyes were still adjusting to the light and he didn't identify the first two, but the third was Margaret.

By the time he made his way to the kitchen there was no sign of them, but all the cooks and maids and serving men wearing tuxedos and holding platters were staring through the far doors, which swung on their hinges. Katterman replaced the gun and raced back outside.

Hossbach stood next to their car, which had finally arrived. The driver was disheveled, his tie undone. Probably drunk, the idiot, hitting the grappa with the other off-duty servants, rather than standing at the ready as commanded.

"Where have you been?" Hossbach snapped. He yanked open the door. "Get in."

"It's a diversion." Katterman looked around, dismayed to see not a single police officer or carabinieri; every one of them had taken off, apparently. He needed help and he needed it quickly.

"What are you talking about?"

"Burnside's sister. Two others. They were trying to slip away while we were distracted. Draw your gun. Stay here, make sure nobody gets past you. I'm going inside to enlist the count, any other officers I can find. Block the driveway with the car. Do you understand me? Nobody leaves."

"Katterman, I'm telling you—"

"I'll find some men. Armed, if possible. Do not let anyone leave under any circumstances. The rest of us will turn the house upside down until we find them."

For a moment it looked like Hossbach would break, but then he shook his head. "No. Forget about the girl. Nigel Burnside—that's our man. We're leaving."

"You're wrong. I'm finding her."

"Come back here! That's an order."

Katterman ignored him and moved to the bottom of the stone staircase in front of the house. Behind him, the car door slammed and he wasn't surprised to hear Hossbach pulling away in the car to pursue Nigel.

Dunleavy's note. It was written like a telegram.

HK knew. Stop. Allowed transfer. Stop. Contact SD in Rome. Stop.

It was handwritten, so Katterman assumed that Dunleavy meant to pass it off for someone else to send. And internationally, he assumed.

HK meant Hossbach and Katterman, no doubt. And the SD in Rome would be the *Sicherheitsdienst*, Reinhard Heydrich's spy service. Was that an order to alert SD agents in Rome, or a question? And what did "allowed transfer" mean?

For a moment it almost came to him, the missing piece of the puzzle that would connect the cover-up of Sturmbannführer Wenck's death, what Katterman learned in his phone calls from Rosario's office, and Hossbach executing the Scottish actor at the theater. And now this bizarre behavior.

But then it was gone, and he returned to the task at hand.

Katterman had to organize a search before Margaret

and her friends realized he was alone and tried to force their way out. He looked up along the balcony, at the crowds still spilling outside.

Count d'Angelo stood to one side with two elderly men weighed down with sashes and medals, while another man, this one younger, pontificated to them about something or other, using broad Italian gestures. Katterman scaled the stairs two at a time and elbowed his way through the crowd until he was at d'Angelo's side.

"What's this, *signore?*" one of the elderly men said with a scowl.

"Your excellency," Katterman said to d'Angelo, uncertain if he was using the right honorific, "we have three fugitives loose in your house. I urgently request your help to apprehend them before they can escape."

The count looked taken aback, but recovered quickly. "Yes, of course. What do you need?"

"First, I want that driveway blocked. Do you understand? Nobody gets in and out."

The count snapped his fingers and gestured impatiently for a butler, who lifted his tray overhead to better maneuver through the crowd.

Katterman didn't wait for him to arrive. "Do you have bodyguards?"

"Two."

"Good. Now listen carefully. Get them. Send them to the bottom of the stairs. Then find me ten more trusted men. Arm them with whatever you can find."

The count licked his lips and nodded. "What then?"

"I want every person in this house herded onto the balcony. Servants, guests, men, women. Even children, if there are any on the premises. I want them under guard. Understand?"

"Si, signore."

D'Angelo turned to his butler and gave him instructions about the car. The butler dropped his tray and ran for the stairs, and then the count spoke in rapid-fire Italian to the men at his side.

Katterman's confidence rose as he looked down at the driveway. No more cars came around from the far side, and no figures ran across the gravel. In spite of Hossbach's shameful abandonment to give chase to their decoy, Katterman would shortly have matters under control. Only moments had passed since he'd chased those three back into the house.

Moments more and he'd catch them.

Jim followed Margaret back through the house with Kovács between them. He expected shouts, maybe even gunfire from their rear, but they seemed to have lost Katterman, at least for the moment. They fled through the kitchen and back up the stairs. The hallway was quiet, with only a single pair of women with lorgnettes held to their eyes as they examined a Renaissance painting of saints surrounding the Virgin and Child. Loud voices came from the ballroom and it sounded as though someone had thrown open the doors to the balcony. Nigel's flight must have attracted attention from the party as well as from Rosario and his men.

"Onto the balcony," Margaret said. "Hurry. We'll take the stairs."

"Let me go back," Jim said. "I'll run out the back doors and make for the olive trees. With any luck they'll chase me, and you can get the car."

"They'll kill you."

Maybe, but if the carabinieri were all gone, all he had to do was occupy the two Germans long enough for Margaret to escape with the Hungarian scientist. He didn't think they'd kill him. Of course they would work him over, and when they discovered his role in matters... well, he didn't want to go there. A good part of him was grateful that she wasn't going to feed him to the wolves for the sake of buying a few precious seconds.

But just when he thought Margaret was trying to protect him, she added, "I can't risk you talking. We are too far from the coast. Too much at stake and we don't know how you hold up to torture."

"Torture?" Kovács said. His face turned pale. He had looked terrified ever since Margaret handed him a cyanide capsule and told him to bite down on it if they caught him. She had one for herself, too, she said, but none for Jim. He didn't know whether he'd have the guts to bite down if they took him, but wished he had one just in case.

"Anyone else we can trust?" Jim asked as they made their way down the hall toward the ballroom. "Weil?"

"Maybe, maybe not. He doesn't know specifics. His ignorance is good for him, good for us. Keep your distance from him if you can — don't let people spot us together." She stopped them outside the ballroom. "You see Katterman and Hossbach, on the other hand, you go up to them, improvise. Hold them while we try to slip past."

They pushed into the ballroom. Much of the party had spilled onto the balcony, the doors now flung open and winter chilling the ballroom in defiance of the huge blaze that guttered in the fireplace. Few people glanced their way. He spotted a knot of actors from the company, including Lula and Weil, standing in one corner, looking worried, speaking in low tones that didn't penetrate the general commotion. Lula spotted them and said something to the others, who then waved for them to come over.

"Don't look at them," Margaret said. "Keep going."

They made it onto the balcony but stopped abruptly. Katterman stood near the stairs, speaking firmly with Count d'Angelo and three other men, all of whom listened intently. A butler shoved his way through the crowd, took instructions from the count and then dropped his tray with a clatter and ran for the stairs.

Margaret let out a hiss. She pulled Jim and Kovács back inside, and the three of them took refuge behind a pair of potted palm trees.

"What now?" she asked.

"Is too late," Kovács said. "We not escape." His voice was flat and he fumbled in his jacket pocket where he'd put the cyanide pill moments earlier.

Margaret grabbed his wrist. "Not yet, not now. Listen to me. No!"

"Only feeling. Only making sure. In case." Kovács removed his hand from his pocket.

"Jim, for God's sake," she said. "Any ideas?"

But Jim was frozen with indecision. As far as he could see, all paths had closed down. Where was Hossbach? Downstairs, guarding the servant's exit, most likely. But even if not, could they make it down before Katterman had these men organized to trap them on the property? No. Other exits, then? The back doors to the gardens and olive groves. Yes, but where to from there?

"We have to make a run for it," he said at last. "I'll

charge Katterman."

"He's a trained officer and he's armed. You'll die."

"If I do, I'll make it good. You two go for the stairs while everyone is looking at me."

"But Jim—"

"No time. Quickly."

He started around the palm, but then someone grabbed his sleeve. He whirled, alarmed, and drew short. It was the contessa. She studied him with a furrowed brow, and then looked to Margaret and Kovács. "You're in trouble."

"Contessa, not now," Jim said.

"I can help. Tell me what to do."

Margaret said, "It's your husband. And the Germans. We have to get past them." She nodded at Kovács. "They'll kill this man. Maybe us, too. What can you do?"

The contessa looked around the palm and toward the balcony. "I am an actress," she said. "That's what I will do, I shall act."

Before they could stop her or ask for clarification, the contessa was leaving them. She staggered through the crowd like a drunk woman, moving toward her husband on the balcony, stopping once to whisper in the ear of a footman, and another time in the ear of a young Italian officer in dress uniform and wearing a sword. The footman nodded and turned in a different direction, the young Italian stiffened and followed her at a distance toward the balcony. But as she moved, her drunk act grew more exaggerated, until it looked like she could barely keep her feet. Once she knocked over someone's drink, and then she crashed into someone with an apology. Already, heads turned and people edged in her direction, as if aware that new excitement was brewing.

As she stepped through the open doors onto the balcony, the contessa called out in a full, piercing stage voice that penetrated the noise of the crowd. *"L'hai fatto? Dimmi che non hai!"* Jim needed no translation to hear the outrage in her voice. A woman scorned.

Count d'Angelo turned toward his wife, alarmed. He lifted his hands in supplication as the contessa came at him, berating him loudly. The elderly men at the count's side shrank back, but they couldn't escape the crush of people crowding in with barely concealed delight as the contessa tore into her husband, the Italian coming out like bullets from a machine gun, words piling onto each other into a single, polysyllabic cry of jealousy and rage. She slapped at his face and he grabbed her wrist. Jim couldn't see what happened next, but suddenly they'd tumbled to the ground and other people tripped over them. The young Italian officer and the footman, Jim saw, were actively herding the crowd into the conflict. More and more people stumbled and fell over the count and the contessa.

"Nein!" Katterman shouted. He was pressed against the railing, but fighting with some success to break free. "Move. All of you. This can wait." He switched to Italian, but nobody paid him any attention.

Back behind the palm trees, Margaret started forward. "Now! Go for the stairs."

The crowd had flowed outside and the three members of the theater company found the way opening toward the stairs in the middle of the balcony. Jim's heart leapt in sudden hope as he looked into the courtyard to see the black Fiat that had brought him to the villa idling below the stairs, the driver standing in front of the open driver's side door. Margaret shoved aside a few people who got in the way and they almost reached the stairs when Katterman looked away from the fray and spotted them.

"You! Halt!"

"Run!" Margaret cried.

She got Kovács onto the stairs and started down. Jim was right behind them when a hand clamped on his shoulder and spun him around. It was Katterman.

Jim swung his fist, but the other man ducked and the blow glanced off the side of his head. Katterman jerked Jim to the ground and then was on top of him, too strong, raining blows onto his head. Jim couldn't protect himself, couldn't push the man away.

Go! he thought in Margaret's direction. *Get away while you can!*

Chapter Twenty-Eight

J IM LIFTED HIS KNEE TO push Katterman away, but another man had Jim by the legs and pinned him. Someone tripped over them, and they were surrounded by churning, stomping legs and feet and angry, frightened cries. Jim couldn't get free, couldn't escape the blows. The only hope was that he could hold off Katterman for a few seconds longer.

"Let go!" a voice cried out in English. "Get your hands off him, you animal."

His defender was Lula Larouche. She threw herself around Katterman's neck. Weil was there, too, and Jergens, Smith, Becher, all rushing to the aid of their fellow actor. They got Katterman off and Jim to his feet. Katterman swung his fist and one man's head snapped back under the blow and he fell. Weil threw his arms around the German and dragged him back to the ground. They disappeared in a sea of legs and evening gowns.

A gunshot. People screamed, ran. Someone crashed into the railing and knocked over a row of vases along the edge. They tumbled end over end and smashed in the courtyard below. The crowd parted to show Katterman on top of Weil, trying to regain his feet, pistol in hand. Weil clutched at his belly and threw his head to one side with a grimace of agony. Blood spread in a crimson stain across the front of his white shirt. Katterman stood over him with his gun outstretched, panting, but already recovering.

"Run!" Lula told Jim. "For God's sake!" She threw herself at Katterman as he spotted Jim and lifted his gun.

Another shot split the air as Jim reached the stairs. He expected a stab of pain, but felt nothing. He didn't look back, but flew down the stairs, half-stumbling, half-running. He reached the driveway, worried he would be too late, that Margaret and Kovács would already be speeding off down the hill, while he stared at a cloud of dust. But the car was still there, and Margaret held the door open.

"Run!" she cried.

The car started to pull away. He ran after it with legs pumping and arms flailing. The tires spit gravel in his face. Another gunshot sounded, and this one whizzed by his ear like an angry wasp. He flinched, almost tripped. The car was pulling away.

"Jim!"

It slowed briefly at the edge of the hill and he caught up. He dove for the open door. Margaret was alone in the back seat, with Kovács and the driver up front, each shouting at him in their respective languages. She got her hands under Jim's arms and wrestled him inside as the car accelerated into the first turn while his legs still kicked outside the car. And then he got in, while Margaret reached over him for the door. She got the handle and used the momentum of the turning car to get it shut.

Gunfire snapped at their back, but then they rounded the corner and left it behind.

"I thought you were going to leave me," Jim said as they reached the bottom of the hill and straightened onto a rutted country lane.

"What do you take me for?" Margaret glanced back over her shoulder. "Dammit, they're still coming."

Already lights circled the hill above them. Their driver better know what he was doing, by God, or they'd be trapped and killed before they reached the open road.

"Weil is dead," Jim said. "Katterman shot him. Might have shot Lula, too."

"Oh," she said. Her hands trembled violently, belying her calm tone of voice.

"Never mind," he said and gave her hands a squeeze. "Let's see if we can keep the rest of Katterman's bullets inside the gun where they belong. Where are we going? The rendezvous with Nigel?"

She leaned forward and said to the driver, "We're going to Vinci, right?"

"*Che cosa?*"

"Ah, let's see. *Andiamo a Vinci, no?*"

"*Si, si, per Vinci. Non ti preoccupare.*"

"Very good." She settled back. "I think that was a yes."

"So long as that last bit doesn't mean 'and when we get there, I'll turn you into the secret police for my reward.'"

"You never know with these smuggler types. This chap looks like a Chicago gangster."

"Kovács, you okay up there, pal?" Jim said.

"Very frightened."

"Yeah, me too. But we made it. A short drive and we'll get you out of this blasted country and somewhere safe." Jim turned to Margaret. "A boat, is that it? We'll load everyone up and make for what? Malta?"

"No idea, but I rather hope not. Malta is seven hundred miles from the Tuscan coast. German planes, Italian cruisers, and the lot—it would be a bloody difficult crossing."

At this point he'd take his chances in the open sea. Maybe the British could send planes to escort them across, or maybe they could slip through, looking to the world like petty smugglers. There must be hundreds, if not thousands, of smugglers plying their age-old trade on the Mediterranean at the moment and surely the Axis forces couldn't track them all, even if they wanted to. In any event, he'd deal with those dangers when they came; at the moment, the seventy miles to the coast concerned him more than the seven hundred off it.

The driver turned down a country lane, followed it for a few bone-jarring miles with his lights out, tires catching ruts and then jerking out again. When they came out the other side he accelerated again onto a flatter, straighter road that had been properly graded. From the back seat at least, the countryside whipped by in near darkness, and how the Italian was keeping them out of a ditch, Jim didn't know. Once the car jerked to a halt when something staggered into the road in front of them. It turned out to be a cow, which stopped in the headlights and stared. They couldn't get around, so Jim jumped out and slapped its bony rump until it ambled across to the ditch on the far side.

"I hope the contessa is all right," Margaret said when he got back in the car and they pulled away again. "That was an awful risk she took. An hour ago I thought she was a silly old fascist wife."

"Turns out she was an actress after all. Played her part

perfectly. And so did Lula, Weil, and the rest of them."

Margaret fell silent. At last she said, "This is wrong, but I can't help thinking about the play."

"How do you mean?"

"That we will never go onstage again, never see the curtain rise, hear the audience take in their breath as the show starts. I should be thinking about Weil and Dunleavy, dead. Instead, my lines are running through my head. All those wonderful Oscar Wilde asides, so silly and contradictory, and yet illuminating at the same time."

"I suppose you're an actress, too. Only secondarily a spy."

"I hate this war. Wasn't 1914 enough of a lesson? Did they have to start up again so soon? Why do they do it?"

"Because they can," Jim said. "And because they're not the ones who pay the price. At the end of the day, Churchill and Hitler will sit down to tea — only they'll call it a peace conference. And Roosevelt and Stalin will be there. Mussolini, too. They'll make big speeches and come home to cheers. Popes and kings will hang medals around their necks and proclaim them great statesmen. Except back home every village green will have a new war monument, a new cemetery. Boys will return from the front with burned-out lungs and missing limbs. That's the way it always happens. The people who start the wars never pay the cost."

"Not this time," she said. "Not after what the Germans are doing in Eastern Europe, not when people learn what's happening to the Jews. Hitler will swing from a rope and all his minions, too, Mussolini included. This war will change everything."

"Maybe," he said, unconvinced.

"Mark my words. This time it is different."

"Anyway, first we have to win the blasted thing or all bets are off."

"Yes, there is that."

They had been zig-zagging through the Tuscan countryside for a good forty-five minutes and Margaret leaned toward the driver. "Where are we going? *Dove?*"

"*Est, est. Non ti preoccupare.*"

"There's that part about the secret police again," Jim muttered.

"I think it means 'don't worry,' actually," Margaret said. "Problem is, I *am* rather worried, at that. Any idea what direction we're going?"

Jim rolled down the window to look outside, but the landscape was a jumble of dark hills and olive groves. A few lights winked in a village to their right, but he saw nothing that looked like Florence or any other city. "I can't tell," he admitted. "Probably west. Kovács, what do you think?"

The Hungarian leaned his own head out and fixed on the half-moon, and then swept his eyes across the star-studded sky. "Southeast."

"Hullo," Margaret said. "That's not toward Vinci. Are you sure?"

"Certain. Approximately one-hundred-twenty-eight degrees on the compass."

"That's all wrong." She leaned forward. "You up there!"

"*Est. Non ti preoccupare.*"

"We bloody well are not going *est*. We're supposed to go toward Vinci. We have to stop the car." She tensed, as if readying herself to make a lunge over the back seat.

"Hold it," Jim said. He pulled her back. "At this speed? We'll go into the ditch."

"We have to take a chance. We have to find Nigel or we'll never get Kovács to the coast in time. And that means we have got to turn around now before it is too late. You grab the driver, I'll get the wheel."

"Yeah, but then what?" he said. "Where the hell are we? We have no idea. Want to drive into the next town and ask for directions? We don't even speak Italian. They'll have the police on us faster than you can say 'Heila Mussolini.'"

Two pairs of headlights flared suddenly in front of them. The driver hit the brakes and stopped only feet before they slammed into the trucks that blocked the road. Two men scrambled out of the vehicles to confront the car with lowered submachine guns.

Jim grabbed the driver's shoulder. "Get us out of here!"

"BANDITOS!" Margaret said. "Back up!"

But flashlights knifed into the road at their rear, and as Jim looked back, half a dozen more men armed with carbines, pistols, and submachine guns surrounded the Fiat's back bumper. Before he could shout another warning to the driver, the man threw himself from the car and thrust his hands into the air, gibbering at top speed. The other doors flew open. Two men dragged Kovács out, while another man grabbed for Margaret. They tried to get Jim, too, but he leaned back and kicked his legs, while backing toward where they'd taken Margaret. She cried for his help.

But they came at him from the other side of the car, yanked him out, and hauled him to his feet. He turned to swing, and came face to face with a man in a peasant jacket, trousers, and a hat pulled low over his eyes. The man shoved a pistol against Jim's forehead.

He stopped struggling.

CHAPTER TWENTY-NINE

Hossbach's voice was tinny through the ancient telephone receiver. "I'm leaving for Livorno and I want you to meet me there. It will take three hours. Tell the count to give you a driver."

Katterman switched the earpiece to his other ear. "Why?"

"No time to explain. You must leave at once."

Outside the telephone booth, the chaos had turned into a messy cleanup. Károly Weil lay dead, and by Katterman's own hand. Another member of the theater company, Lula Larouche, had a gunshot wound to the shoulder, serious enough that she needed medical attention. Various other members of the cast suffered twisted ankles and concussive blows to the head. One other woman had a broken arm, and one of the musicians a broken nose after someone trampled his Stradivarius and a secondary brawl ensued. The fighting had spilled into the hallway and a two-thousand-year-old Roman bust fell off a pedestal and smashed on the marble floor, which set off another round of brawling, this one including d'Angelo's footmen.

Katterman calmed the fighting and then took the entire theater company prisoner and ordered them moved to the library and kept under armed guard by two elderly soldiers armed with swords and hundred-year-old smoothbore muskets. They demanded to be freed, shouted at Katterman to get a doctor for Lula (all in good time, he told them), and threatened to complain to the ministry, even the Gestapo. He ignored them.

He wanted the contessa separated too, suspicious of the timing of her drunken accusations about her husband's philandering, but she had fallen into the count's arms, weeping and begging his forgiveness. The old fool had melted at once. He helped her to a divan, then found her ostrich-feather fan and stood above her, waving the thing himself while his wife fluttered her eyes and passed in and out of consciousness.

Or so she was feigning. Katterman didn't believe any of it. Unfortunately, he had no authority here, except for the moral variety, and that was only good so long as he kept the count on his side. And as far as his wife was concerned, d'Angelo's willpower was as limp as a bowl of overcooked noodles.

"Katterman, are you there?" Hossbach said on the other end of the line.

"I'm here. Why do I need to meet you in Livorno?"

"I told you already—"

"You didn't tell me anything," Katterman interrupted. "You gave me orders. And this after disappearing for mysterious reasons. Because you left, I've lost Heydrich, Burnside's sister, and the other Hungarian. But I do have their confederates in hand and intend to interrogate them and let the Italians comb their own countryside for the fugitives. Unless, that is, you are more forthcoming with information and explain what is so urgent on the Italian coast."

"I can't. The line might be tapped."

"It may be. Nevertheless, I am not leaving here until you share more information. Why Livorno?"

Hossbach hesitated. "It's the Hungarian. Not the one you killed. Kovács. Rosario caught a man, a smuggler. He claims they're trying to get Kovács out of the country."

"Whatever for?"

"He's a scientist, apparently, a physicist who taught at Budapest Technical Institute. He's wanted by the Gestapo."

"This isn't a Jew hunt is it?" Katterman asked. "We have bigger worries. A bigger conspiracy to break. Heydrich's nephew, for a start. If you tell me we want Kovács because he is a Jew..."

"I have no idea if he is or not. It doesn't matter. The Gestapo wants him, so does the enemy. Whatever it is, it's important. Now I need you down here. Getting Kovács is more important than anything, and that includes James Heydrich."

Katterman considered. This new information didn't answer all of his questions, but it did answer some of them. Why they'd created such a scene to escape from the party. Maybe even what that business in the fish market and on the bridge was about. The fish market transfer would have been about a rendezvous at Livorno, and they must have learned it would take place tonight. They'd had no choice but to move now.

A burning curiosity filled him, almost an itch that demanded attention. He wanted nothing more than to get his hands on these people and start digging.

"Very well. I suppose I could leave my prisoners with the count and meet you in Livorno. We'll arrest Heydrich and the rest. Tell me how to find you."

"Excellent. Listen carefully."

When Katterman finished with Hossbach, he hung up but didn't set down the earpiece. Something was niggling in his mind. An answer, or a hint of an answer, that would explain Hossbach's strange behavior. He lifted the phone again and tapped the hook switch. "Operator?"

A woman answered at the switchboard with a clear, bell-like tone, and he imagined an opera singer, out of work and looking for a job where her beautiful voice wouldn't be completely wasted.

"This is Inspector Katterman with the Reich Ministry of Propaganda and Enlightenment. I need the German embassy in Rome."

"Which number, *signore*? There are five separate phone lines at the German embassy."

Five lines? They must have a small army in Rome.

"What are they?" he asked. "The names attached to each number?"

"I am afraid I could not say, *signore*. The numbers are on the red list."

"This is an emergency. Is there a number that is either the Ausland SD or the Gestapo?"

"Perhaps."

"Put me through. I will accept the consequences if this proves to be a mistake."

She patched him through. He counted the rings. It was up to fifteen and Katterman was expecting the operator to cut in with an apologetic tone when a sleepy voice said, "Bloch here."

"This is Wulf Katterman. Is this the SD?"

"Katterman? Who the blazes is that? There's no Katterman registered with the embassy." Bloch's voice was the opposite of the Italian operator's, filled with gravel. If the operator was an unemployed opera singer, he imagined Bloch cut his voice screaming at prisoners in a concentration camp.

"Listen to me, this is important. I am with the Reich Ministry of Propaganda and Enlightenment. I have a priority one security situation on the Tuscan coast." Katterman had no idea if priority one meant a damn thing, but he doubted Bloch would either.

"Is this line secure?" Bloch asked.

"No, it is not. I have no choice, you understand. If I don't get help at once, they are going to escape and do grievous harm to the war effort."

"Who is going to escape?"

"Two British spies and a German traitor. And a fourth man who may possess critical scientific military secrets."

This got Bloch's attention. By the time Katterman hung up the phone with the embassy he had the man's full cooperation.

Jim lifted his hands slowly to the sky while the bandits pushed him with their gun barrels to join Margaret and Kovács in a knot in the middle of the road. There were at least a dozen men, dressed in peasant trousers with dirty wool jackets, patched and repatched and frayed at the cuffs.

Their driver stood in a knot of the bandits, smoking and jabbering in Italian. Not a prisoner. They'd been set up.

"That bastard," Margaret said.

There seemed to be some argument among the men as

to what to do next, and voices rose in pitch and gestures grew more wild. One of the men came toward them with a bowlegged swagger. He had a dirty cap over the top of his head and fingerless gloves. He pinched a stubby cigarette between his thumb and forefinger, took a huge drag that ate up the rest of the cigarette, and then flicked the remnant into the night.

He thumped his chest. "I Nicolo." His words rode on a gasp of smoke exhaled from his lungs. "You come with me, yes?"

"The hell we will," Jim said. "What are you playing at here?"

"You come," he said, more urgently. He gestured toward one of the trucks and a second bandit standing by the open back doors, gesturing for them to come, a short, wiry man with pants cinched too tightly and a German pistol in his hand.

"Not until you tell us what you want." The man grabbed for his arm, but Jim jerked back. "Don't touch me, I'm warning you."

Nicolo returned to the crowd of men, arguing in louder voices.

"Why haven't they robbed us or killed us already?" Margaret asked. "They don't want the car — the driver is with them — so maybe they'll turn us over to the police? Except they haven't even checked us for weapons. Here he comes again. They think you're in charge — play along, don't get us killed. Maybe we can still weasel out of this."

Nicolo's gestures were more urgent now. "Come, come. Friend!" He tapped Jim's chest with a thick index finger. "Friend." He tapped his own chest. "Nicolo friend."

"You're not our friend," Jim said. "And we're not getting in there."

"*Il tuo amico. L'inglese è in attesa.*"

"Hold on," Margaret said. "The Englishman? Is that the friend you're talking about? Nigel?"

"*Si, si!*" He lifted his shirt to point at his side and then grimaced. It was a fair approximation of Nigel's wound. "We have. We have. *Non ti preoccupare.*"

"There's that bit again," Jim said. "You're sure that means 'don't worry'?"

"Let us hope," she said. "Kovács, what do you think? Do we trust these fellows?"

"No good choice," Kovács said. "Yes, we trust."

The Italians were all gesturing now, including their former driver, urging them toward the back of the truck. Reluctantly, the three of them set in motion. The vehicle was a farm truck with a bed in the back concealed beneath a canvas-covered frame. They climbed up inside. His stomach churning, Jim expected to see men emerge from the shadows, holding ropes and guns, maybe truncheons to beat them unconscious.

And so he jumped when something moved in the darkness of the truck. A cough.

"Who is that?" Margaret said. "Who's there?"

"It's me," came a weak voice.

"Nigel?" she said. "Thank God. You're all right? You're not a prisoner?"

"Not a prisoner. Neither am I all right. Kovács is with you?"

"He's here," Jim said. "Right behind me."

"What are we doing?" she said. "I thought we were supposed to meet in Vinci."

"Never mind," Nigel said. "We are back on schedule.

Get back here."

The other three made their way deeper into the truck bed as the truck engine coughed, turned over, and then rumbled into life. As it pulled away, two more men jumped into the back. They sat on the edge of the truck bed with their legs hanging over and carbines propped across their laps. Outside the canvas Jim heard other vehicles start up, including the now-familiar growl of the Fiat that had driven him from Florence and again from the count's villa. A moment later, he heard nothing but their own truck.

It hit a bump and Nigel groaned.

"What's the matter?" Margaret said. "Did someone hurt you?"

"It's that bloody gunshot. The stitches are out. I'm bleeding again."

"Let me have a look," Jim said.

He groped in the darkness until his hands found the man lying in a bed of straw with his shirt off and pressed against his side. It was slick, soaked all the way through with blood. Margaret fumbled with something and a moment later she handed Jim a big mass of cloth.

"What's this?" he asked.

"My dress. It's just getting in the way, anyhow."

"You can't run around in your bloomers."

"No, I bloody well cannot. You stop the blood. I'll worry about trousers."

He used his teeth to rip through the edge of Margaret's dress and then tore off large strips while Margaret went to the two men on the edge of the truck and negotiated for the smaller one's trousers. In different circumstances the exchange would have been hilarious, as the men first thought she'd gone mad, then realized she was without pants and trying to remove the one fellow's own trousers, starting with the belt. There was some laughter, some leering noises, but a couple of slaps and curses later and she got through the man's thick, peasant skull that, strangely enough, she wasn't going to take him back to ravish him in the hay, she just wanted his trousers. He protested some, but by now he already had them off and his friend was openly jeering. She took his boots, too. By the time Margaret came back, the half-naked bandit was burying his legs in the straw to keep them warm. Or perhaps out of shame.

Meanwhile, Jim tied strips of the dress around Nigel's waist and cinched them against the bloody shirt until the man gasped in pain. Jim knotted them off one after another. Nigel needed a doctor — a surgeon, really — not to be bandaged haphazardly in the dark as a truck jounced along country roads. Jim kept wrapping and bandaging until he thought he'd at least slowed the flow of blood.

While he worked, Nigel explained through clenched teeth. He'd left the party on a tear, and as expected, Rosario's men gave chase. They followed him through hilltop villages and across darkened stretches of countryside. Nigel's driver stopped, pushed him into another car — driven by this Nicolo fellow — and they took off in another direction. On two different occasions he thought they'd escaped, only to see lights swing onto the road to their front or rear. Finally, vehicles blocked them on both sides and they abandoned the car and disappeared into the darkness of some vineyards.

"That's how I got re-injured," he said. "There was a wire fence. Nicolo whispered a warning, but I didn't understand what he was saying. I ran straight into it, fell over the other side. When I came up my gut was on fire. I must have ripped open the wound." He paused to take in some ragged breaths. "Or, I might have taken another bullet. They were shooting across the vineyards. I suppose it is possible they hit me in the same spot. It was all a jumble. I don't know how I made the road."

"But you got away," Jim said. "How did that happen?"

"Nicolo half dragged me up the hillside. We got to the road and headlights came on. I thought we were done for. At that point I didn't much care any more. I had a cyanide capsule. I meant to take it. As it turned out, Nicolo had friends. They intercepted your driver before he could run into the carabinieri road block at Vinci."

"Wish someone had explained that to us," Jim said. "We thought they set us up. Who are these friends, anyway?"

"I don't know much about them except that they are not fascists."

"Bandits," Margaret said. "That much is obvious. Although I suppose bandit and partisan might have some overlapping meaning in these parts. What are they planning?"

"The roads are swarming with carabinieri," Nigel said. "Nicolo says—assuming I deciphered the Italian correctly—that the only way we'll make the coast is if we have some diversions. I think they're planning something up by the count's villa, and there's a fascist mayor or minister or some such in one of those villages they mean to assassinate tonight. Or at least that's what I took all the pantomiming to mean. I might be completely mistaken." He stopped again, gasped for air. "Tell me what happened with you."

Jim and Margaret took turns explaining their escape from the villa.

"But you got Kovács, that's good. He is all right? The fellow is awfully quiet up there."

"Kovács is fine," Margaret said. "Weil and Lula are not." She told him about the gunfire.

"Hossbach and Katterman split up. That is curious. Listen—" He interrupted himself with a weak cough. "I don't know if I can make it."

"You'll make it," Jim said. "You haven't come this far to give up now."

"But if I do, if I'm too weak to get on the boat. Or if…if I don't make it to Livorno…I have to tell you everything I know. I don't know what these Italians are up to. Maybe they'll get to Livorno and leave you on your own. You have to be able to find the boat by yourself."

Jim started to protest again, that Nigel was sounding like a defeatist, that he'd soon be in British hands and with a proper surgeon to patch him up, but Margaret cut him off. "Go ahead, tell us everything."

And so Nigel did. A fishing boat waited at the harbor in Livorno. It would leave an hour before dawn, follow the safe channel through the minefields. There, a few miles offshore they would meet a British boat, lurking in the darkness. The signal, in Morse code, was "Shiva."

"Shiva, the Hindu god?" Jim said. "The destroyer of worlds?"

"That's right," Nigel said. "You do know Morse code, right?"

"I'll have to think about it, but yes, I learned it in Boy Scouts. I should be able to remember."

"Only as a last resort. Otherwise, Margaret will send the signal."

"Got it."

"Good," Nigel said. "The fishing boat has a lifeboat

attached — a rowboat. When you get the return signal, abandon the fishing boat, take the rowboat in. If you approach with the fishing vessel, the British ship will sink you. Do you understand?" When they said they did, Nigel added, "And remember, Kovács is the only one who matters. The rest of us must give up our lives to get him on that boat and away to safety."

"It won't come to that," Jim said. "We're all getting on that boat. Alive. Nobody is going to sacrifice anything."

"Are you sure? Do you think Weil and Dunleavy would agree?" Nigel grabbed Jim's wrist and pressed something into his hand. It was a pistol, heavy and solid in his grasp. "Do they teach one how to use *this* in Boy Scouts?" Nigel asked.

"No, but I can manage."

"Make sure that you do."

The implication was clear.

You don't have a cyanide capsule, Nigel was saying, *but now you have a gun. If the time comes, you know what to do.*

CHAPTER THIRTY

THEIR BANDIT GUARDS IN THE back of the truck hid their rifles in the straw and threw open the canvas at the rear of the truck as they pulled into Livorno. Even the gray of predawn made the four fugitives blink after several hours in the darkness. Jim's stomach was unsettled from the bouncing, winding road and no food since lunchtime yesterday. Not that he wanted food at the moment. Coffee, maybe. He'd drifted in and out of sleep since that meeting on the road and his head was stuffed with cotton, his mouth dry as sand.

The truck was too big for the narrow lanes that wound toward the harbor. Instead, Nicolo followed a remnant of the medieval city wall that crumbled under the weight of wisteria vines and fig trees sprouting from cracks in the mortar. Handsome, if neglected stone houses gave way to collapsed buildings with their foundations filled with trash, to wooden shanties crowded with dirty, sullen people. At the sound of the truck, children wrapped in filthy blankets stuck their heads out to stare at them, or toothless old women crawled from piles of crates with tin cups outstretched. A young man without shoes, on the other hand, took one look at them and went running, perhaps thinking it was an army roundup.

"This is the new Roman Empire?" Jim said.

"Mussolini couldn't conquer Greece without Hitler coming to his rescue," Margaret said. "This is where the Axis will fall, here in the weak underbelly. Some countries will fight to the end — Russia, England. But Italy? She'll turn. The knife in Hitler's back. Don't you think, Nigel?"

Nigel only grunted. He had been moving less and less through the night. The bleeding had stopped, but Jim couldn't see how he'd make it out to the harbor in his condition. Not unless he was able to draw on some hidden reserves.

"If this country is a knife," Jim said, "it's a knife with a rubber blade. More dangerous for the man holding it than his enemy. Maybe it's better to leave Italy to the Axis."

Nicolo pulled into a weedy lot in the shadow of the last remaining wall of a collapsed house, the bricks under assault by vines attempting to finish the job. The two bandits jumped down from the back truck, and there was a brief argument with Nicolo about one man's state of undress — his trousers, boots, and belt on Margaret at the moment. Nicolo went down the street, returning a few minutes later with new clothes for his man, a shirt and cap for Margaret, and complete changes of clothing for Nigel, Jim, and Kovács.

"*Ecco, signorina*," Nicolo said as he handed Margaret the shirt and cap. "You man now."

"I most certainly am not a man," she said.

"He means dressed like a man, dear," Nigel said. He swung his legs over the edge of the truck bed with a grimace, hand at his side against the bloody shirt and strips torn from Margaret's ballroom gown.

Jim and Kovács helped Nigel get undressed, get the

pants on, and then turned to their own clothing. Jim shuffled out of the coat and tails he'd put on after the show when he'd dressed once more as Goring's butler, Phipps. The trousers were rough canvas, the shirt had holes at the elbows and a frayed collar and cuffs. It smelled like anchovies. None of the clothes fit, including the boots, which were a half size too small. But it was no more than a mile to the harbor and he figured he could manage. When he finished, Kovács was lacing up his boots and Nigel was dressed, while Margaret struggled to get free of the corset.

"Can't get this blasted knot undone, I'm only making it worse."

Jim slid over. "Move your hands, let me try."

"I don't need help."

"Yes, you do. Come on, there's no shame."

She dropped her hands and let him pick at the knot behind her back. "Stop staring," she said to the Italian bandits, who stood gaping with broken crates in their hands, taken from a stack near the brick wall. Ostensibly they were moving the stack, but they kept stopping to look at Margaret. "Nicolo, make them look away." She waved her hand until the Italians turned.

Jim got the knot undone. "Got it. I'll turn my back."

"I don't care about that, it's those bandits leering at me that I don't fancy. It's no good, my hands are numb from the cold—can you pull the laces out?"

He worked at the laces until he had them out. He pried the corset apart and then pulled it up and over. Corset and sewn-in blouse came off together. Margaret inhaled deeply, as if she'd been holding her breath all night. Nigel looked away and held out the shirt for her to take. Jim should have looked away, too. He meant to.

Instead, his eyes lingered on her figure as she slipped her arms into the shirt. His face flushed and he thought of last night in the dressing room between acts, when they'd torn each other's clothes off. The curve of her body, from her neck to the swell of her breasts, to her waist and belly. The feel of her skin, her smell...

Her fingers worked at the buttons and she looked up to catch him staring. She met his gaze. "Jim, I—"

"*Andiamo!*" Nicolo said. "*Ora!*"

She gave a slight shake of her head, as if to clear it, and then she jumped down from the truck and tucked the shirt into her trousers. The pants hung off her hips, and she tightened the belt again. "Come on, Jim. Hurry."

Jim tucked Nigel's gun into his belt, then took the net Nicolo pushed into his arms. The man gave one to Nigel, too, and baskets for Kovács and Margaret, which he filled with straw and odds and ends gleaned from the rubbish of the vacant lot. He pantomimed holding the baskets up in front of their faces, then retrieved a gaffing hook on a wooden pole, which he draped over one shoulder. A few instructions from Nicolo to the other bandits, who stayed behind with the truck, and then the man led the fugitives back onto the street. Moments later, they'd turned down a winding, staircase-like alley that cut down the hill toward the harbor.

Less than an hour until dawn. Every few minutes they caught a glimpse of the Mediterranean below them, stretching like a rippling sheet of black silk. Under blackout rules, there were no blinking lights to guide ships in and out of the harbor, no lighthouses to warn of treacherous shoals. Every ten seconds one of two tones would sound: a low, deep foghorn and a higher-pitched whining, like the beginning of an air raid siren, abruptly cut off. Jim supposed these served as warnings where lights had once been used. But then, unexpectedly, a light flashed three times on the north edge of the harbor, and from the southern curve of the bay came an answer: two blinks, a pause, and then three blinks. Someone, then, was watching the harbor.

Margaret must have seen it too. "That's the Italians for you. Incompetent when you need them capable, and capable when you're counting on incompetence."

"Never mind," Nigel said. "Means nothing."

He was laboring. Twice he had to lean against one of the houses that crowded the alley. The second time he shook his head when Nicolo urged him to keep moving, but then Margaret took his arm and whispered something in his ear, her tone surprisingly gentle, although Jim couldn't pick out the exact words. He nodded, ashen faced, and hoisted up the net again to set in motion.

The streets were coming awake.

An old man crossed them in an alley, clanking a cowbell to mark six o'clock, and rough, weather-beaten fisherman stepped out of buildings made of crumbling mud bricks and ramshackle huts stacked one against another, nets over their shoulders or strings of hooks in hand, each one the length of a man's thumb and wickedly sharp, but laced together in an interlocking pattern that both kept the barbs safely engaged and the lines untangled. A man pulled a handcart loaded with clay octopus pots. Another man carried two buckets of offal on a pole draped over his shoulders. It smelled like rotting fish guts and attracted an obnoxious cloud of flies that swarmed over the bucket and on and around the man's face. The five companions walked behind him with shirts held up over their mouths. The smell was awful, but wherever the man approached, people shied to the other side of the alley or even turned around to look for another street. The shutters on one house slammed shut ahead of them, as if the smell carried its own warning all the way down the street.

And then they were at the harbor. Rotting docks stretched toward a breakwater that curved around an inner harbor to protect it from waves. Gulls circled overhead, crying out, and several times Jim heard scratching or glimpsed rats scurrying to take refuge in piles of rags or boards or disappear among stacks of empty barrels. The wind carried the smell of brine, rotting fish, and something more subtle, like burning rubber, perhaps the smell of distant battle — a burning ship or bombed-out port.

Fishermen untied boats and set them into the water. Some of the bigger boats had motors, but most were one- or two-man craft, rowed out beyond the breakwater before the fisherman raised sails to catch the breeze. They were rough-looking fellows: grizzled old men without teeth, small dark sorts who looked like Arabs or Moors, and men with skin tanned to leather even to the top of their bald, bare heads. Shoulder muscles like knotted rope showed through torn shirts, together with beefy forearms from years of dragging heavy nets. Grunting, cursing. One man slapped a blond-headed boy who may or may not have been his son. But nobody paid the outsiders any attention.

Nicolo led them toward a pair of rusting trawlers near the end of the docks. He let out a low whistle, and a man emerged from the shadows on one of the trawlers and trotted down the gangplank, then jumped to the dock with a thud of bare feet on wood. He exchanged a few words with Nicolo, who handed over a wad of bills, hastily stuffed into the fisherman's pocket. The fisherman sauntered up the docks toward the town without a backward glance.

Nicolo waved for them to climb in. Kovács went up first, followed by Margaret, who stood at the top of the gangplank and held out her hand. "Come on, Nigel. Take my hand."

Nigel steadied himself against the rope that tied the boat to the dock. He looked ready to puke from the swell of the dock beneath their feet. "You know how to pilot this thing?" he asked Nicolo.

"Come, come," Nicolo said.

"I'm right behind you," Jim said. "And Margaret is up already. You won't fall."

Nigel swallowed hard, let go of the rope and put an unsteady foot on the gangplank. He made it two steps and wobbled, before Jim caught his belt to steady him. A few more steps and Margaret had him by the wrist and the two of them helped Nigel onto the boat. Nicolo untied and coiled the rope, came up after them, and they pulled in the gangplank. He climbed a ladder to the stern deck and a moment later the engine growled to life with a puff of diesel and a rumble beneath their feet.

Margaret and Jim helped Nigel to sit on a metal locker that ran along the starboard side of the ship, beneath a small dinghy suspended from davits over the transom. He was pale and shaking and his wounds were oozing blood again.

Margaret touched Jim's arm. "See if there's a medical kit on board."

He started to rise, but Nigel caught him by the wrist. "No. Sit still. Don't move until we're in open water."

Nigel leaned his head back against the bulwark and closed his eyes. Jim watched, worried. Whatever pitiful bandages were on board this boat they wouldn't be enough. What Nigel needed was a surgeon.

Nicolo steered the boat from the deck above them, threading through the other fishing boats that clogged the inner harbor. They moved at walking pace, inching along. None of the other fishing boats seemed to pay them any attention, and Jim allowed himself to hope that it would really be that easy. Already, Nicolo was swinging around the breakwater and increasing speed. According to Nigel, they had maybe thirty, forty minutes cruising through the water before they'd drop the lifeboat and row to the British vessel and safety. The other boats thinned. The land retreated behind them as they gained the open sea.

"Other ship," Kovács said, unexpectedly. He leaned against the railing on the foredeck. "On left."

A warship sat off port, roughly a half mile distant. It flew the Italian naval flag, a tricolor with a crown and shield in the center, and was covered in dazzle paint, variegated stripes of green and tan. A patrol boat, from the looks of it, maybe a hundred feet long, the kind designed to guard the coast against smugglers. Smaller than a corvette, but big enough to be a menacing figure that could turn and devour them at will. It crept along without lights at maybe three or four knots, moving in the opposite direction as the trawler.

They said nothing, and above them on the stern deck, Nicolo stared straight ahead. The other ship didn't change course. A few more minutes and they'd be past and lost in the fog that grew thicker the farther offshore they traveled.

And then a spotlight knifed across the distance from the patrol boat and bathed the fishing boat in white light. Nicolo cursed in Italian and the motor whined as he revved the engine.

When the light swung away momentarily, Jim saw with horror that the patrol boat was pulling around to fall in behind them. And picking up speed.

CHAPTER THIRTY-ONE

HOSSBACH STOOD AT THE PROW and leaned over the railing with a pair of binoculars at his eyes. "Heydrich, you bastard. Now we have you." He turned to Katterman with a triumphant look. "We have them. Look!"

Katterman took up the binoculars. It was still too dark to pick out details, and the enemy too distant, but he could sense the panic of the figures scrambling across the back of the fishing trawler. Who was piloting the boat, an Italian? And those other four must be Nigel and Margaret Burnside, Vilmos Kovács, and James Heydrich.

The Italian naval ship gave pursuit. Predator and prey, a chase played out in slow motion. They told Katterman the top speed of the patrol boat was nineteen knots, and the fishing boat was maybe fifteen knots. The distance between the two boats was two thousand meters and closing. Ten more minutes to close the gap.

The fishing boat was a puny thing, rusting and belching smoke and laboring to stay above the swells, while the patrol boat knifed through the water like a barracuda bearing down on a wounded sardine. Katterman knew it was an illusion. What if there was a British cruiser wallowing a few kilometers offshore, undetected by incompetent Italian coastal defenses? It was not impossible to imagine that such a ship could have slipped through the German air blockade of Malta and steamed through the night until it came out for the rescue. It might even now be thrusting toward them, ready to smash this little patrol boat to kindling.

Rosario came down from the upper decks. His hair was disheveled, his carabinieri uniform wrinkled, but he had a gleam in his eyes that erased any exhaustion from the night's chase and search. "The captain says we can fire at any time. He suggests the 6.45 centimeter, to give us a chance of picking up survivors."

"No," Hossbach said. "No shooting."

"We could knock out the engine."

"Too dangerous. I need them alive. The *Reich* needs them. Make that clear. No shooting."

"As you wish." Rosario climbed the metal staircase back up to the deck.

Two sailors sat in swivel chairs behind a pair of guns on the stern, the 6.45 centimeters. They may have been the smaller guns on board, but against the fishing boat they may as well have been the biggest guns of the German battleship Bismark.

"Tell those men to stand down," Hossbach told Katterman.

"These Italians are touchy. Better let the captain handle it. They won't shoot without his orders."

"I suppose you're right. Give me those."

Katterman handed back the binoculars and studied his partner. "We could have taken them at the docks, you understand."

"Too dangerous. Who knows how many bandits these men had lurking around town? Rosario was itching for a fight — our fugitives might have died in the crossfire.

Anyway, I wanted to see what they were planning. More evidence."

"What more evidence do we need?"

"Look at that," Hossbach said. "The fools intend to fight back."

Katterman took the binoculars a second time. Condensation formed on the lenses, and he wiped them off before lifting them to his eyes. It was true; two men struggled to mount what looked like a 12.7-millimeter machine gun to the back of the trawler. A third, slimmer figure carted over ammunition cans. It was still too dark to pick out faces, but he guessed it was the girl.

"Very good," he said. "They wouldn't shoot if they didn't recognize their situation is hopeless."

The boat was growing in size as they drew closer. He could see the figures on the deck without the binoculars now. Light flared from the muzzle of their gun. Hossbach grabbed Katterman and pulled him down. Bullets pinged against the side of the patrol boat, like hail against a tin roof. The Italians at the guns kept their aim, but did not shoot back. They looked jittery, anxiously waiting the command.

Eight hundred meters now, maybe less. A few minutes longer. More enemy gunfire, but this was no more effective than before. Katterman watched the enemy boat through his binoculars, his confidence growing.

The trawler banked sharply to starboard. His first thought was that this would only cut the time until they caught their prey, but then Hossbach cursed.

Katterman dropped the binoculars. He saw why dawn was so sluggish in arriving this morning. They were passing into a fog bank. The fog lay thickest to the right, like a wall of fleece. The trawler penetrated the wall and then disappeared.

As soon as Nicolo penetrated the fog bank, he swiveled to port again, then cut the engine and let them drift while he raced down from the stern deck. "Here!" he said, voice tight and panicked. "This! Here!"

Jim abandoned the gun, where he'd been squeezing off bursts in an attempt to slow the Italian patrol boat. It hadn't worked, but it might make them more cautious coming into the fog.

"Is this it?" Nigel asked. He roused himself from where he'd slumped on the deck with his back to the cabin door. Fog clung to his face like cobwebs, lending a corpse-like air to his pallid complexion.

"You sit back down," Margaret ordered Nigel as he wobbled to his feet. "Until we get the boat out, I don't want you to move."

As the fishing boat slowed, they wrestled the rowboat over the edge. It fell into the water with a splash. The rope drew taut and the rowboat dragged along by their side. Nicolo climbed down, helped Kovács into the lifeboat, and then took the oars from Margaret and Jim.

"*Andiamo!*"

Jim and Margaret turned to help Nigel, only to discover him struggling up the ladder to the stern deck.

Jim grabbed for his ankle. "What the hell are you doing?"

"Go," he said. "Leave me."

He kicked free, but they followed him up to the deck and caught him as he reached the wheel.

"Nigel, for God's sake, what are you doing?"

Margaret said.

"I'm giving you cover, what do you think?"

They tried to pry his fingers from the wheel, but he held on with a death grip. Nicolo and Kovács were begging them in Italian and Hungarian and broken English, and Jim was afraid they'd cut loose and take their chances on the open sea instead of waiting for the patrol boat to come out of the fog.

"What will I say," Margaret said, "that I left you behind? Hurry, we don't have time for this."

Lights swung through the fog off port. The patrol boat was close, no more than a few hundred meters. Too close. Any moment now.

"Listen to me," Nigel said. "You know the signal. Morse code. Shiva. But I need to get that boat away so you have a chance."

"Nigel!"

"That's a goddamned order!"

Jim grabbed Margaret and pulled her away. She cried and struggled, but only until he got her to the ladder, and then she went down. On reaching the bottom, he pushed her to the edge, where Nicolo and Kovács grabbed her arms and hauled her into the boat. Nicolo took a fishing knife to the rope. He sawed until it broke free. Jim jumped and landed sprawling. To their side the trawler motor revved and then it was banking away. More lights. They ducked down in the rowboat.

The patrol boat emerged from the fog. It cut the fog no more than fifty yards to the left of the rowboat, following, Jim saw with a mixture of dread and hope, the path cut by Nigel moments earlier.

"No," Margaret whispered. "Let him get away. Please."

Nicolo pulled out a compass and pointed to their

right. Jim threaded the oars through the oarlocks and rowed in the direction that he was pointing.

"Margaret, the signal," he said.

She tore her gaze from the fog to their rear, and then took out the flashlight and pointed it forward. She pulsed it into the fog. Nothing.

Gunfire sounded behind them, the chatter of a machine gun. What was Nigel doing? They must have come up to him and he was trying to buy more time. Jim redoubled his effort. His muscles ached. Nicolo tapped him on the shoulder, gestured a slight course correction. Margaret flashed the light again. Still nothing.

The gunfire stopped, then started up again. He was holding them off, earning them precious seconds.

Thump. Thump.

It was a heavier gun this time, firing two shells. A split second of silence passed and then an explosion tore the air. Light flared.

Margaret threw a hand over her mouth to stifle a cry.

"The signal," Jim said, gasping. "Margaret! For God's sake!"

She lifted the flashlight again with shaking hands. It blinked its Morse code. Nothing.

What was wrong? It was the right time, the right place, according to Nigel. But here they were and no British ship came out of the fog to rescue them and fight off the Italian patrol boat that would surely discover within moments that a rowboat and four of the five passengers were missing from the wrecked trawler.

He was almost spent. Time to give Nicolo a turn at the oars, but even a few seconds in the transfer would be too many. They had to keep going, they had to —

And then it came. An answering flash. It was bright,

not a flashlight, but a signal beacon. So bright, in fact, that it attracted attention. A searchlight cut the fog to their rear. It swung back and forth through the gloom until it fixed upon them. The dark shape of the patrol boat came toward them. With his back to the prow Jim could see it looming closer moment by moment.

"*Andiamo!*" Nicolo cried. "*Più veloce!*"

Jim rowed for all he was worth. It was reflex now, a gritty, gut-check of his reserves. Lean, pull. Lean, pull.

"There!" Margaret cried.

He glanced over his shoulder to see a ship in front of them, dark and low to the waterline. Three men stood on the deck at a gun that swiveled toward them. A flash of light from the muzzle.

He braced himself for the explosion, but the ship was firing overhead and targeting the Italians. Two shots fired in response from the patrol boat. Gouts of water shot into the sky and landed spray on the rowboat. But the Italians now veered to one side, as if afraid of a direct confrontation. Already, though, he could see them changing course yet again in order to bring their guns to bear. Whatever this ship was ahead of them, it didn't have the firepower to drive off the patrol boat for good.

Men swarmed over the deck of the boat in front of them. A second gun, this one a machine gun, snarled from the other side of a conning tower. It was a submarine, Jim realized with surprise as he hazarded another glance. That explained the low profile, the inability to fight off the Italians with deck guns. Did they have torpedoes? Could they fire them while at the surface? He had no idea. He kept rowing.

Margaret grabbed his shoulders. "Look out!"

He ducked as something clanked at the bottom of

the boat. A grappling hook tossed from the submarine. Nicolo snagged it on the bow of the rowboat and the rope went taut and jerked the boat forward. The men on deck were pulling the rope hand over hand to drag them in. Jim tried to row as well, but his arms and shoulders had collapsed and he gave up and sank back with chest heaving.

Moments later strong hands hauled them out of the rowboat and onto the submarine. Young men stared down, their faces pinched, their voices high and excited. English. British sailors.

The patrol boat fired through the fog. Spouts of water shot skyward and bullets hissed through the air. The submarine deck guns fired back, but it wasn't enough and they weren't intending to give battle. Instead, they abandoned the guns and shoved crates of ammo overboard, where they sank with a splash into the Mediterranean. The sailors ran for the open hatch. The four survivors from the rowboat joined them. Moments later, they were scrambling down a long metal ladder into the bowels of the ship. They emerged from the ladder into a narrow, too-short passageway, where the sailors hurried them along. Jim bent himself through the restricted openings that led from one compartment to the other. A yellow light strobed at every corner and a klaxon blared.

The sailors hustled them into a small, rounded room, crammed with empty bunks. A man shut the door behind them, and they found themselves in complete blackness. Jim groped for one of the bunks. The siren stopped abruptly. The hull groaned and there were popping sounds like coals in a fire snapping and crackling.

Several seconds passed and then an explosion boomed

through the hull. The room shuddered and almost pitched Jim from his seat. And then quiet. Moments later, a second, more distant boom.

Kovács was breathing heavily. Nicolo whispered in rapid-fire Italian what sounded like a prayer. Jim found Margaret, where she'd taken one of the bunks. She was crying softly.

"Margaret?"

"Shh. They're listening."

"It's okay," he whispered in her ear. "We're going to make it."

She turned her mouth to his ear. "Nigel is dead."

"I'm sorry."

Boom!

The room gave a violent jerk. He grabbed at Margaret as she flew forward, but then he lost his balance and fell. The entire room seemed to roll and he thought they were going belly up, a hole torn through the hull. But then it rolled back. Several seconds of silence passed with only the groaning of the hull as the pressure increased. Another explosion, this one farther away.

Nobody came for them. Instead, they sat in the darkness, the air growing hotter and hotter with every passing minute. They'd turned off all ventilation, Margaret explained, any system that might produce sound, while they crept away from the coast. At full speed, the batteries could only run for sixty minutes, she whispered, and then they'd be forced to surface to get air for the diesel engines. But sea planes would be circling overhead, looking for them. If they surfaced, they'd come under attack at once.

However, at minimal speed, the submarine could continue on battery power for hours. Until nightfall.

Gradually, the explosions grew more and more distant. A light came on overhead. Margaret lay on her bunk, stony faced, with no more tears. Nicolo panted, face red. Kovács lay on his belly with his face buried in his hands.

Another hour passed in silence before the door opened. A man in a civilian suit, with a bushy mustache and lamb chops that wouldn't have looked out of place on a Victorian stage, stood in the doorway. He'd loosened his tie and sweat trickled down his forehead.

"Well now," he said in a precise, upper-class diction. "That was a jolly good adventure, if I do say."

CHAPTER THIRTY-TWO

KATTERMAN WATCHED HOSSBACH WARILY AS the patrol boat returned to the harbor. Three hours in hopeless, frustrating search since the gun battle with the submarine, and Hossbach had grown more agitated with every passing moment, until he paced back and forth, wringing his hands.

From the open water to their rear came the continued thump of muffled explosions. Two corvettes—the pride of the Italian navy, though he doubted they wandered from littoral waters to brave the wrath of the British fleet—had sped south from the larger naval base up the Tuscan coast, but had arrived too late to stop the enemy submarine from diving. These larger ships cruised back and forth, still searching.

"Hammering away with active sonar," Hossbach had said, "for all the good it will do them."

And dropping depth charges, as well, but had nothing to show for it but a raft of dead fish bobbing on the surface and a sea cleared of fishing boats as the locals gave the action a wide berth and hugged the coastline to wait for it to end. Another thump sounded.

Hossbach looked up from his pacing. "Ridiculous. We lost a long time ago, right when those first charges failed. Why do they insist on continuing the search?"

"Maybe they wounded it," Katterman said.

"Then you would see an oil slick, it would be forced to surface." He cursed for several seconds. "It's that captain's fault. I yelled at him, told him to fire straight ahead. Those submarine guns were weak, no more than 12 centimeters. We could have engaged them with our eighteens and sunk those bastards. Where is Rosario? I want the name of the commander of this vessel. Dereliction of duty."

Katterman assumed that Hossbach knew what he was talking about. Supposing the British submarine had escaped the coast, it would never be seen again, and neither would the Hungarian scientist and the surviving fugitives. They had found Nigel Burnside's body amid the wreckage of the fishing boat, but none of the others. The assumption was that the rest had taken the rowboat and arrived safely at the submarine.

"Look at you," Hossbach said. "Calm, uncaring. Standing there like a goddamned statue."

"On the contrary, I am rather distressed. I wish I had picked up the clues earlier."

"Clues. Hah!" Hossbach lit a cigarette and took long, nervous drags. "Damn this!" He slammed his other hand against the railing.

"It is not entirely a loss. In fact, there may be a victory to salvage."

"What the hell is that supposed to mean?"

Katterman turned back around to look toward the harbor and the dozens of fishing boats tacking against the wind to get out of the way of the speedily moving patrol boat. They had been loitering outside the breakwater, as if expecting the operation to end at any moment and let them return to their livelihood.

"A few things to work out yet," Katterman said, "but it is all coming to me."

He felt the weight of the gun, tucked inside his jacket to rest against his chest. Was Hossbach armed? He thought not.

The boat slowed as it swung around the breakwater. They glided past the rotting wooden piers, docks, and wharves of the fishing port and to the heavier dock and the slips of the naval base. Concrete pillboxes guarded the entrance and the Italians had dropped a submarine net to let the ship into a small inner bay big enough to hold half a dozen patrol boats, but not so large as to hold anything approaching the size of the corvettes.

Several men waited on the dock as the patrol boat pulled in. Katterman studied Hossbach for a reaction, but the man stared out to sea, scowling, as if watching and listening for gunfire or explosions. Hoping, somehow, that the enemy would still be caught. Hossbach lit another cigarette.

Rosario and his fellow carabinieri came down from the poop deck and gave Katterman a significant look. The patrol boat reversed its motor and eased to a stop. Men lashed ropes to cleats on the dock, and two more sailors heaved over the gangplank.

Hossbach turned around at last. His eyes found the men waiting at the bottom of the gangplank and the cigarette fell from his lips. He turned to Katterman.

"What the devil is this?"

Katterman stood a few feet away, hand tucked into his jacket. Rosario and his man trained their pistols on the other German. Hossbach's eyes widened.

"No sudden moves," Katterman said. "Get on the gangplank. Let's go down and meet our friends. Hands out where I can see them."

Hossbach obeyed. He reached the bottom and the mixture of Italian secret service, carabinieri armed with carbines, and SD agents in trench coats and black leather jackets. One of them stepped forward, a tall man with blond hair cut close to the scalp and thinning on top.

"Hans Bloch?" Katterman said.

A nod. "You must be Katterman. Is this Hossbach?"

"Assuming that is his real name, yes."

"My real name?" Hossbach said, sputtering.

"Klaus Hossbach," Katterman said. "You are under arrest for high treason, for crimes against the Reich and the Führer, and for knowingly abetting enemies of the state."

"Under arrest? How dare you!" He turned to Bloch and held up his skull ring as the Italians swarmed him, and shoved their hands into his pockets, removing a billfold, a few papers, a pen, and finally, his pistol. "I have the rank of Obersturmbannführer, and I answer only to Heinrich Himmler himself. If you know you what is good for you—"

"Arrest is unnecessary," Bloch said with a smile. He paid no attention to Hossbach's protests. "We don't stand on formalities, and it doesn't carry much weight down here anyway. Protective custody is sufficient."

"I do not care much for protective custody," Katterman said. "Even when the guilt is so obvious."

Hossbach was still threatening, but Bloch nodded at Rosario, and the Italian captain stepped forward and pistol-whipped their prisoner across the side of the head. He fell to his knees with a cry. Katterman looked away.

"Still," Bloch said. "We will need to turn him over to the Italians for a few hours before we bring him home.

These Italians are prickly, and they demand their rights."

"I suppose that would be necessary," Katterman said with some reluctance.

"So let's hear if this man has an answer to your accusation before they haul him away. I would hate to punish an innocent man."

The Italians dragged Hossbach to his feet. He bled from a cut above his eye and stared back defiantly. Katterman, guessing at the man's motives, felt almost sorry for him, serious crimes or no.

"What accusations?" Hossbach said. "It's all lies."

"Something bothered me from the first," Katterman said. "Why bring in a small-town police officer from Saxony? The Gestapo is filled with competent investigators. I was flattered by the attention, but once I thought critically, I realized there must be a good reason."

"Heydrich..."

"Yes, I know your story. You needed to be quiet to investigate Reinhard Heydrich's nephew. And you didn't trust the Gestapo leadership. But that story fell apart. You didn't work for the Gestapo at all—they knew nothing about Wenck's death, had no record of your membership in the SS. And you do not work for the Ministry of Public Enlightenment and Propaganda, either. I checked that as well. Yet you have freedom to move around Europe. You produced my papers so quickly I thought they must be official. Now I know they were forged."

"Are you saying he is an enemy agent?" Bloch asked.

"An agent, but not the sort you're thinking of. We shall revisit that in a moment."

"But what about his ring?" Bloch held up his own right hand to show a similar death's head ring. "You can't stop in at the local jeweler and pick one up. Himmler gives them out personally. You must be vetted, initiated into the SS."

"Yes, that is exactly what Hossbach told me." Katterman grabbed Hossbach's hand and twisted off the man's ring. He showed it to Bloch. "Look at the scratch. This is the very one taken from Sturmbannführer Fritz Wenck when Hossbach manipulated me into shooting him. Wenck fell, struck his hand against the brick fireplace, and scratched the silver. Hossbach confiscated the ring, said Himmler would want it back."

"I can explain," Hossbach said. "It's because I lost the other one."

"I am an observant man," Katterman said. "When you shook my hand—shook, I'll note, instead of saluting—you were not wearing a ring. Not that first time. No, you're not SS."

"Then he *must* be a spy," Bloch said, triumphant. "There's something about that face. It's not quite Aryan. He's a Russian, isn't he?"

"He's German. And he even considers himself a patriot, of sorts. He genuinely wanted to capture Heydrich and the others, at least at the end. Before then, he missed every opportunity. When Rosario arrested Heydrich, for instance, and Margaret Burnside. I set the trap perfectly—we had them. Hossbach ordered them freed, let them move around more or less freely. He murdered Dunleavy, and why? Did you reach Berlin?"

"I called, but couldn't reach anyone useful," Bloch said. "We'll soon get word."

"Dunleavy's unsent telegram read 'HK knew. Allowed transfer. Contact SD in Rome.' HK is Hossbach and Katterman of course—although he was wrong about me, since I didn't know at the time. Allowed transfer must refer to the note the British spies picked up in the fish market. And the last bit was advice to have the SD come up from Rome to arrest us."

"So who is Dunleavy?" Bloch asked.

"A mole in the theater company. SS, either Gestapo or SD. Perhaps SS-Obergruppenführer Heydrich's own man, keeping an eye on his nephew. Hossbach must have found out. Decided to kill Dunleavy before he could spread his information."

Hossbach's jaw tightened.

"And then at the villa, he acted foolishly—no, let us say deliberately—to allow our fugitives to escape during an obvious diversion. Somehow, he knew they meant to take the Hungarian to Livorno, but he did not act in time to arrest them before they slipped onto the fishing boat. We could have sealed the inner harbor and questioned anyone appearing at the docks. We didn't. In the end, when he grew anxious, it was too late."

"I thought we had them," Hossbach said. "I swear it."

"Yes, but capturing them was not your main priority. Not until you had made the attempted escape and arrest into an international incident. Something that would be sure to get back to Berlin, sure to have repercussions."

"You don't understand."

"I *do* understand. You couldn't get to the SS-Obergruppenführer, could you? Reinhard Heydrich is one of the most powerful, ruthless men in the Reich, military dictator of half of Europe and with an army of ruthless men beneath him. No, you couldn't touch him. But you could get to his nephew. A nephew unwittingly stumbling around Europe, protecting and protected by enemy agents. This was your chance, your opportunity. When it came out that Heydrich's own nephew was in the company of enemies, you expected to pounce, to finish him off." When Hossbach said nothing, Katterman prodded. "Those are the facts, aren't they?"

"The facts," Hossbach said. "Is that all you care about?"

"The facts," he said. "And the law. That's what I told you from the beginning."

"The law is bringing an enemy of the Reich to justice! You were supposed to help me. You were supposed to bring down that bastard. Do you understand? Do you know what Heydrich will do to our country, what ruin he will bring to us? Have you given that any thought at all?"

"Reinhard Heydrich is not my concern. His nephew was. And you aided his escape."

"Damn you!"

"But how did he know?" Bloch said. "If Hossbach figured out that some of the actors were spies, why didn't we? Who is this man?"

"Klaus Hossbach seems to know a good deal about naval operations," Katterman said. "If I were you I would check with military intelligence."

"The Abwehr," Bloch said. "Of course. Those traitors."

Hossbach stopped his struggles. Once again, he stared straight ahead.

The Abwehr was the other German spy network. It was controlled not by men like Himmler and Heydrich, but stood as an independent secret service, an organization that directed its attentions outward, toward the British, the Americans, the Russians. Fiercely independent, under the command of Admiral Canaris. Not as pervasive nor as all-powerful as the Gestapo or the SD, but not without resources, either. And apparently some men in the Abwehr had determined that Reinhard Heydrich and his ilk were a bigger threat to the nation than an enemy spy network passing freely through the heart of German-occupied Europe.

"I've heard enough," Bloch said.

He said a few words in passable, if grammatically incorrect Italian, and the Italian secret service officers and Captain Rosario started arguing about which one of them would take Hossbach into custody. It almost turned into a wrestling match until Rosario got the upper hand, at least for the moment. Hossbach's defiance was gone now and he looked terrified as they marched him off toward the cars parked at the edge of the naval base, just up from the docks. Katterman watched them go with a hard feeling settling into his gut. Now that it was done, he had no stomach for the aftermath.

The Italians shoved Hossbach into the back of Rosario's black Fiat and pulled away. The Italian secret police dispersed as well, leaving only the Germans and a few Italian sailors watching from the deck of the patrol boat.

Bloch gave Katterman an approving nod. "Well then," he said. "Not bad work for a village police officer."

"Hmm, yes. I had begun to think of myself as an agent of the Reich. I suppose I had better adjust my expectations downward again."

The German agent smiled. "I wouldn't do that just yet." He turned to the other men. "We are done here."

Hands flew skyward, salutes and return salutes, and when their eyes fell on him, Katterman hastily lifted his own to join. And then he fell behind Hans Bloch as the man led them up the docks toward the waiting cars.

CHAPTER THIRTY-THREE

WULF KATTERMAN ENTERED THE STONE holding cell in the Wewelsburg Castle and took a seat on the bench, where he removed his clothing item by item. He folded his trousers and shirt into a neat pile, and then rolled his socks and tucked them into his shoes. He slid the old clothes beneath the bench as he'd been instructed, and then picked up the new pile of clothing, measured and cut to his figure.

He put on the black socks first, then the black trousers, the black shirt, starched and stiff. He put on the shoes, their leather polished to obsidian, and then the necktie. He tightened the black belt over the top of his jacket and fixed the swastika armband into place, and finally straightened the hat on his head. It held a straight-winged eagle that gripped a swastika and perched above a grinning death's head. Only when the hat was in place did he turn to look in the mirror that hung on the wall to his right.

The face that looked back at him was severe, firm-jawed. A man in the prime of his life, handsome and arrogant in an SS uniform, protected by runes and totems: skulls and swastikas, double lightning slashes and the *wolfsangel* — the wolf hook.

You will join a proud and ancient German order, the

summons read.

He had arrived in Westphalia only yesterday, disgorged from a train in the village of Marsberg. He'd found the town clean and neat, the people well-dressed and orderly. Food and goods were abundant in the shops and except for the large number of uniformed SS officers, it had been hard to believe that a war was raging — a terrible siege at Leningrad, air and sea battles at Malta, fighting from Burma to North Africa. Here, all was calm, with the church bell tolling the hours above the red roofs of the village. The winter sky was clear and cold, and the sky a perfect shade of blue.

Nevertheless, a gnawing hollow opened in his gut when they picked him up in the black Mercedes and drove him to Wewelsburg Castle. The car crossed hills covered with rows of pine and fir, sometimes planted in varying shades of green in the shape of swastikas. The castle itself was triangular, imposing, a mountain fortress rumored to be the last defense of the country should Huns ever invade from the east. Ten men stood at attention outside the castle. None of them spoke as he stepped beneath the portcullis, crossed the central courtyard, and entered the double oak doors of the castle. His footsteps rang across the flagstones as he proceeded down the hallway and entered a vast central hall, perhaps thirty meters by forty meters in dimension. Several SS officers sat around a huge oak table in the middle of the room, chatting or reading from *Der Stürmer* while smoking pipes or cigarettes. A beautiful young woman with her blond hair pulled into a bun brought in snifters of whiskey on a silver platter, the only woman Katterman had seen since leaving the village.

One of the officers rose from the table and approached

Katterman at a stroll, his features arrogant behind an icy blue gaze. Katterman recognized the face. It was SS-Obergruppenführer Reinhard Heydrich, one of the five most powerful men in the Reich. The two men shared salutes.

"So you are the one who exposed the treachery in the Abwehr," Heydrich said. He led Katterman away from the table and beyond the envious stares of the SS officers. "It originated in the navy — thanks to your effort we have crushed the entire operation. You know they have always hated me in the Kriegsmarine. Ever since I was drummed out on falsified charges. No doubt you have heard rumors."

"A few," Katterman admitted.

Indeed, he had. Heydrich, dismissed from the navy for "conduct unbecoming to an officer and a gentleman." That is, sleeping with the wrong woman.

"That is to be expected," Heydrich said. "We're poised for a final victory, but the communists, the Jews, the inferior men, the traitors will not give up. Let them try. We will see every last enemy hang." He shook his head, and a darker look came over his face. "What I was not expecting was treachery within my own family."

"I am sorry the young man escaped."

"Did he? Well, perhaps." A thin, dangerous smile. "And perhaps he will find he is not so safe as he supposes."

"You mean when England falls?"

"Then, too, of course. But more immediately, my nephew may have slipped out of our hands, but his friends haven't. We will extract justice from the remainder of his theater company, from their sponsors in the government. And what about his family? We have his mother, his father, his young sisters. They will pay and I shall make sure James hears every last detail of their fate."

Katterman blinked. But these people were *Heydrich's* family, too. Surely he wouldn't arrest and torture his own brother, sister-in-law, nieces, because his nephew had fallen into bad company.

Heydrich studied his face. "Yes, I can be a hard man. I can see what you are thinking. You should come east, you'd see what we're dealing with. You'd see this isn't the time for caution or mercy. If we hesitate, if we blink instead of stiffening to the task at hand, our enemies will devour us. I don't know what Himmler has planned for you, but maybe I will see you in Prague and then you'll see. To survive, we need intelligent men like you. Ruthless men."

Ruthless, Katterman thought, looking into the mirror as he dressed that evening for the SS ceremony. Was that his character? Hadn't he twinged when the Italians drove Hossbach away for interrogation? And then, two days later, when Katterman and Bloch took the beaten, broken man into German custody to transport him north, hadn't he felt a deeper, more poignant twist at his gut? The man was guilty, he knew that without a doubt, but did that justify torture?

He fingered the shoulder patches on his jacket. Twin lightening bolts for the SS, and the rank of Hauptsturmführer, or captain. The pin on the lapel indicated the Ausland-SD — Foreign Intelligence, General Government and the Protectorate of Bohemia and Moravia. Not the Kripo then, the Suppression of Crime, as he had hoped. But assigned to the military government of Eastern Europe, a territory formed from the torn-apart nations of Poland, Czechoslovakia, the Ukraine, Russia, and the Baltics. It was here that SS-Obergruppenführer Reinhard Heydrich acted as military dictator able to command, kill, and torture as he saw fit.

He had guessed as much. After Heydrich's comments in the great hall, he had *known* it.

Katterman thought about his wife and son, packing in Saxony, readying the move. Not certain where. Brigitte hoped for Berlin. France, if required to move to the occupied territories. Like many Germans, she dreaded the east.

A knock came at the door of the chamber. He adjusted his cuffs, straightened his belt and stepped into the hallway. Several other young men in black lined up outside, feet shuffling, licking lips and swallowing hard. Torches lined the hallway, casting banners with Germanic runes in red and orange light. A bronze eagle hung over the far doorway, a wreathed swastika clutched in its talons and rays of light beaming from the tips of its feathers. A man in a black uniform with no rank or insignia save for a Nazi armband stepped up to the wooden door at the end of hallway. He lifted the ring that hung from the mouth of a huge iron wolf head on the oak door and let it fall with a bang. The door creaked open. The men marched through with their boots ringing on the flagstone floor.

Two more unranked men in black led the initiates into the great hall. Torches guttered on the wall. There were a dozen silver plates set at the table, their mirrored surfaces decorated with eagles and swastikas. Silverware, crystal wine goblets, fine linen. Ten initiates and the two men who stood at the head of the table: the severe-looking Reinhard Heydrich and the bookish Heinrich Himmler, with his thin mustache and round glasses. One by one the initiates approached the two men. For each one, Himmler read from an open book, some incantation in an archaic, incomprehensible Germanic tongue, and then Heydrich slipped a totenkopf ring onto the man's right ring finger.

When it was his turn, Katterman bowed his head at the reading, and then looked up as Heydrich slid the leering skull ring onto his finger. "You earned this ring, Hauptsturmführer," Heydrich said. "More than any other man here. Wear it with pride and dignity."

Himmler and Heydrich thrust out their arms and flattened palms like lances braced against enemy cavalry. "Heil Hitler!"

"Heil Hitler!" Katterman said.

As he filed around the table, Katterman rubbed his thumb against the underside of the ring, against the scratch in the silver, where Fritz Wenck struck it against the brick fireplace as he fell with Katterman's bullet in his chest. He glanced over his shoulder at Himmler and Heydrich, the later watching through eyes half closed.

And then Katterman turned away and took his seat at the banquet table.

CHAPTER THIRTY-FOUR

JIM HEYDRICH ROSE FROM HIS seat in second class and recovered his bag as the train screeched into the station in Cambusdaroch. It was a gray, soggy day in northern Scotland, a temporary retreat of warmer weather during the back and forth of the approaching spring and the declining winter. The train shuddered to a stop. It belched smoke from the stack and spewed passengers from the cars. They stepped onto a platform already crowded with uniformed soldiers on leave, old men with battered suitcases, pretty young nurses, and women in smart wool dresses with bits of ribbon sewn as honorifics into their collars. One of these women, trim and pretty, looked so much like Margaret that he pushed his way roughly through the crowd to reach her side, but as he drew closer he saw that her jawline was wrong and she held the hands of two young children. His heart fell and an ache returned like a nagging injury.

Among the crowd waiting to board were two or three dozen children, chattering with the accents of London and Birmingham, so out of place in this wet, windswept place far from the cities. The bombing of coastal cities had eased, and the government was encouraging families to retrieve their children evacuated to the countryside. In the meanwhile, the Germans had taken to bombing historic sites: Exeter, Canterbury, Bath, York. It only served to enrage the English people. There were reports of British aerial bombardments in Germany too in Hamburg and Rostock, and reports that the Russians were holding at Leningrad and relieving pressure on Moscow, perhaps even counterattacking.

A military car waited in the street outside the station. Jim put up his umbrella against the drizzle and approached the window. It rolled down to reveal an officer in a tan uniform behind the wheel. "Jim Hyde?" the man said, using Jim's assumed surname.

Even in the Ministry of Information, where they knew better, he went by Hyde now. That was fine as far as he was concerned; the one time he'd let out that he was German, after downing too many beers in a pub and sharing too much information in an attempt to shake off the crushing loneliness, the bartender punched him in the face, and two old men drove him into the street with their canes.

"That's right," he said. He eyed the man's rank insignia. "They sent a major?"

"Apparently so." The man cocked his head. "American, is it? It's high time you Yanks showed up to the fight. We can't bloody well do it alone."

Jim didn't correct the man about his nationality. He didn't feel like chatting, in any event. He was coming off a cold, and last night he'd spent three hours reading in German for the European broadcasts until he was hoarse. They had him on a regular schedule, working twelve hours a day, with half days every other Sunday. An hour broadcast in the late morning, then translating intercepted German military broadcasts from North Africa with lunch taken at his desk, and then more reading for radio in the evening. They never told him what was real and what was propaganda, what messages were meant for actual partisans, and which were fake, meant to fool the Gestapo. He never identified himself on air as Reinhard Heydrich's nephew, but he guessed they were keeping this in reserve, ready to spring it at a moment of maximum effectiveness. Meanwhile, he affected the accent of a Prussian Junker for his radio persona and claimed he was a Wehrmacht general who had defected to "save the German people from the Austrian Ape."

The manor house sat several miles from the train station. They passed through a tiny village on the way, with houses snugged against the road, a steepled church, and stone bridges that returned them to the countryside and the green, sheep-covered hills. A loch glistened beneath a frowning mountain with its top crowned in fog. But the sun was out now, the clouds parting to show blue, and with a final swish, the driver turned off the wipers.

The road hugged the loch along the eastern side before disappearing into a pine forest. As soon as the car turned into the forest soldiers appeared from hidden guard posts. The driver showed his papers, and then showed them again as they exited the trees and approached the center of the estate.

A stately manor house sat in the middle of a broad, grassy field, with the forest to the west and south, and formal gardens to the north. The tower of a ruined castle thrust above the trees near the lake. The house was smaller than those of the English countryside, and he saw no visible guard posts, pillboxes, or anti-aircraft defenses, but he assumed they were present.

The car crunched to a stop on the crushed gravel

driveway. Jim opened the door, but turned to the driver before he stepped out. "What now?"

"Into the gardens."

"And that's where I will find—" He stopped himself before he said it: Capuchin. That was classified. "—the fellow I'm supposed to contact?"

"I have no more information. Sorry, Yank, you're on your own."

Jim climbed out and shut the door, and the major turned the car and left the estate the way he'd come. A moment later and Jim was alone. He walked around the side of the house until he found the path that led into the gardens. It sloped through rhododendrons, just starting to bud, down a flagstone staircase, and into a secret garden, enclosed with ivy-covered brick walls. A woman sat on a stone bench in front of a fountain that poured water from a stone urn and into a surrounding basin of water. She wore a gray wool dress and a wool felt cap, with brown leather gloves tucked in her lap and an umbrella propped at her side. She sat on a Mackintosh spread over the bench to keep herself dry. She turned as he approached and one corner of her mouth lifted in an enigmatic smile.

Margaret. He stopped, heart pounding.

"Germans are moving freely about the country?" Her eyebrow rose. "I am aghast."

"I am regularly frisked for sauerkraut and lederhosen." He sat down next to her, close so as to share the dry underside of her Mackintosh. He forced himself not to stare.

"Heard your broadcast. Didn't sound like you at all. What's that accent?"

"I had a headmaster in Halle who spoke like that. From

an old Junker family. He wore a monocle and paddled naughty boys. Every time I go on air I put his voice in my head. 'Heydrich, you are an incorrigible miscreant. Step to the head of the class and bare your buttocks!'"

She laughed.

"They didn't tell me you'd be here," Jim said. "So when do we meet this guy?"

"Who do you mean?"

"Capuchin. The head of the mission."

"That would be me, Jim. I'm Capuchin."

"You're Capuchin? Isn't that a monkey?"

"Don't look so smug. Your alias is Gibbon. I suggested Baboon, but that was already taken."

He laughed and looked into her sparkling eyes. Here she was, so close he could smell peaches from whatever she'd used to wash her hair. And she was the leader of the operation. She must have chosen him.

"You have clearance," she said. "I won't hold anything back, so if you have any questions..."

"Is it true?" he said. "We're going to Eastern Europe?"

"Czechoslovakia, to meet a pair of Czech NCOs we infiltrated in late December but who have been unable to meet their objective. You have three weeks to rehearse your part. Three weeks to learn weapons and explosives, and how to jump out of a plane late at night with a parachute strapped to your back."

His mouth felt dry, but he managed a nod. "And what are we doing when we get there?"

"We are going after the Hangman of Prague. We are going to assassinate your uncle."

Jim's fear dissolved. A grim knot of resolve formed deep in his gut. Yes, this was it. This was his chance.

"Who else is dropping with us?" he asked.

"Nobody. You and I. We're it." Margaret studied his face. "Jim, there is something I need to clarify before we leave this garden and go into the house for your first briefing. It is about us. You and me, I mean, and what happened in Florence."

"You don't have to clarify anything. I understand."

"But I do. I've been thinking about this since Malta. No, before then. From the submarine crossing, as soon as I stopped worrying, as soon as I could think about something other than Nigel's death." She hesitated. "I thought about what you said. Do you remember?"

Of course he did. He had exposed his emotions for her to see, and yes, it had been a moment of stress, but if anything, his feelings had sharpened these past several weeks, as he had a chance to run through everything that had happened between them again and again, starting with the night they hid beneath the Ponte Vecchio, and then that moment between scenes in the dressing room. His mouth on hers, the feel of her breasts, her skin, her hot breath in his ear.

"You probably wonder why I haven't contacted you," she said. "Why I disappeared in Gibraltar."

"It's a war. We're all busy. And the important thing was Kovács, getting him into American hands so they could...well, do whatever it is they need to do with a Hungarian physicist. You had bigger things to think about than coddling a German turncoat."

She winced. "Don't talk like that, please. It makes me sound so cold, unfeeling. And that isn't right anyway. I needed to get a handle on my own feelings before I saw you again."

"I thought you had a handle. You told me definitively what you were thinking at d'Angelo's villa."

"Yes, I know. About danger pushing us together. And I still wish I hadn't thrown myself on you like that during the middle of the show."

Jim said nothing. Whatever else, he didn't regret that.

"But I was wrong," she continued. She picked up her gloves and twisted them between her hands. "There *is* something. Something real. Only I can't...I mean, we can't. Not right now, not with so much at stake."

"What are you saying?"

"You know what I mean, don't you?"

"Not entirely," he said. She looked upset, like she was going to stand up and walk off and he'd never get it out of her and so he added, "You might have to use simple words. I'm not very bright and I speak a funny dialect of English called Canadian."

Margaret laughed, although it caught in her throat. Her eyes glistened when she looked at him again. "You were brave enough, so why can't I be brave, too?"

"I don't understand."

"You took a chance. Opened yourself to ridicule. I can do it now. It's my turn." She took a deep breath and put her hands over the top of his. "Here goes. Jim, I love you. Do you love me, too?"

He stared, unable to speak. For a moment it was too much to take in, but at last he squeezed her hands and gave a big, dopey nod. She laughed.

Margaret leaned back and that smile came over her face again. "We have a role to play in Prague. Are you ready for it?"

"Don't tell me you're playing my spoiled little sister."

"I wrote the script! Do you think I'd put that in? Heavens, no." She slipped her hand into the right pocket of her jacket and came out with something that glittered. "No, I'm playing the new wife of a young German businessman. The Reich is at war, so there is no time or permission to take a honeymoon, but he is taking her with him to Prague where he has an important meeting with Wehrmacht requisitions. With any luck, the young couple will be able to slip to a mountain spa for a day or two of passionate lovemaking." She handed him the diamond ring and then held out her hand. "Now, won't you put this on me?"

He took the ring and stared at it. This was insane. He wanted to put it on her, yes, and then marry her for real and run away to South America or somewhere safe, not back into that den of vipers and asps. And then he had another, even deeper worry as he stared at her shining eyes, that she was acting. That this whole thing was a feint as she got into character. She needed him to play the part of the devoted husband and so she was helping him get into the role. No, of course not. Not if he knew anything. He dismissed the idea as one last worry of an aching heart, unable to believe that it has found happiness.

Jim took her hand and with all the solemnity he could muster said, "With this ring, I thee wed."

She held up her hand and admired the diamond. "Excellent work. I really believed that." She glanced back to the house and then at her wristwatch. "Now, we have five minutes before we're expected inside. There's one other thing I want to rehearse before we go in."

"What's that?"

"It has to look real. That means we need to practice."

"Practice?" he tried to say, but he didn't get a chance.

She threw her arms around his neck.

And if there was any doubt left about her intentions, the hunger in her kiss erased it.

Thank you for reading Wolf Hook. Visit http://michaelwallaceauthor.com/ to sign up for my new releases list and receive a free copy of my Righteous novella, Trial by Fury. This mailing list is not used for any other purpose. If you enjoyed the book, I always appreciate a quick review at Amazon, Barnes and Noble, or wherever you purchased the book, which helps readers discover my work. Also, you might check out my other novels, such as my World War II thriller, The Red Rooster.

Author's note: In general, I like to be as accurate as possible with known historic details. However, I did take one notable artistic liberty when I created a fictional older brother for Nazi mastermind Reinhard Heydrich. Heydrich did have a *younger* brother, Heinz Heydrich, but the brother worked to help Jews escape by forging identity documents, and I didn't want to impugn the man's legacy.

About the Author:

Michael Wallace has trekked across the Sahara on a camel, ridden an elephant through a tiger preserve in Southeast Asia, eaten fried guinea pig, and been licked on the head by a skunk. In a previous stage of life he programmed nuclear war simulations, smuggled refugees out of a war zone, and milked cobras for their venom. He speaks Spanish and French and grew up in a religious community in the desert. His suspense/thrillers include The Devil's Deep, State of Siege, Implant, and The Righteous, and he is also the author of collections of travel stories and fantasy books for children. His work has appeared in print more than a hundred times, including publication in markets such as The Atlantic and The Magazine of Fantasy and Science Fiction.

Made in the USA
Middletown, DE
21 October 2015